SO-AZD-768

3 4028 05353 5010

DISCARDS

Kip SS
Kipling, Rudyard,
The man who would be king,
    and other stories

$22.95
ocm08772061

DISCARD

The Man Who
Would Be King
and other stories

The Man Who Would Be King
and other stories

---

by
Rudyard Kipling

Amereon House

To the Reader
It is our pleasure to keep available uncommon
titles and to this end, at the time of publication,
we have used the best available sources. To aid
catalogers and collectors, this is printed in an
edition limited to 400 copies. ——— Enjoy!

Library of Congress Catalog Card Number 82-71909
International Standard Book Number 0-88411-995-5

To order contact:
Amereon House, the publishing division of
Amereon Ltd.
Post Office Box 1200
Mattituck, New York 11952-9500

Manufactured in the United States of America

CONTENTS

The Man Who
Would Be King
and other stories

THE MAN WHO
WOULD BE KING

❧

Brother to a prince and fellow to a beggar if
he be found worthy.

The law, as quoted, lays down a fair conduct of life, and
one not easy to follow. I have been fellow to a beggar
again and again under circumstances which prevented either of us finding out whether the other was worthy. I
have still to be brother to a prince, though I once came
near to kinship with what might have been a veritable
king, and was promised the reversion of a kingdom—
army, law-courts, revenue, and policy all complete. But
today, I greatly fear that my king is dead, and if I want a
crown I must go hunt it for myself.

The beginning of everything was in a railway train
upon the road to Mhow from Ajmer. There had been a
deficit in the budget, which necessitated travelling, not
second-class, which is only half as dear as first-class, but
by intermediate, which is very awful indeed. There are no
cushions in the intermediate class, and the population are
either intermediate, which is Eurasian, or native, which
for a long night journey is nasty, or loafer, which is
amusing though intoxicated. Intermediates do not buy

from refreshment-rooms. They carry their food in bundles and pots, and buy sweets from the native sweetmeat-sellers, and drink the roadside water. That is why in hot weather intermediates are taken out of the carriages dead, and in all weathers are most properly looked down upon.

My particular intermediate happened to be empty till I reached Nasirabad, when a big black-browed gentleman in shirt-sleeves entered, and, following the custom of intermediates, passed the time of day. He was a wanderer and a vagabond like myself, but with an educated taste for whisky. He told tales of things he had seen and done, of out-of-the-way corners of the empire into which he had penetrated, and of adventures in which he risked his life for a few days' food.

"If India was filled with men like you and me, not knowing more than the crows where they'd get their next day's rations, it isn't seventy millions of revenue the land would be paying—it's seven hundred millions," said he; and as I looked at his mouth and chin I was disposed to agree with him.

We talked politics—the politics of loaferdom, that sees things from the underside where the lath and plaster are not smoothed off; and we talked postal arrangements because my friend wanted to send a telegram back from the next station to Ajmer, the turning-off place from the Bombay to the Mhow line as you travel westward. My friend had no money beyond eight annas, which he wanted for dinner, and I had no money at all owing to the hitch in the budget before mentioned. Further, I was going into a wilderness where, though I should resume touch with the treasury, there were no telegraph offices. I was, therefore, unable to help him in any way.

"We might threaten a station-master and make him send a wire on tick," said my friend, "but that'd mean inquiries for you and for me, and I've got my hands full these days. Did you say you were travelling back along this line within any days?"

"Within ten," I said.

"Can't you make it eight?" said he. "Mine is rather urgent business."

"I can send your telegram within ten days if that will serve you," I said.

"I couldn't trust the wire to fetch him now I think of it. It's this way. He leaves Delhi on the twenty-third for Bombay. That means he'll be running through Ajmer about the night of the twenty-third."

"But I'm going into the Indian desert," I explained.

"Well *and* good," said he. "You'll be changing at Marwar Junction to get into Jodhpur territory—you must do that—and he'll be coming through Marwar Junction in the early morning of the twenty-fourth by the Bombay mail. Can you be at Marwar Junction on that time? 'Twon't be inconveniencing you, because I know that there's precious few pickings to be got out of these Central India States—even though you pretend to be correspondent of the *Backwoodsman*."

"Have you ever tried that trick?" I asked.

"Again and again, but the residents find you out, and then you get escorted to the border before you've time to get your knife into them. But about my friend here. I *must* give him a word o' mouth to tell him what's come to me, or else he won't know where to go. I would take it more than kind of you if you was to come out of Central India in time to catch him at Marwar Junction and say to him: 'He has gone south for the week.' He'll know what that means. He's a big man with a red beard, and a great swell he is. You'll find him sleeping like a gentleman with all his luggage round him in a second-class apartment. But don't you be afraid. Slip down the window and say: 'He has gone South for the week,' and he'll tumble. It's only cutting your time of stay in those parts by two days. I ask you as a stranger—going to the West," he said with emphasis.

"Where have *you* come from?" said I.

"From the East," said he, "and I am hoping that you will give him the message on the Square—for the sake of my mother as well as your own."

Englishmen are not usually softened by appeals to the memory of their mothers, but for certain reasons, which will be fully apparent, I saw fit to agree.

"It's more than a little matter," said he, "and that's why I asked you to do it; and now I know that I can depend on you doing it. A second-class carriage at Marwar Junction, and a red-haired man asleep in it. You'll be sure to remember. I get out at the next station, and I must hold on there till he comes or sends me what I want."

"I'll give the message if I catch him," I said, "and for the sake of your mother as well as mine I'll give you a word of advice. Don't try to run the Central India States just now as the correspondent of the *Backwoodsman*. There's a real one knocking about here, and it might lead to trouble."

"Thank you," said he simply, "and when will the swine be gone? I can't starve because he's ruining my work. I wanted to get hold of the Degumber Rajah down here about his father's widow, and give him a jump."

"What did he do to his father's widow, then?"

"Filled her up with red pepper and slippered her to death as she hung from a beam. I found that out myself, and I'm the only man that would dare going into the state to get hush-money for it. They'll try to poison me, same as they did in Chortumna when I went on the loot there. But you'll give the man at Marwar Junction my message?"

He got out at a little roadside station, and I reflected. I had heard more than once of men personating correspondents of newspapers and bleeding small native states with threats of exposure, but I had never met any of the caste before. They lead a hard life, and generally die with great suddenness. The native states have a wholesome horror of English newspapers, which may throw light on their peculiar methods of government, and do their best to choke correspondents with champagne, or drive them out of their mind with four-in-hand barouches. They do not understand that nobody cares a straw for the internal administration of native states so long as oppression and crime are kept within decent limits and the ruler is not drugged, drunk, or diseased from one end of the year to the other. They are the dark places of the earth, full of unimaginable cruelty, touching the railway and the telegraph on one side, and on the other the days of Harunal-Raschid. When I left the train I did business with divers kings, and in eight days passed through many changes of life. Sometimes I wore dress-clothes and consorted with princes and politicals, drinking from crystal and eating from silver. Sometimes I lay out upon the ground and devoured what I could get from a plate made of leaves, and drank the running water, and slept under the same rug as my servant. It was all in the day's work.

Then I headed for the great Indian desert upon the proper date, as I had promised, and the night mail set me down at Marwar Junction, where a funny little happy-go-lucky native-managed railway runs to Jodhpur. The Bombay mail from Delhi makes a short halt at Marwar. She arrived as I got in, and I had just time to hurry to her platform and go down the carriages. There was only one second-class on the train. I slipped the window and looked down upon a flaming red beard, half covered by a railway rug. That was my man, fast asleep, and I dug him gently in the ribs. He woke with a grunt, and I saw his face in the light of the lamps. It was a great and shining face.

"Tickets again?" said he.

"No," said I. "I am to tell you that he is gone south for the week. He has gone south for the week!"

The train had begun to move out. The red man rubbed his eyes. "He has gone south for the week," he repeated. "Now that's just like his impidence. Did he say that I was to give you anything? 'Cause I won't.'"

"He didn't," I said, and dropped away, and watched the red lights die out in the dark. It was horribly cold because the wind was blowing off the sands. I climbed into my own train—not an intermediate carriage this time— and went to sleep.

If the man with the beard had given me a rupee I should have kept it as a memento of a rather curious affair. But the consciousness of having done my duty was my only reward.

Later on I reflected that two gentlemen like my friends could not do any good if they foregathered and personated correspondents of newspapers, and might, if they blackmailed one of the little rat-trap states of Central India or southern Rajputana, get themselves into serious difficulties. I therefore took some trouble to describe them as accurately as I could remember to people who would be interested in deporting them, and succeeded, so I was later informed, in having them headed back from the Degumber borders.

Then I became respectable, and returned to an office where there were no kings and no incidents outside the daily manufacture of a newspaper. A newpaper office seems to attract every conceivable sort of person, to the prejudice of discipline. Zenana-mission ladies arrive and beg that an editor will instantly abandon all his duties to describe a Christian prize-giving in a back slum of a perfectly inaccessible village; colonels who had been overpassed for command sit down and sketch the outline of a series of ten, twelve, or twenty-four leading articles on "Seniority versus Selection"; missionaries wish to know why they have not been permitted to escape from their regular vehicles of abuse and swear at a brother-missionary under special patronage of the editorial "we"; stranded theatrical companies troop up to explain that they cannot pay for their advertisements, but on their return from New Zealand or Tahiti will do so with interest; inventors of patent punkah-pulling machines, carriage couplings, and unbreakable swords and axle-trees call with specifications in their pockets and hours at their disposal; tea-companies enter and elaborate their prospectuses with the office pens; secretaries of ball-committees clamour to have the glories of their last dance more fully described; strange ladies rustle in and say, "I want a hundred lady's cards printed *at once,* please," which is manifestly part of an editor's duty; and every dissolute ruffian that ever tramped the Grand Trunk Road makes it his business to ask for employment as a proof-reader. And, all the time, the telephone-bell is ringing madly, and kings are being killed on the Continent, and empires are saying, "You're another," and Mr. Gladstone is calling down brimstone upon the British dominions and the little black copy-boys are whining, *"kaa-pi chay-ha-yeh"* (copy wanted) like tired bees, and most of the paper is as blank as Modred's shield.

But that is the amusing part of the year. There are six other months when none ever come to call, and the thermometer walks inch by inch up to the top of the glass, and the office is darkened to just above reading-light, and the press-machines are red-hot of touch, and nobody writes anything but accounts of amusements in the hill-stations or obituary notices. Then the telephone becomes a tinkling terror, because it tells you of the sudden deaths of men and women that you knew intimately, and the prickly-heat covers you with a garment, and you sit down and write: "A slight increase of sickness is reported from the Khuda Janta Khan district. The outbreak is purely sporadic in its nature, and, thanks to the energetic efforts of the district authorities, is now almost at an end. It is, however, with deep regret we record the death, etc."

Then the sickness really breaks out, and the less recording and reporting the better for the peace of the subscribers. But the empires and the kings continue to divert themselves as selfishly as before, and the foreman thinks that a daily paper really ought to come out once in twenty-four hours, and all the people at the hill-stations in the middle of their amusements say: "Good gracious! Why can't the paper be sparkling? I'm sure there's plenty going on up here."

That is the dark half of the moon, and as the advertisements say, "must be experienced to be appreciated."

It was in that season, and a remarkably evil season, that the paper began running the last issue of the week on Saturday night, which is to say Sunday morning, after the custom of a London paper. This was a great convenience, for immediately after the paper was put to bed, the dawn would lower the thermometer from ninety-six degrees to almost eighty-four degrees for half an hour, and in that chill—you have no idea how cold is eighty-four degrees on the grass until you begin to pray for it—a very tired man could get off to sleep ere the heat roused him.

One Saturday night it was my pleasant duty to put the paper to bed alone. A king or courtier or a courtesan or a community was going to die or get a new constitution or do something that was important on the other side of the world, and the paper was to be held open till the latest possible minute in order to catch the telegram.

It was a pitchy-black night, as stifling as a June night can be, and the *loo,* the red-hot wind from the westward, was booming among the tinder-dry trees and pretending that the rain was on its heels. Now and again a spot of almost boiling water would fall on the dust with the flop of a frog, but all our weary world knew that was only pretence. It was a shade cooler in the press-room than the office, so I sat there while the type ticked and clicked, and the night-jars hooted at the windows, and the all but naked compositors wiped the sweat from their foreheads and called for water. The thing that was keeping us back, whatever it was, would not come off, though the *loo* dropped, and the last type was set, and the whole round earth stood still in the choking heat, with its finger on its lip, to wait the event. I drowsed and wondered whether the telegraph was a blessing and whether this dying man or struggling people might be aware of the inconvenience the delay was causing. There was no special reason beyond the heat and worry to make tension, but as the clock-hands crept up to three o'clock and the machines spun their fly-wheels two and three times to see that all was in order before I said the word that would set them off, I could have shrieked aloud.

Then the roar and rattle of the wheels shivered the quiet into little bits. I rose to go away, but two men in white clothes stood in front of me. The first one said, "It's him!" The second said, "So it is!" And they both laughed almost as loudly as the machinery roared, and mopped their foreheads. "We seed there was a light burning across the road, and we were sleeping in that ditch there for coolness, and I said to my friend here, 'The office is open. Let's come along and speak to him as turned us back from the Degumber State,'" said the smaller of the two. He was the man I had met in the Mhow train, and his fellow was the red-bearded man of Marwar Junction. There was no mistaking the eyebrows of the one or the beard of the other.

I was not pleased, because I wished to go to sleep, not to squabble with loafers. "What do you want?" I asked.

"Half an hour's talk with you, cool and comfortable, in the office," said the red-bearded man. "We'd *like* some drink—the contrack doesn't begin yet, Peachey, so you needn't look—but what we really want is advice. We don't want money. We ask you as a favour, because we found out you did us a bad turn about Degumber State."

I led from the press-room to the stifling office with the maps on the walls, and the red-haired man rubbed his hands. "That's something like," said he. "This was the proper shop to come to. Now, sir, let me introduce to you

Brother Peachey Carnehan, that's him, and Brother Daniel Dravot, that is *me*, and the less said about our profes-
sions the better, for we have been most things in our time.
Soldier, sailor, compositor, photographer, proof-reader,
street-preacher, and correspondents of the *Backwoodsman*
when we thought the paper wanted one. Carnehan is sober, and so am I. Look at us first, and see that's sure. It
will save you cutting into my talk. We'll take one of your
cigars apiece, and you shall see us light up."

I watched the test. The men were absolutely sober, so I
gave them each a tepid whisky and soda.

"Well *and* good," said Carnehan of the eyebrows,
wiping the froth from his moustache. "Let me talk now,
Dan. We have been all over India, mostly on foot. We
have been boiler-fitters, engine-drivers, petty contractors,
and all that, and we have decided that India isn't big
enough for such as us."

They certainly were too big for the office. Dravot's
beard seemed to fill half the room and Carnehan's shoulders the other half, as they sat on the big table. Carnehan
continued: "The country isn't half worked out because
they that governs it won't let you touch it. They spend all
their blessed time in governing it, and you can't lift a
spade, nor chip a rock, nor look for oil, nor anything like
that without all the government saying, 'Leave it alone,
and let us govern.' Therefore, such *as* it is, we will let it
alone and go away to some other place where a man isn't
crowded and can come to his own. We are not little men,
and there is nothing that we are afraid of except drink,
and we have signed a contrack on that. *Therefore,* we are
going away to be kings."

"Kings in our own right," muttered Dravot.

"Yes, of course," I said. "You've been tramping in the
sun, and it's a very warm night, and hadn't you better
sleep over the notion? Come tomorrow."

"Neither drunk nor sunstruck," said Dravot. "We have
slept over the notion half a year and require to see books
and atlases, and we have decided that there is only one
place now in the world that two strong men can Sar-a-
whack. They call it Kafiristan. By my reckoning it's the
top right-hand corner of Afghanistan, not more than three
hundred miles from Peshawar. They have two and thirty

heathen idols there, and we'll be the thirty-third and
-fourth. It's a mountaineous country, and the women of
those parts are very beautiful."

"But that is provided against in the contrack," said
Carnehan. "Neither woman nor liqu-or, Daniel."

"And that's all we know, except that no one has gone
there, and they fight, and in any place where they fight, a
man who knows how to drill men can always be a king.
We shall go to those parts and say to any king we find—
'D'you want to vanquish your foes?' and we will show
him how to drill men, for that we know better than anything else. Then we will subvert that king and seize his
throne and establish a dy-nasty."

"You'll be cut to pieces before you're fifty miles across
the border," I said. "You have to travel through Afghanistan to get to that country. It's one mass of mountains
and peaks and glaciers, and no Englishman has been
through it. The people are utter brutes, and even if you
reached them you couldn't do anything."

"That's more like," said Carnehan. "If you could think
us a little more mad we would be more pleased. We have
come to you to know about this country, to read a book
about it, and to be shown maps. We want you to tell us
that we are fools and to show us your books." He turned
to the bookcases.

"Are you at all in earnest?" I said.

"A little," said Dravot sweetly. "As big a map as you
have got, even if it's all blank where Kafiristan is, and any
books you've got. We can read, though we aren't very
educated."

I uncased the big thirty-two-miles-to-the-inch map of
India, and two smaller frontier maps, hauled down volume INF–KAN of the "Encyclopaedia Britannica," and
the men consulted them.

"See here!" said Dravot, his thumb on the map. "Up to
Jagdallak, Peachey and me know the road. We was there
with Roberts' army. We'll have to turn off to the right at
Jagdallak through Laghmann territory. Then we get
among the hills—fourteen thousand feet—fifteen thousand—it will be cold work there, but it don't look very far
on the map."

I handed him Wood on the "Sources of the Oxus." Carnehan was deep in the encyclopaedia.

"They're a mixed lot," said Dravot reflectively; "and it won't help us to know the names of their tribes. The more tribes, the more they'll fight, and the better for us. From Jagdallak to Ashang. H'mm!"

"But all the information about the country is as sketchy and inaccurate as can be," I protested. "No one knows anything about it really. Here's the file of the United Services' Institute. Read what Bellew says."

"Blow Bellew!" said Carnehan. "Dan, they're a stinkin' lot of heathens, but this book here says they think they're related to us English."

I smoked while the men pored over Raverty, Wood, the maps, and the encyclopaedia.

"There is no use your waiting," said Dravot politely. "It's about four o'clock now. We'll go before six o'clock if you want to sleep, and we won't steal any of the papers. Don't you sit up. We're two harmless lunatics, and if you come tomorrow evening down to the Serai we'll say good-bye to you."

"You *are* two fools," I answered. "You'll be turned back at the frontier or cut up the minute you set foot in Afghanistan. Do you want any money or a recommendation down-country? I can help you to the chance of work next week."

"Next week we shall be hard at work ourselves, thank you," said Dravot. "It isn't so easy being a king as it looks. When we've got our kingdom in going order we'll let you know, and you can come up and help us to govern it."

"Would two lunatics make a contrack like that?" said Carnehan with subdued pride, showing me a greasy half-sheet of notepaper on which was written the following. I copied it, then and there, as a curiosity:

This Contract between me and you persuing witnesseth in the name of God—Amen and so forth.

(One)   That me and you will settle this matter together, i. e., to be Kings of Kafiristan.

(Two)   That you and me will not, while this matter is being settled, look at any Liquor, nor any

Woman black, white, or brown, so as to get
mixed up with one or the other harmful.

(Three)   That we conduct ourselves with Dignity and
Discretion, and if one of us gets into trouble
the other will stay by him.

Signed by you and me this day.
Peachey Taliaferro Carnehan
Daniel Dravot
Both Gentlemen at Large

"There was no need for the last article," said Carnehan, blushing modestly, "but it looks regular. Now you
know the sort of men that loafers are—we *are* loafers,
Dan, until we get out of India—and *do* you think that we
would sign a contrack like that unless we was in earnest?
We have kept away from the two things that make life
worth having."

"You won't enjoy your lives much longer if you are going to try this idiotic adventure. Don't set the office on
fire," I said, "and go away before nine o'clock."

I left them still poring over the maps and making notes
on the back of the "contrack." "Be sure to come down to
the Serai tomorrow," were their parting words.

The Kumharsen Serai is the great four-square sink of
humanity where the strings of camels and horses from the
North load and unload. All the nationalities of Central
Asia may be found there, and most of the folk of India
proper. Balkh and Bokhara there meet Bengal and Bombay and try to draw eye-teeth. You can buy ponies,
turquoises, Persian pussy-cats, saddle-bags, fat-tailed
sheep, and musk in the Kumharsen Serai, and get many
strange things for nothing. In the afternoon I went down
to see whether my friends intended to keep their word or
were lying there drunk.

A priest attired in fragments of ribbons and rags
stalked up to me, gravely twisting a child's paper whirligig.
Behind him was his servant, bending under the load of a
crate of mud toys. The two were loading up two camels,
and the inhabitants of the Serai watched them with
shrieks of laughter.

"The priest is mad," said a horse-dealer to me. "He is
going up to Kabul to sell toys to the amir. He will either

be raised to honour or have his head cut off. He came in
here this morning and has been behaving madly ever
since."

"The witless are under the protection of God," stam-
mered a flat-cheeked Usbeg in broken Hindi. "They fore-
tell future events."

"Would they could have foretold that my caravan
would have been cut up by the Shinwaris almost within
shadow of the pass!" grunted the Eusufzai agent of a
Rajputana trading-house whose goods had been diverted
into the hands of other robbers just across the border, and
whose misfortunes were the laughing-stock of the bazaar.
"Ohé, priest, whence come you and whither do you go?"

"From Roum have I come," shouted the priest, waving
his whirligig; "from Roum, blown by the breath of a
hundred devils across the sea! O thieves, robbers, liars,
the blessing of Pir Khan on pigs, dogs, and perjurers!
Who will take the protected of God to the North to sell
charms that are never still to the amir? The camels shall
not gall, the sons shall not fall sick, and the wives shall
remain faithful while they are away, of the men who give
me place in their caravan. Who will assist me to slipper
the king of the Roos with a golden slipper with a silver
heel? The protection of Pir Khan be upon his labours!"
He spread out the skirts of his gaberdine and pirouetted
between the lines of tethered horses.

"There starts a caravan from Peshawar to Kabul in
twenty days, *Huzrut,*" said the Eusufzai trader. "My
camels go therewith. Do thou also go and bring us good
luck."

"I will go even now!" shouted the priest. "I will depart
upon my winged camels and be at Peshawar in a day! Ho!
Hazar Mir Khan," he yelled to his servant, "drive out the
camels, but let me first mount my own."

He leapt on the back of his beast as it knelt, and, turning round to me, cried, "Come thou also, Sahib, a little
along the road, and I will sell thee a charm—an amulet
that shall make thee king of Kafiristan."

Then the light broke upon me, and I followed the two
camels out of the Serai till we reached open road and the
priest halted.

"What d'you think o' that?" said he in English. "Carnehan can't talk their patter, so I've made him my servant. He makes a handsome servant. 'Tisn't for nothing that I've been knocking about the country for fourteen years. Didn't I do that talk neat? We'll hitch on to a caravan at Peshawar till we get to Jagdallak, and then we'll see if we can get donkeys for our camels and strike into Kafiristan. Whirligigs for the amir, O Lor! Put your hand under the camel-bags and tell me what you feel."

I felt the butt of a Martini, and another and another.

"Twenty of 'em," said Dravot placidly. "Twenty of 'em, and ammunition to correspond, under the whirligigs and the mud dolls."

"Heaven help you if you are caught with those things!" I said. "A Martini is worth her weight in silver among the Pathans."

"Fifteen hundred rupees of capital—every rupee we could beg, borrow, or steal—are invested on these two camels," said Dravot. "We won't get caught. We're going through the Khyber with a regular caravan. Who'd touch a poor mad priest?"

"Have you got everything you want?" I asked, overcome with astonishment.

"Not yet, but we shall soon. Give us a memento of your kindness, *brother*. You did me a service yesterday, and that time in Marwar. Half my kingdom shall you have, as the saying is." I slipped a small charm compass from my watch-chain and handed it up to the priest.

"Good-bye," said Dravot, giving me his hand cautiously. "It's the last time we'll shake hands with an Englishman these many days. Shake hands with him, Carnehan," he cried as the second camel passed me.

Carnehan leaned down and shook hands. Then the camels passed away along the dusty road, and I was left alone to wonder. My eye could detect no failure in the disguises. The scene in the Serai proved that they were complete to the native mind. There was just the chance, therefore, that Carnehan and Dravot would be able to wander through Afghanistan without detection. But beyond, they would find death—certain and awful death.

Ten days later a native correspondent, giving me the news of the day from Peshawar, wound up his letter with: "There has been much laughing here on account of a certain mad priest who is going in his estimation to sell petty gauds and insignificant trinkets which he ascribes as great charms to H. H., the amir of Bokhara. He passed through Peshawar and associated himself to the Second Summer caravan that goes to Kabul. The merchants are pleased because through superstition they imagine that such mad fellows bring good fortune."

The two, then, were beyond the border. I would have prayed for them, but that night a real king died in Europe and demanded an obituary notice.

The wheel of the world swings through the same phases again and again. Summer passed and winter thereafter, and came and passed again. The daily paper continued, and I with it, and upon the third summer there fell a hot night, a night issue, and a strained waiting for something to be telegraphed from the other side of the world, exactly as had happened before. A few great men had died in the past two years, the machines worked with more clatter, and some of the trees in the office garden were a few feet taller. But that was all the difference.

I passed over to the press-room, and went through just such a scene as I have already described. The nervous tension was stronger than it had been two years before, and I felt the heat more acutely. At three o'clock I cried, "Print off," and turned to go, when there crept to my chair what was left of a man. He was bent into a circle, his head was sunk between his shoulders, and he moved his feet one over the other like a bear. I could hardly see whether he walked or crawled—this rag-wrapped, whining cripple who addressed me by name, crying that he was come back. "Can you give me a drink?" he whimpered. "For the Lord's sake, give me a drink!"

I went back to the office, the man following with groans of pain, and I turned up the lamp.

"Don't you know me?" he gasped, dropping into a chair, and he turned his drawn face, surmounted by a shock of grey hair, to the light.

I looked at him intently. Once before had I seen eyebrows that met over the nose in an inch-broad black band, but for the life of me I could not tell where.

"I don't know you," I said, handing him the whisky. "What can I do for you?"

He took a gulp of the spirit raw and shivered in spite of the suffocating heat.

"I've come back," he repeated; "and I was the king of Kafiristan—me and Dravot—crowned kings we was! In this office we settled it—you setting there and giving us the books. I am Peachey—Peachey Taliaferro Carnehan, and you've been setting here ever since—O Lord!"

I was more than a little astonished, and expressed my feelings accordingly.

"It's true," said Carnehan with a dry cackle, nursing his feet, which were wrapped in rags. "True as gospel. Kings we were, with crowns upon our heads—me and Dravot—poor Dan—oh, poor, poor Dan, that would never take advice, not though I begged of him!"

"Take the whisky," I said, "and take your own time. Tell me all you can recollect of everything from beginning to end. You got across the border on your camels. Dravot dressed as a mad priest and you his servant. Do you remember that?"

"I ain't mad—yet, but I shall be that way soon. Of course I remember. Keep looking at me, or maybe my words will go all to pieces. Keep looking at me in my eyes, and don't say anything."

I leaned forward and looked into his face as steadily as I could. He dropped one hand upon the table and I grasped it by the wrist. It was twisted like a bird's claw, and upon the back was a ragged, red, diamond-shaped scar.

"No, don't look there. Look at *me*," said Carnehan. "That comes afterwards, but for the Lord's sake don't distrack me! We left with that caravan, me and Dravot playing all sorts of antics to amuse the people we were with. Dravot used to make us laugh in the evenings when all the people was cooking their dinners—cooking their dinners, and—What did they do then? They lit little fires with sparks that went into Dravot's beard, and we all laughed—fit to die. Little red fires they was, going into Dravot's big red beard—so funny." His eyes left mine, and he smiled foolishly.

"You went as far as Jagdallak with that caravan," I

said at a venture, "after you had lit those fires. To Jagdallak, where you turned off to try to get into Kafiristan."

"No, we didn't neither. What are you talking about?
We turned off before Jagdallak, because we heard the
roads was good. But they wasn't good enough for our two
camels—mine and Dravot's. When we left the caravan,
Dravot took off his clothes, and mine too, and said we
would be heathen, because the Kafirs didn't allow
Muhammadans to talk to them. So we dressed betwixt
and between, and such a sight as Daniel Dravot I never
saw yet nor expect to see again. He burned half his beard,
and slung a sheepskin over his shoulder, and shaved his
head into patterns. He shaved mine too, and made me
wear outrageous things to look like a heathen. That was
in a most mountaineous country, and our camels couldn't
go along anymore because of the mountains. They were
tall and black, and coming home I saw them fight like
wild goats—there are lots of goats in Kafiristan. And
these mountains, they never keep still, no more than the
goats. Always fighting they are, and don't let you sleep at
night."

"Take some more whisky," I said very slowly. "What
did you and Daniel Dravot do when the camels could go
no further because of the rough roads that led into Kafiristan?"

"What did which do? There was a party called Peachey
Taliaferro Carnehan that was with Dravot. Shall I tell you
about him? He died out there in the cold. Slap from the
bridge fell old Peachey, turning and twisting in the air like
a penny whirligig that you can sell to the amir. No; they
was two for three ha'pence, those whirligigs, or I am
much mistaken and woeful sore. And then these camels
were no use, and Peachey said to Dravot, 'For the Lord's
sake let's get out of this before our heads are chopped
off,' and with that they killed the camels all among the
mountains, not having anything in particular to eat, but
first they took off the boxes with the guns and the ammunition, till two men came along driving four mules. Dravot
up and dances in front of them, singing, 'Sell me four
mules.' Says the first men, 'If you are rich enough to buy,
you are rich enough to rob'; but before ever he could put
his hand to his kinfe, Dravot breaks his neck over his

knee, and the other party runs away. So Carnehan loaded the mules with the rifles that was taken off the camels, and together we starts forward into those bitter cold mountaineous parts, and never a road broader than the back of your hand."

He paused for a moment, while I asked him if he could remember the nature of the country through which he had journeyed.

"I am telling you as straight as I can, but my head isn't as good as it might be. They drove nails through it to make me hear better how Dravot died. The country was mountaineous and the mules were most contrary and the inhabitants was dispersed and solitary. They went up and up, and down and down, and that other party, Carnehan, was imploring of Dravot not to sing and whistle so loud, for fear of bringing down the tremenjus avalanches. But Dravot says that if a king couldn't sing it wasn't worth being king, and whacked the mules over the rump, and never took no heed for ten cold days. We came to a big level valley all among the mountains, and the mules were near dead, so we ki'led them, not having anything in special for them or us to eat. We sat upon the boxes and played odd and even with the cartridges that was jolted out.

"Then ten men with bows and arrows ran down that valley, chasing twenty men with bows and arrows, and the row was tremenjus. They was fair men—fairer than you or me—with yellow hair and remarkable well built. Says Dravot, unpacking the guns, 'This is the beginning of the business. We'll fight for the ten men,' and with that he fires two rifles at the twenty men, and drops one of them at two hundred yards from the rock where he was sitting. The other men began to run, but Carnehan and Dravot sits on the boxes picking them off at all ranges, up and down the valley. Then we goes up to the ten men that had run across the snow too, and they fires a footy little arrow at us. Dravot, he shoots above their heads, and they all falls down flat. Then he walks over them and kicks them, and then he lifts them up and shakes hands all round to make them friendly like. He calls them and gives them the boxes to carry, and waves his hand for all the world as though he was king already. They takes the

boxes and him across the valley and up the hill into a
pine wood on the top, where there was half a dozen big
stone idols. Dravot, he goes to the biggest—a fellow they
call Imbra—and lays a rifle and a cartridge at his feet,
rubbing his nose respectful with his own nose, patting him
on the head, and saluting in front of it. He turns round to
the men and nods his head and says, 'That's all right. I'm
in the know too, and all these old jim-jams are my
friends.' Then he opens his mouth and points down it,
and when the first man brings him food, he says, 'No';
and when the second man brings him food he says 'No';
but when one of the old priests and the boss of the village
brings him food, he says, 'Yes,' very haughty, and eats it
slow. That was how we came to our first village, without
any trouble, just as though we had tumbled from the
skies. But we tumbled from one of those damned rope-
bridges, you see, and—you couldn't expect a man to
laugh much after that?"

"Take some more whisky and go on," I said. "That
was the first village you came into. How did you get to be
king?"

"I wasn't king," said Carnehan. "Dravot, he was the
king, and a handsome man he looked with the gold crown
on his head, and all. Him and the other party stayed in
that village, and every morning Dravot sat by the side of
old Imbra, and the people came and worshipped. That
was Dravot's order. Then a lot of men came into the valley, and Carnehan and Dravot picks them off with the
rifles before they knew where they was, and runs down
into the valley and up again the other side and finds another village, same as the first one, and the people all falls
down flat on their faces, and Dravot says, 'Now what is
the trouble between you two villages?' and the people
points to a woman, as fair as you or me, that was carried
off, and Dravot takes her back to the first village and
counts up the dead—eight there was. For each dead man
Dravot pours a little milk on the ground and waves his
arms like a whirligig, and 'That's all right,' says he. Then
he and Carnehan takes the big boss of each village by the
arm and walks them down into the valley, and shows
them how to scratch a line with a spear right down the
valley, and gives each a sod of turf from both sides of the

line. Then all the people comes down and shouts like the
devil and all, and Dravot says, 'Go and dig the land, and
be fruitful and multiply,' which they did, though they
didn't understand. Then we asks the names of things in
their lingo—bread and water and fire and idols and
such—and Dravot leads the priest of each village up to
the idol and says he must sit there and judge the people,
and if anything goes wrong he is to be shot.

"Next week they was all turning up the land in the valley as quiet as bees and much prettier, and the priests
heard all the complaints and told Dravot in dumb show
what it was about. 'That's just the beginning,' says Dravot. 'They think we're gods.' He and Carnehan picks out
twenty good men and shows them how to click off a rifle,
and form fours, and advance in line, and they was very
pleased to do so, and clever to see the hang of it. Then he
takes out his pipe and his baccy-pouch and leaves one at
one village, and one at the other, and off we two goes to
see what was to be done in the next valley. That was all
rock, and there was a little village there, and Carnehan
says, 'Send 'em to the old valley to plant,' and takes 'em
there and gives 'em some land that wasn't took before.
They were a poor lot, and we blooded 'em with a kid before letting 'em into the new kingdom. That was to
impress the people, and then they settled down quiet, and
Carnehan went back to Dravot, who had got into another
valley, all snow and ice and most mountaineous. There
was no people there, and the army got afraid, so Dravot
shoots one of them, and goes on till he finds some people
in a village, and the army explains that unless the people
wants to be killed they had better not shoot their little
matchlocks; for they had matchlocks. We make friends
with the priest, and I stays there alone with two of the
army, teaching the men how to drill; and a thundering big
chief comes across the snow with kettledrums and horns
twanging, because he heard there was a new god kicking
about. Carnehan sights for the brown of the men half a
mile across the snow and wings one of them. Then he
sends a message to the chief that unless he wished to be
killed, he must come and shake hands with me and leave
his arms behind. The chief comes alone first, and Carnehan shakes hands with him and whirls his arms about,

same as Dravot used, and very much surprised that chief
was, and strokes my eyebrows. Then Carnehan goes alone
to the chief and asks him in dumb show if he had an enemy he hated. 'I have,' says the chief. So Carnehan weeds
out the pick of his men and sets the two of the army to
show them drill, and at the end of two weeks the men can
manoeuvre about as well as volunteers. So he marches
with the chief to a great big plain on the top of a mountain, and the chief's men rushes into a village and takes it,
we three Martinis firing into the brown of the enemy. So
we took that village too, and I gives the chief a rag from
my coat and says, 'Occupy till I come,' which was
scriptural. By way of a reminder, when me and the army
was eighteen hundred yards away, I drops a bullet near
him standing on the snow, and all the people falls flat on
their faces. Then I sends a letter to Dravot wherever he be
by land or by sea."

At the risk of throwing the creature out of train, I interrupted: "How could you write a letter up yonder?"

"The letter? Oh! The letter! Keep looking at me between the eyes, please. It was a string-talk letter, that
we'd learned the way of it from a blind beggar in the
Punjab."

I remember that there had once come to the office a
blind man with a knotted twig and a piece of string which
he wound round the twig according to some cipher
of his own. He could, after the lapse of days or hours, repeat the sentence which he had reeled up. He had
reduced the alphabet to eleven primitive sounds, and he
tried to teach me his method, but I could not understand.

"I sent that letter to Dravot," said Carnehan, "and told
him to come back because this kingdom was growing too
big for me to handle, and then I struck for the first valley,
to see how the priests were working. They called the
village we took, along with the chief, Bashkai, and the
first village we took Er-Heb. The priests at Er-Heb was
doing all right, but they had a lot of pending cases about
land to show me, and some men from another village had
been firing arrows at night. I went out and looked for that
village and fired four rounds at it from a thousand yards.
That used all the cartridges I cared to spend, and I waited

for Dravot, who had been away two or three months, and I kept my people quiet.

"One morning I heard the devil's own noise of drums and horns, and Dan Dravot marches down the hill with his army and a tail of hundreds of men, and, which was the most amazing, a great gold crown on his head. 'My Gord, Carnehan,' says Daniel, 'this is a tremenjus business, and we've got the whole country as far as it's worth having. I am the son of Alexander by Queen Semiramis, and you're my younger brother and a god too! It's the biggest thing we've ever seen. I've been marching and fighting for six weeks with the army, and every footy little village for fifty miles has come in rejoiceful; and more than that, I've got the key of the whole show, as you'll see, and I've got a crown for you! I told 'em to make two of 'em at a place called Shu, where the gold lies in the rock like suet in mutton. Gold I've seen, and turquoise I've kicked out of the cliffs, and there's garnets in the sands of the river, and here's a chunk of amber that a man brought me. Call up all the priests and, here, take your crown.'

"One of the men opens a black hair bag, and I slips the crown on. It was too small and too heavy, but I wore it for the glory. Hammered gold it was—five pound weight, like a hoop of a barrel.

" 'Peachey,' says Dravot, 'we don't want to fight no more. The craft's the trick, so help me!' and he brings forward that same chief that I left at Bashkai—Billy Fish we called him afterwards, because he was so like Billy Fish that drove the big tank-engine at Mach on the Bolan in the old days. 'Shake hands with him,' says Davot, and I shook hands and nearly dropped, for Billy Fish gave me the grip. I said nothing, but tried him with the fellow craft grip. He answers all right, and I tried the master's grip, but that was a slip. 'A fellow craft he is!' I says to Dan. 'Does he know the word?' 'He does,' says Dan, 'and all the priests know. It's a miracle! The chiefs and the priests can work a fellow craft lodge in a way that's very like ours, and they've cut the marks on the rocks, but they don't know the third degree, and they've come to find out. It's Gord's truth. I've known these long years that the Afghans knew up to the fellow craft degree, but this is a miracle. A god and a grand-master of the craft am I, and a lodge in the third degree I will open, and we'll raise the head priests and the chiefs of the villages.'

" 'It's against all the law,' I says, 'holding a lodge without warrant from anyone; and you know we never held office in any lodge.'

" 'It's a master-stroke o' policy,' says Dravot. 'It means running the country as easy as a four-wheeled bogie on a down grade. We can't stop to inquire now, or they'll turn against us. I've forty chiefs at my heels, and passed and raised according to their merit they shall be. Billet these men on the villages, and see that we run up a lodge of some kind. The temple of Imbra will do for the lodge-room. The women must make aprons as you show them. I'll hold a levee of chiefs tonight and lodge tomorrow.'

"I was fair run off my legs, but I wasn't such a fool as not to see what a pull this craft business gave us. I showed the priests' families how to make aprons of the degrees, but for Dravot's apron the blue border and marks was made of turquoise lumps on white hide, not cloth. We took a great square stone in the temple for the master's chair, and little stones for the officers' chairs, and painted the black pavement with white squares, and did what we could to make things regular.

"At the levee which was held that night on the hillside with big bonfires, Dravot gives out that him and me were gods and sons of Alexander, and past grand-masters in the craft, and was come to make Kafiristan a country where every man should eat in peace and drink in quiet, and specially obey us. Then the chiefs come round to shake hands, and they were so hairy and white and fair it was just shaking hands with old friends. We gave them names according as they was like men we had known in India—Billy Fish, Holly Dilworth, Pikky Kergan, that was bazaar-master when I was at Mhow, and so on, and so on.

"*The* most amazing miracles was at lodge next night. One of the old priests was watching us continuous, and I felt uneasy, for I knew we'd have to fudge the ritual, and I didn't know what the men knew. The old priest was a stranger come in from beyond the village of Bashkai. The minute Dravot puts on the master's apron that the girls had

made for him, the priest fetches a whoop and a howl and
tries to overturn the stone that Dravot was sitting on. 'It's
all up now,' I says. 'That comes of meddling with the
craft without warrant!' Dravot never winked an eye, not
when ten priests took and tilted over the grand-master's
chair—which was to say the stone of Imbra. The priest
begins rubbing the bottom end of it to clear away the
black dirt, and presently he shows all the other priests the
master's mark, same as was on Dravot's apron, cut into
the stone. Not even the priests of the temple of Imbra
knew it was there. The old chap falls flat on his face at
Dravot's feet and kisses 'em. 'Luck again,' says Dravot
across the lodge to me; 'they say it's the missing mark
that no one could understand the why of. We're more
than safe now.' Then he bangs the butt of his gun for a
gavel and says, 'By virtue of the authority vested in me by
my own right hand and the help of Peachey, I declare
myself grand-master of all free-masonry in Kafiristan in
this the mother lodge o' the country, and king of Kafiristan equally with Peachey!' At that he puts on his crown
and I puts on mine—I was doing senior warden—and we
opens the lodge in most ample form. It was a amazing
miracle! The priests moved in lodge through the first two
degrees almost without telling, as if the memory was
coming back to them. After that Peachey and Dravot
raised such as was worthy—high priests and chiefs of
far-off villages. Billy Fish was the first, and I can tell you
we scared the soul out of him. It was not in any way according to ritual, but it served our turn. We didn't raise
more than ten of the biggest men, because we didn't want
to make the degree common. And they was clamouring to
be raised.

" 'In another six months,' says Dravot, 'we'll hold another communication and see how you are working.' Then
he asks them about their villages, and learns that they was
fighting one against the other, and were sick and tired of
it. And when they wasn't doing that they was fighting
with the Muhammadans. 'You can fight those when they
come into our country,' says Dravot. 'Tell off every tenth
man of your tribes for a frontier guard, and send two
hundred at a time to this valley to be drilled. Nobody is
going to be shot or speared anymore so long as he does

well, and I know that you won't cheat me, because you're white people—sons of Alexander—and not like common black Muhammadans. You are *my* people, and by God,' says he, running off into English at the end, 'I'll make a damned fine nation of you, or I'll die in the making!'

"I can't tell all we did for the next six months, because Dravot did a lot I couldn't see the hang of, and he learned their lingo in a way I never could. My work was to help the people plough, and now and again go out with some of the army and see what the other villages were doing, and make 'em throw rope-bridges across the ravines which cut up the country horrid. Dravot was very kind to me, but when he walked up and down in the pine wood pulling that bloody red beard of his with both fists, I knew he was thinking plans I could not advise about, and I just waited for orders.

"But Dravot never showed me disrespect before the people. They were afraid of me and the army, but they loved Dan. He was the best of friends with the priests and the chiefs, but anyone could come across the hills with a complaint and Dravot would hear him out fair and call four priests together and say what was to be done. He used to call in Billy Fish from Bashkai, and Pikky Kergan from Shu, and an old chief we called Kafuzelum—it was like enough to his real name—and hold councils with 'em when there was any fighting to be done in small villages. That was his council of war, and the four priests of Bashkai, Shu, Khawak, and Madora was his privy council. Between the lot of 'em they sent me, with forty men and twenty rifles, and sixty men carrying turquoises, into the Ghorband country to buy those hand-made Martini rifles, that come out of the amir's workshops at Kabul, from one of the amir's Herati regiments that would have sold the very teeth out of their mouths for turquoises.

"I stayed in Ghorband a month, and gave the governor there the pick of my baskets for hush-money, and bribed the colonel of the regiment some more; and between the two and the tribespeople, we got more than a hundred hand-made Martinis, a hundred good Kohat Jezails that'll throw to six hundred yards, and forty man-loads of very bad ammunition for the rifles. I came back with what I had and distributed 'em among the men that the chiefs sent in to me to drill. Dravot was too busy to attend to those things, but the old army that we first made helped me, and we turned out five hundred men that could drill and two hundred that knew how to hold arms pretty straight. Even those corkscrewed, hand-made guns was a miracle to them. Dravot talked big about powder-shops and factories, walking up and down in the pine wood when the winter was coming on.

" 'I won't make a nation,' says he; 'I'll make an empire! These men aren't Niggers; they're English! Look at their eyes, look at their mouths. Look at the way they stand up. They sit on chairs in their own houses. They're the Lost Tribes, or something like it, and they've grown to be English. I'll take a census in the spring if the priests don't get frightened. There must be a fair two million of 'em in these hills. The villages are full o' little children. Two million people, two hundred and fifty thousand fighting men—and all English! They only want the rifles and a little drilling. Two hundred and fifty thousand men ready to cut in on Russia's right flank when she tries for India! Peachey, man,' he says, chewing his beard in great hunks, 'we shall be emperors—emperors of the earth! Rajah Brooke will be a suckling to us. I'll treat with the viceroy on equal terms. I'll ask him to send me twelve picked English—twelve that I know of—to help us govern a bit. There's Mackray, sergeant-pensioner at Segowli—many's the good dinner he's given me, and his wife a pair of trousers. There's Donkin, the warder of Tounghoo jail; there's hundreds that I could lay my hand on if I was in India. The viceroy shall do it for me; I'll send a man through in the spring for those men, and I'll write for a dispensation from the grand lodge for what I've done as grand-master. That—and all the Sniders that'll be thrown out when the native troops in India take up the Martini. They'll be worn smooth, but they'll do for fighting in these hills. Twelve English, a hundred thousand Sniders run through the amir's country in driblets—I'd be content with twenty thousand in one year—and we'd be an empire. When everything was shipshape, I'd hand over the crown—this crown I'm wearing now—to Queen Victoria, on my knees, and she'd say, "Rise up, Sir Danial Dravot." Oh, it's big! It's big, I tell you! But there's so much to be

done in every place—Bashkai, Khawak, Shu, and everywhere else.'

" 'What is it?' I says. 'There are no more men coming
in to be drilled this autumn. Look at those fat black
clouds. They're bringing the snow.'

" 'It isn't that,' says Daniel, putting his hand very hard
on my shoulder; 'and I don't wish to say anything that's
against you, for no other living man would have followed
me and made me what I am as you have done. You're a
first-class commander-in-chief, and the people know you;
but—it's a big country, and somehow you can't help me,
Peachey, in the way I want to be helped.'

" 'Go to your blasted priests then!' I said, and I was
sorry when I made that remark, but it did hurt me sore to
find Daniel talking so superior when I'd drilled all the
men and done all he told me.

" 'Don't let's quarrel, Peachey,' says Daniel, without
cursing. 'You're a king too, and the half of this kingdom
is yours; but can't you see, Peachey, we want cleverer
men than us now—three or four of 'em that we can scat-
ter about for our deputies. It's a hugeous great state, and
I can't always tell the right thing to do, and I haven't time
for all I want to do, and here's the winter coming on, and
all.' He put half his beard into his mouth, all red like the
gold of his crown.

" 'I'm sorry, Daniel,' says I. 'I've done all I could. I've
drilled the men and shown the people how to stack their
oats better; and I've brought in those tinware rifles from
Ghorband—but I know what you're driving at. I take it
kings always feel oppressed that way.'

" 'There's another thing too,' says Dravot, walking up
and down. 'The winter's coming, and these people won't
be giving much trouble, and if they do we can't move
about. I want a wife.'

" 'For Gord's sake leave the women alone!' I says.
'We've both got all the work we can, though I *am* a fool.
Remember the contrack, and keep clear o' women.'

" 'The contrack only lasted till such time as we was
kings; and kings we have been these months past,' says
Dravot, weighing his crown in his hand. 'You go get a
wife too, Peachey—a nice, strappin', plump girl that'll
keep you warm in the winter. They're prettier than English

girls, and we can take the pick of 'em. Boil 'em once or
twice in hot water, and they'll come out like chicken and
ham.'

" 'Don't tempt me!' I says. 'I will not have any dealings
with a woman, not till we are a damn side more settled
than we are now. I've been doing the work o' two men,
and you've been doing the work of three. Let's lie off a
bit and see if we can get some better tobacco from Afghan country and run in some good liquor; but no
women.'

" 'Who's talking o' *women?*' says Dravot. 'I said
wife—a queen to breed a king's son for the king. A queen
out of the strongest tribe, that'll make them your blood-
brothers and that'll lie by your side and tell you all the
people thinks about you and their own affairs. That's
what I want.'

" 'Do you remember that Bengali woman I kept at
Mogul Serai when I was a plate-layer?' says I. 'A fat lot
o' good she was to me. She taught me the lingo and one
or two other things; but what happened? She ran away
with the station-master's servant and half my month's
pay. Then she turned up at Dadur Junction in tow of a
half-caste, and had the impidence to say I was her husband—all among the drivers in the running-shed too!'

" 'We've done with that,' says Dravot; 'these women
are whiter than you or me, and a queen I will have for
the winter months.'

" 'For the last time o' asking, Dan, do *not*,' I says. 'It'll
only bring us harm. The Bible says that kings ain't to
waste their strength on women, 'specially when they've
got a new raw kingdom to work over.'

" 'For the last time of answering, I will,' said Dravot,
and he went away through the pine-trees looking like a
big red devil, the sun being on his crown and beard and
all.

"But getting a wife was not as easy as Dan thought. He
put it before the council, and there was no answer till
Billy Fish said that he'd better ask the girls. Dravot
damned them all round. 'What's wrong with me?' he
shouts, standing by the idol Imbra. 'Am I a dog or am I
not enough of a man for your wenches? Haven't I put the
shadow of my hand over this country? Who stopped the

last Afghan raid?' It was me really, but Dravot was too angry to remember. 'Who bought your guns? Who repaired the bridges? Who's the grand-master of the sign cut in the stone?' says he, and he thumped his hand on the block that he used to sit on in lodge and at council, which opened like lodge always. Billy Fish said nothing, and no more did the others. 'Keep your hair on, Dan,' said I; 'and ask the girls. That's how it's done at home, and these people are quite English.'

" 'The marriage of the king is a matter of state,' says Dan in a white-hot rage, for he could feel, I hope, that he was going against his better mind. He walked out of the council-room, and the others sat still, looking at the ground.

" 'Billy Fish,' says I to the chief of Bashkai, 'what's the difficulty here? A straight answer to a true friend.'

" 'You know,' says Billy Fish. 'How should a man tell you who knows everything? How can daughters of men marry gods or devils? It's not proper.'

"I remembered something like that in the Bible; but if, after seeing us as long as they had, they still believed we were gods, it wasn't for me to undeceive them.

" 'A God can do anything,' says I. 'If the king is fond of a girl, he'll not let her die.'

" 'She'll have to,' said Billy Fish. 'There are all sorts of gods and devils in these mountains, and now and again a girl marries one of them and isn't seen anymore. Besides, you two know the mark cut in the stone. Only the gods know that. We thought you were men till you showed the sign of the master.'

"I wished then that we had explained about the loss of the genuine secrets of a master-mason at the first go-off, but I said nothing. All that night there was a blowing of horns in a little dark temple halfway down the hill and I heard a girl crying fit to die. One of the priests told us that she was being prepared to marry the king.

" 'I'll have no nonsense of that kind,' says Dan. 'I don't want to interfere with your customs, but I'll take my own wife.'

" 'The girl's a little bit afraid,' says the priest. 'She thinks she's going to die, and they are a-heartening of her up down in the temple.'

" 'Hearten her very tender, then,' says Dravot, 'or I'll
hearten you with the butt of a gun so you'll never want to
be heartened again.' He licked his lips, did Dan, and
stayed up walking about more than half the night, thinking of the wife that he was going to get in the morning. I
wasn't any means comfortable, for I knew that dealings
with a woman in foreign parts, though you was a crowned
king twenty times over, could not but be risky. I got up
very early in the morning while Dravot was asleep, and I
saw the priests talking together in whispers, and the chiefs
talking together too, and they looked at me out of the
corners of their eyes.

" 'What is up, Fish?' I says to the Bashkai man, who
was wrapped up in his furs and looked splendid to behold.

" 'I can't rightly say,' says he; 'but if you can make the
king drop all this nonsense about marriage, you'll be doing him and me and yourself a great service.'

" 'That I do believe,' says I. 'But sure, you know, Billy,
as well as me, having fought against and for us, that the
king and me are nothing more than two of the finest men
that God Almighty ever made. Nothing more, I do assure
you.'

" 'That may be,' says Billy Fish, 'and yet I should be
sorry if it was.' He sinks his head upon his great fur cloak
for a minute and thinks. 'King,' says he, 'be you man or
god or devil, I'll stick by you today. I have twenty of my
men with me, and they will follow me. We'll go to
Bashkai until the storm blows over.'

"A little snow had fallen in the night, and everything
was white except the greasy fat clouds that blew down
and down from the north. Dravot came out with his
crown on his head, swinging his arms, and stamping his
feet, and looking more pleased than Punch.

" 'For the last time, drop it, Dan,' says I in a whisper;
'Billy Fish here says that there will be a row.'

" 'A row among my people!' says Dravot. 'Not much.
Peachey, you're a fool not to get a wife too. Where's the
girl?' says he with a voice as loud as the braying of a
jackass. 'Call up all the chiefs and priests, and let the emperor see if his wife suits him.'

"There was no need to call anyone. They were all there
leaning on their guns and spears round the clearing in the

centre of the pine wood. A lot of priests went down to the little temple to bring up the girl, and the horns blew fit to wake the dead. Billy Fish saunters round and gets as close to Daniel as he could, and behind him stood his twenty men with matchlocks. Not a man of them under six feet. I was next to Dravot, and behind me was twenty men of the regular army. Up comes the girl, and a strapping, wench she was, covered with silver and turquoises, but white as death, and looking back every minute at the priests.

" 'She'll do,' said Dan, looking her over. 'What's to be afraid of, lass? Come and kiss me.' He puts his arm round her. She shuts her eyes, gives a bit of a squeak, and down goes her face in the side of Dan's flaming red beard.

" 'The slut's bitten me!' says he, clapping his hand to his neck, and, sure enough, his hand was red with blood. Billy Fish and two of his matchlock-men catches hold of Dan by the shoulders and drags him into the Bashkai lot, while the priests howls in their lingo, 'Neither god nor devil, but a man!' I was all taken aback, for a priest cut at me in front, and the army behind began firing into the Bashkai men.

" 'God A'mighty!' says Dan. 'What is the meaning o' this?'

" 'Come back! Come away!' says Billy Fish. 'Ruin and mutiny is the matter. We'll break for Bashkai if we can.'

"I tried to give some sort of orders to my men—the men o' the regular army—but it was no use, so I fired into the brown of 'em with an English Martini and drilled three beggars in a line. The valley was full of shouting, howling creatures, and every soul was shrieking, 'Not a god nor a devil, but only a man!' The Bashkai troops stuck to Billy Fish all they were worth, but their matchlocks wasn't half as good as the Kabul breech-loaders, and four of them dropped. Dan was bellowing like a bull, for he was very wrathy; and Billy Fish had a hard job to prevent him running out of the crowd.

" 'We can't stand,' says Billy Fish. 'Make a run for it down the valley! The whole place is against us.' The matchlock-men ran, and we went down the valley in spite of Dravot. He was swearing horrible and crying out he was a king. The priests rolled great stones on us, and the regular army fired hard, and there wasn't more than six men, not counting Dan, Billy Fish, and me, that came down to the bottom of the valley alive.

"Then they stopped firing, and the horns in the temple blew again. 'Come away—for Gord's sake come away!' says Billy Fish. 'They'll send runners out to all the villagers before ever we get to Bashkai. I can protect you there, but I can't do anything now.'

"My own notion is that Dan began to go mad in his head from that hour. He stared up and down like a stuck pig. Then he was all for walking back alone and killing the priests with his bare hands, which he could have done. 'An emperor am I,' says Daniel, 'and next year I shall be a knight of the queen.'

" 'All right, Dan,' says I, 'but come along now while there's time.'

" 'It's your fault,' says he, 'for not looking after your army better. There was mutiny in the midst, and you didn't know—you damned engine-driving, plate-laying, missionary's pass-hunting hound!' He sat upon a rock and called me every foul name he could lay tongue to. I was too heart-sick to care, though it was all his foolishness that brought the smash.

" 'I'm sorry, Dan,' says I, 'but there's no accounting for natives. This business is our fifty-seven. Maybe we'll make something out of it yet, when we've got to Bashkai.'

" 'Let's get to Bashkai, then,' says Dan, 'and, by God, when I come back here again I'll sweep the valley so there isn't a bug in a blanket left!'

"We walked all that day, and all that night Dan was stumping up and down on the snow, chewing his beard, and muttering to himself.

" 'There's no hope o' getting clear,' said Billy Fish. 'The priests will have sent runners to the villages to say that you are only men. Why didn't you stick on as gods till things was more settled? I'm a dead man,' says Billy Fish, and he throws himself down on the snow and begins to pray to his gods.

"Next morning we was in a cruel bad country—all up and down, no level ground at all, and no food either. The six Bashkai men looked at Billy Fish hungry-way as if they wanted to ask something, but they said never a word.

At noon we came to the top of a flat mountain all covered with snow, and when we climbed up into it, behold, there was an army in position waiting in the middle!

" 'The runners have been very quick,' says Billy Fish with a little bit of a laugh. 'They are waiting for us.'

"Three or four men began to fire from the enemy's side, and a chance shot took Daniel in the calf of the leg. That brought him to his senses. He looks across the snow at the army, and sees the rifles that we had brought into the country.

" 'We're done for,' says he. 'They are Englishmen, these people, and it's my blasted nonsense that has brought you to this. Get back, Billy Fish, and take your men away; you've done what you could, and now cut for it. Carnehan,' says he, 'shake hands with me and go along with Billy. Maybe they won't kill you. I'll go and meet 'em alone. It's me that did it. Me, the king!'

" 'Go!' says I. 'Go to hell, Dan. I'm with you here. Billy Fish, you clear out, and we two will meet those folk.'

" 'I'm a chief,' says Billy Fish, quite quiet. 'I stay with you. My men can go.'

"The Bashkai fellows didn't wait for a second word, but ran off; and Dan and me and Billy Fish walked across to where the drums were drumming and the horns were horning. It was cold—awful cold. I've got that cold in the back of my head now. There's a lump of it there."

The punkah-coolies had gone to sleep. Two kerosene lamps were blazing in the office, and the perspiration poured down my face and splashed on the blotter as I leaned forward. Carnehan was shivering, and I feared that his mind might go. I wiped my face, took a fresh grip of the piteously mangled hands, and said, "What happened after that?"

The momentary shift of my eyes had broken the clear current.

"What was you pleased to say?" whined Carnehan. "They took them without any sound. Not a little whisper all along the snow, not though the king knocked down the first man that set hand on him—not though old Peachey fired his last cartridge into the brown of 'em. Not a single solitary sound did those swines make. They just closed up tight, and I tell you their furs stunk. There was a man called Billy Fish, a good friend of us all, and they cut his throat, sir, then and there, like a pig; and the king kicks up the bloody snow and says, 'We've had a dashed fine run for our money. What's coming next?' But Peachey, Peachey Taliaferro, I tell you, sir, in confidence as betwixt two friends, he lost his head, sir. No, he didn't, neither. The king lost his head, so he did, all along o' one of those cunning rope-bridges. Kindly let me have the paper-cutter, sir. It tilted this way. They marched him a mile across that snow to a rope-bridge over a ravine with a river at the bottom. You may have seen such. They prodded him behind like an ox. 'Damn your eyes!' says the king. 'D'you suppose I can't die like a gentleman?' He turns to Peachey—Peachey that was crying like a child. 'I've brought you to this, Peachey,' says he. 'Brought you out of your happy life to be killed in Kafiristan, where you was late commander-in-chief of the emperor's forces. Say you forgive me, Peachey.' 'I do,' says Peachey. 'Fully and freely do I forgive you, Dan.' 'Shake hands, Peachey,' says he. 'I'm going now.' Out he goes, looking neither right nor left, and when he was plumb in the middle of those dizzy dancing ropes. 'Cut, you beggars,' he shouts; and they cut, and old Dan fell, turning round and round and round, twenty thousand miles, for he took half an hour to fall till he struck the water, and I could see his body caught on a rock with the gold crown close beside.

"But do you now what they did to Peachey between two pine-trees? They crucified him, sir, as Peachey's hands will show. They used wooden pegs for his hands and his feet; and he didn't die. He hung there and screamed, and they took him down next day and said it was a miracle that he wasn't dead. They took him down—poor old Peachey that hadn't done them any harm—that hadn't done them any—"

He rocked to and fro and wept bitterly, wiping his eyes with the back of his scarred hands and moaning like a child for some ten minutes.

"They was cruel enough to feed him up in the temple, because they said he was more of a god than old Daniel that was a man. Then they turned him out on the snow and told him to go home, and Peachey came home in about a

year, begging along the roads quite safe; for Daniel Dra-
vot, he walked before and said: 'Come along, Peachey.
It's a big thing we're doing.' The mountains, they danced
at night, and the mountains, they tried to fall on
Peachey's head, but Dan, he held up his hand, and
Peachey came along bent double. He never let go of
Dan's hand, and he never let go of Dan's head. They gave
it to him as a present in the temple to remind him not to
come again, and though the crown was pure gold, and
Peachey was starving, never would Peachey sell the same.
You knew Dravot, sir! You knew Right Worshipful
Brother Dravot! Look at him now!"

He fumbled in the mass of rags round his bent waist,
brought out a black horsehair bag embroidered with silver
thread, and shook therefrom onto my table the dried,
withered head of Daniel Dravot! The morning sun that
had long been paling the lamps struck the red beard and
blind, sunken eyes; struck, too, a heavy circlet of gold
studded with raw turquoises, that Carnehan placed ten-
derly on the battered temples.

"You be'old now," said Carnehan, "the emperor in his
'abit as he lived—the king of Kafiristan with his crown
upon his head. Poor old Daniel that was a monarch
once!"

I shuddered, for in spite of defacements manifold, I
recognized the head of the man of Manwar Junction.
Carnehan rose to go. I attempted to stop him. He was not
fit to walk abroad. "Let me take away the whisky, and give
me a little money," he gasped. "I was a king once. I'll go
to the deputy commissioner and ask to set in the
poorhouse till I get my health. No, thank you, I can't wait
till you get a carriage for me. I've urgent private affairs—in the South—at Marwar."

He shambled out of the office and departed in the
direction of the deputy commissioner's house. That day at
noon I had occasion to go down the blinding hot mall,
and I saw a crooked man crawling along the white dust of
the roadside, his hat in his hand, quavering dolorously after the fashion of street-singers at home. There was not a
soul in sight, and he was out of all possible earshot of the
houses. And he sang through his nose, turning his head
from right to left:

The son of man goes forth to war,
A golden crown to gain;
His blood-red banner streams afar—
Who follows in his train?

I waited to hear no more, but put the poor wretch into my carriage and drove him off to the nearest missionary for eventual transfer to the asylum. He repeated the hymn twice while he was with me, whom he did not in the least recognize, and I left him singing it to the missionary.

Two days later I inquired after his welfare of the superintendent of the asylum.

"He was admitted suffering from sun-stroke. He died early yesterday morning," said the superintendent. "Is it true that he was half an hour bare-headed in the sun at midday?"

"Yes," said I, "but do you happen to know if he had anything upon him by any chance when he died?"

"Not to my knowledge," said the superintendent.

And there the matter rests.

[First published in 1888–1890.]

WITHOUT BENEFIT
OF CLERGY

Before my Spring I garnered Autumn's gain,
Out of her time my field was white with grain,
   The year gave up her secrets to my woe.
Forced and deflowered each sick season lay,
In mystery of increase and decay;
I saw the sunset ere men saw the day,
   Who am too wise in that I should not know.

                             Bitter Waters

I

"But if it be a girl?"

"Lord of my life, it cannot be. I have prayed for so
many nights, and sent gifts to Sheikh Badl's shrine so
often, that I know God will give us a son—a man-child
that shall grow into a man. Think of this and be glad. My
mother shall be his mother till I can take him again, and
the mullah of the Pattan mosque shall cast his nativity—
God send he be born in an auspicious hour!—and then,
and then thou wilt never weary of me, thy slave."

"Since when hast thou been a slave, my queen?"

"Since the beginning—till this mercy came to me. How could I be sure of thy love when I knew that I had been bought with silver?"

"Nay, that was the dowry. I paid it to thy mother."

"And she has buried it, and sits upon it all day long like a hen. What talk is yours of dower! I was bought as though I had been a Lucknow dancing-girl instead of a child."

"Art thou sorry for the sale?"

"I have sorrowed, but today I am glad. Thou wilt never cease to love me now? Answer, my king."

"Never—never. No."

"Not even though the *mem-log*—the white women of thy own blood—love thee? And remember, I have watched them driving in the evening; they are very fair."

"I have seen fire-balloons by the hundred. I have seen the moon, and—then I saw no more fire-balloons."

Ameera clapped her hands and laughed. "Very good talk," she said. Then with an assumption of great stateliness, "It is enough. Thou hast my permission to depart—if thou wilt."

The man did not move. He was sitting on a low red-lacquered couch in a room furnished only with a blue and white floor-cloth, some rugs, and a very complete collection of native cushions. At his feet sat a woman of sixteen, and she was all but all the world in his eyes. By every rule and law she should have been otherwise, for he was an Englishman and she a Mussulman's daughter bought two years before from her mother, who, being left without money, would have sold Ameera shrieking to the Prince of Darkness if the price had been sufficient.

It was a contract entered into with a light heart; but even before the girl had reached her bloom she came to fill the greater portion of John Holden's life. For her, and the withered hag her mother, he had taken a little house overlooking the great red-walled city, and found—when the marigolds had sprung up by the well in the courtyard and Ameera had established herself according to her own ideas of comfort, and her mother had ceased grumbling at the inadequacy of the cooking-places, the distance from the daily market, and at matters of housekeeping in general—that the house was to him his home. Anyone could enter his bachelor's bungalow by day or night, and the life that he led there was an unlovely one. In the house in the city his feet only could pass beyond the outer courtyard to the women's rooms; and when the big wooden gate was bolted behind him he was king in his own territory, with Ameera for queen. And there was going to be added to this kingdom a third person, whose arrival Holden felt inclined to resent. It interfered with his perfect happiness. It disarranged the orderly peace of the house that was his own. But Ameera was wild with delight at the thought of it, and her mother not less so. The love of a man, and particularly a white man, was at the best an inconstant affair, but it might, both women argued, be held fast by a baby's hands. "And then," Ameera would always say, "then he will never care for the white *mem-log*. I hate them all—I hate them all."

"He will go back to his own people in time," said the mother; "but by the blessing of God that time is yet afar off."

Holden sat silent on the couch thinking of the future, and his thoughts were not pleasant. The drawbacks of a double life are manifold. The government, with singular care, had ordered him out of the station for a fortnight on special duty in the place of a man who was watching by the bedside of a sick wife. The verbal notification of the transfer had been edged by a cheerful remark that Holden ought to think himself lucky in being a bachelor and a free man. He came to break the news to Ameera.

"It is not good," she said slowly, "but it is not all bad. There is my mother here, and no harm will come to me—unless indeed I die of pure joy. Go thou to thy work and think no troublesome thoughts. When the days are done I believe—nay, I am sure. And—and then I shall lay *him* in thy arms, and thou wilt love me forever. The train goes tonight, at midnight is it not? Go now, and do not let thy heart be heavy by cause of me. But thou wilt not delay in returning? Thou wilt not stay on the road to talk to the bold white *mem-log*. Come back to me swiftly, my life."

As he left the courtyard to reach his horse that was tethered to the gate-post, Holden spoke to the white-haired old watchman who guarded the house and bade him un-

der certain contingencies dispatch the filled-up telegraph-
form that Holden gave him. It was all that could be done,
and with the sensations of a man who has attended his
own funeral Holden went away by the night mail to his
exile. Every hour of the day he dreaded the arrival of the
telegram, and every hour of the night he pictured to
himself the death of Ameera. In consequence his work for
the state was not of first-rate quality, nor was his temper
towards his colleagues of the most amiable. The fortnight
ended without a sign from his home, and torn to pieces by
his anxieties, Holden returned to be swallowed up for two
precious hours by a dinner at the club, wherein he heard,
as a man hears in a swoon, voices telling him how execra-
bly he had performed the other man's duties and how he
had endeared himself to all his associates. Then he fled on
horseback through the night with his heart in his mouth.
There was no answer at first to his blows on the gate, and
he had just wheeled his horse round to kick it in when Pir
Khan appeared with a lantern and held his stirrup.

"Has aught occurred?" said Holden.

"The news does not come from my mouth, Protector of
the Poor, but—" He held out his shaking hand as befitted
the bearer of good news who is entitled to a reward.

Holden hurried through the courtyard. A light burned
in the upper room. His horse neighed in the gateway, and
he heard a shrill little wail that sent all the blood into the
apple of his throat. It was a new voice, but it did not
prove that Ameera was alive.

"Who is there?" he called up the narrow brick staircase.

There was a cry of delight from Ameera, and then the
voice of the mother, tremulous with old age and pride:
"We be two women and—the—man—thy—son."

On the threshold of the room Holden stepped on a
naked dagger that was laid there to avert ill luck, and it
broke at the hilt under his impatient heel.

"God is great!" cooed Ameera in the half light. "Thou
hast taken his misfortunes on thy head."

"Aye, but how is it with thee, life of my life? Old
woman, how is it with her?"

"She has forgotten her sufferings for joy that the child

is born. There is no harm; but speak softly," said the mother.

"It only needed thy presence to make me all well," said Ameera. "My king, thou hast been very long away. What gifts hast thou for me? Ah, ah! It is I that bring gifts this time. Look, my life, look. Was there ever such a babe? Nay, I am too weak even to clear my arm from him."

"Rest, then, and do not talk. I am here, *bachari* [little woman]."

"Well said, for there is a bond and a heel-rope [*peecharee*] between us now that nothing can break. Look—canst thou see in this light? He is without spot or blemish. Never was such a man-child. *Ya illah!* He shall be a pundit—no, a trooper of the queen. And, my life, dost thou love me as well as ever, though I am faint and sick and worn? Answer truly."

"Yea. I love as I have loved, with all my soul. Lie still, pearl, and rest."

"Then do not go. Sit by my side here—so. Mother, the lord of this house needs a cushion. Bring it." There was an almost imperceptible movement on the part of the new life that lay in the hollow of Ameera's arm. "Aho!" she said, her voice breaking with love. "The babe is a champion from his birth. He is kicking me in the side with mighty kicks. Was there ever such a babe? And he is ours to us—thine and mine. Put thy hand on his head, but carefully, for he is very young, and men are unskilled in such matters."

Very cautiously Holden touched with the tips of his fingers the downy head.

"He is of the faith," said Ameera, "for lying here in the night-watches I whispered the call to prayer and the profession of faith into his ears. And it is most marvellous that he was born upon a Friday, as I was born. Be careful of him, my life; but he can almost grip with his hands."

Holden found one helpless little hand that closed feebly on his finger. And the clutch ran through his body till it settled about his heart. Till then his sole thought had been for Ameera. He began to realize that there was someone else in the world, but he could not feel that it was a veritable son with a soul. He sat down to think, and Ameera dozed lightly.

"Get hence, Sahib," said her mother under her breath. "It is not good that she should find you here on waking. She must be still."

"I go," said Holden submissively. "Here be rupees. See that my *baba* gets fat and finds all that he needs."

The chink of the silver roused Ameera. "I am his mother, and no hireling," she said weakly. "Shall I look to him more or less for the sake of money? Mother, give it back. I have borne my lord a son."

The deep sleep of weakness came upon her almost before the sentence was completed. Holden went down to the courtyard very softly with his heart at ease. Pir Khan, the old watchman, was chuckling with delight. "This house is now complete," he said, and without further comment thrust into Holden's hands, the hilt of a sabre worn many years ago when he, Pir Khan, served the queen in the police. The bleat of a tethered goat came from the well-kerb.

"There be two," said Pir Khan, "two goats of the best. I bought them, and they cost much money; and since there is no birth-party assembled their flesh will be all mine. Strike craftily, Sahib! 'Tis an ill-balanced sabre at the best. Wait till they raise their heads from cropping the marigolds."

"And why?" said Holden, bewildered.

"For the birth-sacrifice. What else? Otherwise the child being unguarded from fate may die. The Protector of the Poor knows the fitting words to be said."

Holden had learned them once with little thought that he would ever speak them in earnest. The touch of the cold sabre-hilt in his palm turned suddenly to the clinging grip of the child upstairs—the child that was his own son—and a dread of loss filled him.

"Strike!" said Pir Khan. "Never life came into the world but life was paid for it. See, the goats have raised their heads. Now! With a drawing cut!"

Hardly knowing what he did, Holden cut twice as he muttered the Muhammadan prayer that runs: "Almighty! In place of this my son I offer life for life, blood for blood, head for head, bone for bone, hair for hair, skin for skin." The waiting horse snorted and bounded in his pickets at the smell of the raw blood that spurted over Holden's riding-boots.

"Well smitten!" said Pir Khan, wiping the sabre. "A swordsman was lost in thee. Go with a light heart, Heaven-born. I am thy servant, and the servant of thy son. May the Presence live a thousand years and—the flesh of the goats is all mine?" Pir Khan drew back richer, by a month's pay. Holden swung himself into the saddle and rode off through the low-hanging wood smoke of the evening. He was full of riotous exultation, alternating with a vast vague tenderness directed towards no particular object, that made him choke as he bent over the neck of his uneasy horse. "I never felt like this in my life," he thought. "I'll go to the club and pull myself together."

A game of pool was beginning, and the room was full of men. Holden entered, eager to get to the light and the company of his fellows, singing at the top of his voice:

"In Baltimore a-walking, a lady I did meet!"

"Did you?" said the club secretary from his corner. "Did she happen to tell you that your boots were wringing wet? Great goodness, man, it's blood!"

"Bosh!" said Holden, picking his cue from the rack. "May I cut in? It's dew. I've been riding through high crops. My faith! My boots are in a mess though!

"And if it be a girl she shall wear a wedding-ring,
  And if it be a boy he shall fight for his king,
  With his dirk, and his cap, and his little jacket blue,
  He shall walk the quarter-deck——"

"Yellow on blue—green next player," said the marker monotonously.

" 'He shall walk the quarter-deck—' Am I green, marker? 'He shall walk the quarter-deck—' Eh! That's a bad shot. 'As his daddy used to do!' "

"I don't see that you have anything to crow about," said a zealous junior civilian acidly. "The government is not exactly pleased with your work when you relieved Sanders."

"Does that mean a wigging from headquarters?" said Holden with an abstracted smile. "I think I can stand it."

The talk beat up round the ever-fresh subject of each man's work and steadied Holden till it was time to go to his dark empty bungalow, where his butler received him as one who knew all his affairs. Holden remained awake for the greater part of the night, and his dreams were pleasant ones.

II

"How old is he now?"

"*Ya illah!* What a man's question! He is all but six weeks old; and on this night I go up to the housetop with thee, my life, to count the stars. For that is auspicious. And he was born on a Friday under the sign of the Sun, and it has been told to me that he will outlive us both and get wealth. Can we wish for aught better, beloved?"

"There is nothing better. Let us go up to the roof, and thou shalt count the stars—but a few only, for the sky is heavy with cloud."

"The winter rains are late, and maybe they come out of season. Come, before all the stars are hid. I have put on my richest jewels."

"Thou hast forgotten the best of all."

"*Ai!* Ours. He comes also. He has never yet seen the skies."

Ameera climbed the narrow staircase that led to the flat roof. The child, placid and unwinking, lay in the hollow of her right arm, gorgeous in silver-fringed muslin with a small skull-cap on his head. Ameera wore all that she valued most—the diamond nose-stud that takes the place of the Western patch in drawing attention to the curve of the nostril, the gold ornament in the centre of the forehead studded with tallow-drop emeralds and flawed rubies, the heavy circlet of beaten gold that was fastened round her neck by the softness of the pure metal, and the chinking curb-patterned silver anklets hanging low over the rosy ankle-bone. She was dressed in jade-green muslin as befitted a daughter of the faith, and from shoulder to elbow and elbow to wrist ran bracelets of silver tied with floss silk, frail glass bangles slipped over the wrist in proof of the slenderness of the hand, and certain heavy gold bracelets that had no part in her country's ornaments, but, since they were Holden's gift and fastened with a cunning European snap, delighted her immensely.

They sat down by the low white parapet of the roof, overlooking the city and its lights.

"They are happy down there," said Ameera. "But I do not think that they are as happy as we. Nor do I think the white *mem-log* are as happy. And thou?"

"I know they are not."

"How dost thou know?"

"They give their children over to the nurses."

"I have never seen that," said Ameera with a sigh, "nor do I wish to see. *Ahi!*" She dropped her head on Holden's shoulder. "I have counted forty stars, and I am tired. Look at the child, love of my life; he is counting too."

The baby was staring with round eyes at the dark of the heavens. Ameera placed him in Holden's arms, and he lay there without a cry.

"What shall we call him among ourselves?" she said. "Look! Art thou ever tired of looking? He carries thy very eyes. But the mouth——"

"Is thine, most dear. Who should know better than I?"

"'Tis a feeble mouth. Oh, so small! And yet it holds my heart between its lips. Give him to me now. He has been too long away."

"Nay, let him lie; he has not yet begun to cry."

"When he cries thou wilt give him back—eh? What a man of mankind thou art! If he cried he were only the dearer to me. But, my life, what little name shall we give him?"

The small body lay close to Holden's heart. It was utterly helpless and very soft. He scarcely dared to breathe for fear of crushing it. The caged green parrot that is regarded as a sort of guardian spirit in most native households moved on its perch and fluttered a drowsy wing.

"There is the answer," said Holden. "Mian Mittu has spoken. He shall be the parrot. When he is ready he will talk mightily and run about. Mian Mittu is the parrot in thy—in the Mussulman tongue, is it not?"

"Why put me so far off?" said Ameera fretfully. "Let it

be like unto some English name—but not wholly. For he is mine."

"Then call him Tota, for that is likest English."

"Aye, Tota, and that is still the parrot. Forgive me, my lord, for a minute ago, but in truth he is too little to wear all the weight of Mian Mittu for name. He shall be Tota—our Tota to us. Hearest thou, O small one? Littlest, thou art Tota." She touched the child's cheek, and he waking wailed, and it was necessary to return him to his mother, who soothed him with the wonderful rhyme of *Aré koko, Jaré koko!* which says:

> Oh, crow! Go, crow! Baby's sleeping sound,
> And the wild plums grow in the jungle,
>   only a penny a pound.
> Only a penny a pound, *baba*, only a penny a pound.

Reassured many times as to the price of those plums, Tota cuddled himself down to sleep. The two sleek white well-bullocks in the courtyard were steadily chewing the cud of their evening meal; old Pir Khan squatted at the head of Holden's horse, his police sabre across his knees, pulling drowsily at a big water-pipe that croaked like a bull-frog in a pond. Ameera's mother sat spinning in the lower veranda, and the wooden gate was shut and barred. The music of a marriage procession came to the roof above the gentle hum of the city, and a string of flying foxes crossed the face of the low moon.

"I have prayed," said Ameera after a long pause, "I have prayed for two things. First, that I may die in thy stead if thy death is demanded, and in the second that I may die in the place of the child. I have prayed to the Prophet and to Beebee Miriam [the Virgin Mary]. Thinkest thou either will hear?"

"From thy lips who would not hear the lightest word?"

"I asked for straight talk, and thou hast given me sweet talk. Will my prayers be heard?"

"How can I say? God is very good."

"Of that I am not sure. Listen now. When I die, or the child dies, what is thy fate? Living, thou wilt return to the bold white *mem-log*, for kind calls to kind."

"Not always."

"With a woman, no; with a man it is otherwise. Thou wilt in this life, later on, go back to thine own folk. That I could almost endure, for I should be dead. But in thy very death thou wilt be taken away to a strange place and a paradise that I do not know."

"Will it be paradise?"

"Surely, for who would harm thee? But we two—I and the child—shall be elsewhere, and we cannot come to thee, nor canst thou come to us. In the old days, before the child was born, I did not think of these things; but now I think of them always. It is very hard talk."

"It will fall as it will fall. Tomorrow we do not know, but today and love we know well. Surely we are happy now."

"So happy that it were well to make our happiness assured. And thy Beebee Miriam should listen to me, for she is also a woman. But then she would envy me! It is not seemly for men to worship a woman."

Holden laughed aloud at Ameera's little spasm of jealousy.

"Is it not seemly? Why didst thou not turn me from worship of thee, then?"

"Thou a worshipper! And of me? My king, for all thy sweet words, well I know that I am thy servant and thy slave, and the dust under thy feet. And I would not have it otherwise. See!"

Before Holden could prevent her she stooped forward and touched his feet; recovering herself with a little laugh, she hugged Tota closer to her bosom. Then, almost savagely: "Is it true that the bold white *mem-log* live for three times the length of my life? Is it true that they make their marriages not before they are old women?"

"They marry as do others, when they are women."

"That I know, but they wed when they are twenty-five. Is that true?"

"That is true."

"*Ya illah!* At twenty-five! Who would of his own will take a wife even of eighteen? She is a woman—aging every hour. Twenty-five! I shall be an old woman at that age, and— Those *mem-log* remain young forever. How I hate them!"

"What have they to do with us?"

"I cannot tell. I know only that there may now be alive on this earth a woman ten years older than I who may come to thee and take thy love ten years after I am an old woman, grey-headed, and the nurse of Tota's son. That is unjust and evil. They should die too."

"Now, for all thy years thou art a child, and shalt be picked up and carried down the staircase."

"Tota! Have a care for Tota, my lord! Thou at least art as foolish as any babe!" Ameera tucked Tota out of harm's way in the hollow of her neck, and was carried downstairs laughing in Holden's arms, while Tota opened his eyes and smiled after the manner of the lesser angels.

He was a silent infant, and almost before Holden could realize that he was in the world, developed into a small gold-coloured little god and unquestioned despot of the house overlooking the city. Those were months of absolute happiness to Holden and Ameera—happiness withdrawn from the world, shut in behind the wooden gate that Pir Khan guarded. By day Holden did his work with an immense pity for such as were not so fortunate as himself, and a sympathy for small children that amazed and amused many mothers at the little station-gatherings. At nightfall he returned to Ameera—Ameera, full of the wondrous doings of Tota: how he had been seen to clap his hands together and move his fingers with intention and purpose—which was manifestly a miracle—how later he had of his own initiative crawled out of his low bedstead on to the floor and swayed on both feet for the space of three breaths.

"And they were long breaths, for my heart stood still with delight," said Ameera.

Then Tota took the beasts into his councils—the well-bullocks, the little grey squirrels, the mongoose that lived in a hole near the well, and especially Mian Mittu, the parrot, whose tail he grievously pulled, and Mian Mittu screamed till Ameera and Holden arrived.

"O villain! Child of strength! This to thy brother on the housetop! *Tobah, tobah!* Fie! Fie! But I know a charm to make him wise as Suleiman and Aflatoun [Solomon and Plato]. Now look," said Ameera. She drew from an embroidered bag a handful of almonds. "See! We count seven. In the name of God!"

She placed Mian Mittu, very angry and rumpled, on the top of his cage, and seating herself between the babe and the bird, she cracked and peeled an almond less white than her teeth. "This is a true charm, my life, and do not laugh. See! I give the parrot one half and Tota the other." Mian Mittu with careful beak took his share from between Ameera's lips, and she kissed the other half into the mouth of the child, who ate it slowly with wondering eyes. "This I will do each day of seven, and without doubt he who is ours will be a bold speaker and wise. Eh, Tota, what wilt thou be when thou art a man and I am grey-headed?" Tota tucked his fat legs into adorable creases. He could crawl, but he was not going to waste the spring of his youth in idle speech. He wanted Mian Mittu's tail to tweak.

When he was advanced to the dignity of a silver belt— which, with a magic square engraved on silver and hung round his neck, made up the greater part of his clothing—he staggered on a perilous journey down the garden to Pir Khan and proffered him all his jewels in exchange for one little ride on Holden's horse, having seen his mother's mother chaffering with pedlars in the veranda. Pir Khan wept and set the untired feet on his own grey head in sign of fealty, and brought the bold adventurer to his mother's arms, vowing that Tota would be a leader of men ere his beard was grown.

One hot evening while he sat on the roof between his father and mother watching the never-ending warfare of the kites that the city boys flew, he demanded a kite of his own with Pir Khan to fly it, because he had a fear of dealing with anything larger than himself; and when Holden called him a spark, he rose to his feet and answered slowly in defence of his new-found individuality, *"Hum 'park nahin hai. Hum admi hai* [I am no spark, but a man]."

The protest made Holden choke and devote himself very seriously to a consideration of Tota's future. He need hardly have taken the trouble. The delight of that life was too perfect to endure. Therefore it was taken away as many things are taken away in India—suddenly and without warning. The little lord of the house, as Pir Khan called him, grew sorrowful and complained of pains who had never known the meaning of pain. Ameera, wild with terror, watched him through the night, and in the dawning of the second day the life was shaken out of him by fever—the seasonal autumn fever. It seemed altogether impossible that he could die, and neither Ameera nor Holden at first believed the evidence of the little body on the bedstead. Then Ameera beat her head against the wall and would have flung herself down the well in the garden had Holden not restrained her by main force.

One mercy only was granted to Holden. He rode to his office in broad daylight and found waiting him an unusually heavy mail that demanded concentrated attention and hard work. He was not, however, alive to this kindness of the gods.

III

The first shock of a bullet is no more than a brisk pinch. The wrecked body does not send in its protest to the soul till ten or fifteen seconds later. Holden realized his pain slowly, exactly as he had realized his happiness, and with the same imperious necessity for hiding all trace of it. In the beginning he only felt that there had been a loss and that Ameera needed comforting, where she sat with her head on her knees shivering as Mian Mittu from the housetop called "Tota! Tota! Tota!" Later all his world and the daily life of it rose up to hurt him. It was an outrage that any one of the children at the bandstand in the evening should be alive and clamourous when his own child lay dead. It was more than mere pain when one of them touched him, and stories told by overfond fathers of their children's latest performances cut him to the quick. He could not declare his pain. He had neither help, comfort, nor sympathy; and Ameera at the end of each weary day would lead him through the hell of self-questioning reproach which is reserved for those who have lost a child and believe that with a little—just a little—more care it might have been saved.

"Perhaps," Ameera would say, "I did not take sufficient heed. Did I, or did I not? The sun on the roof that day when he played so long alone and I was—*ahi!* braiding my hair—it may be that the sun then bred the fever.

If I had warned him from the sun he might have lived. But, O my life, say that I am guiltless! Thou knowest that I loved him as I love thee. Say that there is no blame on me, or I shall die—I shall die!"

"There is no blame—before God, none. It was written and how could we do aught to save? What has been, has been. Let it go, beloved."

"He was all my heart to me. How can I let the thought go when my arm tells me every night that he is not here? *Ahi! Ahi!* O Tota, come back to me—come back again, and let us be all together as it was before!"

"Peace, peace! For thine own sake, and for mine also, if thou lovest me—rest."

"By this I know thou dost not care; and how shouldst thou? The white men have hearts of stone and souls of iron. Oh, that I had married a man of mine own people—though he beat me—and had never eaten the bread of an alien!"

"Am I an alien—mother of my son?"

"What else, Sahib? Oh, forgive me—forgive! The death has driven me mad. Thou art the life of my heart and the light of my eyes and the bread of my life, and—and I have put thee from me, though it was but for a moment. If thou goest away, to whom shall I look for help? Do not be angry. Indeed, it was the pain that spoke, and not thy slave."

"I know, I know. We be two who were three. The greater need therefore that we should be one."

They were sitting on the roof as of custom. The night was a warm one in early spring, and sheet-lightning was dancing on the horizon to a broken tune played by far-off thunder. Ameera settled herself in Holden's arms.

"The dry earth is lowing like a cow for the rain, and I—I am afraid. It was not like this when we counted the stars. But thou lovest me as much as before, though a bond is taken away? Answer!"

"I love more because a new bond has come out of the sorrow that we have eaten together, and that thou knowest."

"Yea, I knew," said Ameera in a very small whisper. "But it is good to hear thee say so, my life, who art so strong to help. I will be a child no more, but a woman and an aid to thee. Listen! Give me my *sitar* and I will sing bravely."

She took the light silver-studded *sitar* and began a song of the great hero Rajah Rasalu. The hand failed on the strings, the tune halted, checked, and at a low note turned off to the poor little nursery rhyme about the wicked crow:

> And the wild plums grow in the jungle,
>   only a penny a pound.
> Only a penny a pound, *baba* — only—

Then came the tears, and the piteous rebellion against fate till she slept, moaning a little in her sleep, with the right arm thrown clear of the body as though it protected something that was not there. It was after this night that life became a little easier for Holden. The ever-present pain of loss drove him into his work, and the work repaid him by filling up his mind for nine or ten hours a day. Ameera sat alone in the house and brooded, but grew happier when she understood that Holden was more at ease, according to the custom of women. They touched happiness again, but this time with caution.

"It was because we loved Tota that he died. The jealousy of God was upon us," said Ameera. "I have hung up a large black jar before our window to turn the evil eye from us, and we must make no protestations of delight, but go softly underneath the stars, lest God find us out. Is that not good talk, worthless one?"

She had shifted the accent on the word that means beloved, in proof of the sincerity of her purpose. But the kiss that followed the new christening was a thing that any deity might have envied. They went about henceforward saying, "It is naught, it is naught," and hoping that all the Powers heard.

The Powers were busy on other things. They had allowed thirty million people four years of plenty wherein men fed well and the crops were certain, and the birth-rate rose year by year; the districts reported a purely agricultural population varying from nine hundred to two thousand to the square mile of the overburdened earth; and the member for Lower Tooting, wandering about In-

dia in pot-hat and frock-coat, talked largely of the bene-
fits of British rule and suggested as the one thing needful
the establishment of a duly qualified electoral system and
a general bestowal of the franchise. His long-suffering
hosts smiled and made him welcome, and when he paused
to admire with pretty picked words the blossom of the
blood-red *dhak*-tree that had flowered untimely for a sign
of what was coming, they smiled more than ever.

It was the deputy commissioner of Kot-Kumharsen,
staying at the club for a day, who lightly told a tale that
made Holden's blood run cold as he overheard the end.

"He won't bother anyone anymore. Never saw a man
so astonished in my life. By Jove, I thought he meant to
ask a question in the House about it. Fellow passenger in
his ship—dined next him—bowled over by cholera and
died in eighteen hours. You needn't laugh, you fellows.
The member for Lower Tooting is awfully angry about it,
but he's more scared. I think he's going to take his en-
lightened self out of India."

"I'd give a good deal if he were knocked over. It might
keep a few vestrymen of his kidney to their own parish.
But what's this about cholera? It's fully early for anything
of that kind," said the warden of an unprofitable salt-lick.

"Don't know," said the deputy commissioner reflectively. "We've got locusts with us. There's sporadic cholera
all along the north—at least we're calling it sporadic for
decency's sake. The spring crops are short in five districts,
and nobody seems to know where the rains are. It's
nearly March now. I don't want to scare anybody, but it
seems to me that Nature's going to audit her accounts
with a big red pencil this summer."

"Just when I wanted to take leave, too!" said a voice
across the room.

"There won't be much leave this year, but there ought
to be a great deal of promotion. I've come in to persuade
the government to put my pet canal on the list of famine-
relief works. It's an ill wind that blows no good. I shall
get that canal finished at last."

"Is it the old programme then," said Holden; "famine,
fever, and cholera?"

"Oh, no. Only local scarcity and an unusual prevalence
of seasonal sickness. You'll find it all in the reports if you

live till next year. You're a lucky chap. *You* haven't got a wife to send out of harm's way. The hill stations ought to be full of women this year."

"I think you're inclined to exaggerate the talk in the bazaars," said a young civilian in the Secretariat. "Now, I have observed——"

"I daresay you have," said the deputy commissioner, "but you've a great deal more to observe, my son. In the meantime, I wish to observe to you——" And he drew him aside to discuss the construction of the canal that was so dear to his heart. Holden went to his bungalow and began to understand that he was not alone in the world, and also that he was afraid for the sake of another, which is the most soul-satisfying fear known to man.

Two months later, as the deputy had foretold, Nature began to audit her accounts with a red pencil. On the heels of the spring reapings came a cry for bread, and the government, which had decreed that no man should die of want, sent wheat. Then came the cholera from all four quarters of the compass. It struck a pilgrim-gathering of half a million at a sacred shrine. Many died at the feet of their god; the others broke and ran over the face of the land, carrying the pestilence with them. It smote a walled city and killed two hundred a day. The people crowded the trains, hanging on to the footboards and squatting on the roofs of the carriages, and the cholera followed them, for at each station they dragged out the dead and the dying. They died by the roadside, and the horses of the Englishmen shied at the corpses in the grass. The rains did not come, and the earth turned to iron lest man should escape death by hiding in her. The English sent their wives away to the hills and went about their work, coming forward as they were bidden to fill the gaps in the fighting-line. Holden, sick with fear of losing his chiefest treasure on earth, had done his best to persuade Ameera to go away with her mother to the Himalayas.

"Why should I go?" said she one evening on the roof.

"There is sickness, and people are dying, and all the white *mem-log* have gone."

"All of them?"

"All—unless perhaps there remain some old scald-head who vexes her husband's heart by running risk of death."

"Nay; who stays is my sister, and thou must not abuse her, for I will be a scald-head too. I am glad all the bold *mem-log* are gone."

"Do I speak to a woman or a babe? Go to the hills and I will see to it that thou goest like a queen's daughter. Think, child. In a red-lacquered bullock-cart, veiled and curtained, with brass peacocks upon the pole and red cloth hangings. I will send two orderlies for guard, and——"

"Peace! Thou art the babe in speaking thus. What use are those toys to me? *He* would have patted the bullocks and played with the housings. For his sake, perhaps—thou hast made me very English—I might have gone. Now I will not. Let the *mem-log* run."

"Their husbands are sending them, beloved."

"Very good talk. Since when hast thou been my husband to tell me what to do? I have but borne thee a son. Thou art only all the desire of my soul to me. How shall I depart when I know that if evil befall thee by the breadth of so much as my littlest fingernail—is that not small?—I should be aware of it though I were in paradise. And here, this summer thou mayest die—*ai, janee*, die!—and in dying they might call to tend thee a white woman, and she would rob me in the last of thy love!"

"But love is not born in a moment or on a death-bed!"

"What dost thou know of love, stoneheart? She would take thy thanks at least, and by God and the Prophet and Beebee Miriam the mother of thy Prophet, that I will never endure. My lord and my love, let there be no more foolish talk of going away. Where thou art, I am. It is enough." She put an arm round his neck and a hand on his mouth.

There are not many happinesses so complete as those that are snatched under the shadow of the sword. They sat together and laughed, calling each other openly by every pet name that could move the wrath of the gods. The city below them was locked up in its own torments. Sulphur fires blazed in the streets; the conchs in the Hindu temples screamed and bellowed, for the gods were inattentive in those days. There was a service in the great Muhammadan shrine, and the call to prayer from the minarets was almost unceasing. They heard the wailing in the houses of the dead, and once the shriek of a mother who had lost a child and was calling for its return. In the grey dawn they saw the dead borne out through the city gates, each litter with its own little knot of mourners. Wherefore they kissed each other and shivered.

It was a red and heavy audit, for the land was very sick and needed a little breathing-space ere the torrent of cheap life should flood it anew. The children of immature fathers and undeveloped mothers made no resistance. They were cowed and sat still, waiting till the sword should be sheathed in November if it were so willed. There were gaps among the English, but the gaps were filled. The work of superintending famine-relief, cholera-sheds, medicine-distribution, and what little sanitation was possible went forward because it was so ordered.

Holden had been told to keep himself in readiness to move to replace the next man who should fall. There were twelve hours in each day when he could not see Ameera, and she might die in three. He was considering what his pain would be if he could not see her for three months, or if she died out of his sight. He was absolutely certain that her death would be demanded—so certain that when he looked up from the telegram and saw Pir Khan breathless in the doorway he laughed aloud. "And?" said he.

"When there is a cry in the night and the spirit flutters into the throat, who has a charm that will restore? Come swiftly, Heaven-born! It is the black cholera."

Holden galloped to his home. The sky was heavy with clouds, for the long-deferred rains were near and the heat was stifling. Ameera's mother met him in the courtyard, whimpering, "She is dying. She is nursing herself into death. She is all but dead. What shall I do, Sahib?"

Ameera was lying in the room in which Tota had been born. She made no sign when Holden entered, because the human soul is a very lonely thing and, when it is getting ready to go away, hides itself in a misty borderland where the living may not follow. The black cholera does its work quietly and without explanation. Ameera was being thrust out of life as though the Angel of Death had himself put his hand upon her. The quick breathing seemed to show that she was either afraid or in pain, but neither eyes nor mouth gave any answer to Holden's kisses. There was nothing to be said or done. Holden could only wait and suffer. The first drops of the rain began to fall on the roof, and he could hear shouts of joy in the parched city.

The soul came back a little and the lips moved. Holden bent down to listen. "Keep nothing of mine," said Ameera. "Take no hair from my head. *She* would make thee burn it later on. That flame I should feel. Lower! Stoop lower! Remember only that I was thine and bore thee a son. Though thou wed a white woman tomorrow, the pleasure of receiving in thy arms thy first son is taken from thee forever. Remember me when thy son is born— the one that shall carry thy name before all men. His misfortunes be on my head. I bear witness—I bear witness"—the lips were forming the words on his ear— "that there is no God but—thee, beloved!"

Then she died. Holden sat still, and all thought was taken from him till he heard Ameera's mother lift the curtain.

"Is she dead, Sahib?"

"She is dead."

"Then I will mourn, and afterwards take an inventory of the furniture in this house. For that will be mine. The Sahib does not mean to resume it? It is so little, so very little, Sahib, and I am an old woman. I would like to lie softly."

"For the mercy of God be silent awhile. Go out and mourn where I cannot hear."

"Sahib, she will be buried in four hours."

"I know the custom. I shall go ere she is taken away. That matter is in thy hands. Look to it, that the bed on which—on which she lies——"

"Aha! That beautiful red-lacquered bed. I have long desired——"

"That the bed is left here untouched for my disposal. All else in the house is thine. Hire a cart, take everything, go hence, and before sunrise let there be nothing in this house but that which I have ordered thee to respect."

"I am an old woman. I would stay at least for the days

of mourning, and the rains have just broken. Whither shall I go?"

"What is that to me? My order is that there is a going. The house gear is worth a thousand rupees, and my orderly shall bring thee a hundred rupees tonight."

"That is very little. Think of the cart-hire."

"It shall be nothing unless thou goest, and with speed. O woman, get hence and leave me with my dead!"

The mother shuffled down the staircase, and in her anxiety to take stock of the house-fittings forgot to mourn. Holden stayed by Ameera's side and the rain roared on the roof. He could not think connectedly by reason of the noise, though he made many attempts to do so. Then four sheeted ghosts glided dripping into the room and stared at him through their veils. They were the washers of the dead. Holden left the room and went out to his horse. He had come in a dead, stifling calm through ankle-deep dust. He found the courtyard a rain-lashed pond alive with frogs; a torrent of yellow water ran under the gate, and a roaring wind drove the bolts of rain like buckshot against the mud walls. Pir Khan was shivering in his little hut by the gate and the horse was stamping uneasily in the water.

"I have been told the Sahib's order," said Pir Khan. "It is well. This house is now desolate. I go also, for my monkey-face would be a reminder of that which has been. Concerning the bed, I will bring that to thy house yonder in the morning; but remember, Sahib, it will be to thee a knife turning in a green wound. I go upon a pilgrimage, and I will take no money. I have grown fat in the protection of the Presence whose sorrow is my sorrow. For the last time I hold his stirrup."

He touched Holden's foot with both hands and the horse sprang out into the road, where the creaking bamboos were whipping the sky and all the frogs were chuckling.

Holden could not see for the rain in his face. He put his hands before his eyes and muttered, "Oh, you brute! You utter brute!"

The news of his trouble was already in his bungalow. He read the knowledge in his butler's eyes when Ahmed Khan brought in food, and for the first and last time in

his life laid a hand upon his master's shoulder, saying,
"Eat, Sahib, eat. Meat is good against sorrow. I also have
known. Moreover, the shadows come and go, Sahib; the
shadows come and go. These be curried eggs."

Holden could neither eat nor sleep. The heavens sent
down eight inches of rain in that night and washed the
earth clean. The waters tore down walls, broke roads, and
scoured open the shallow graves on the Muhammadan
burying-ground. All next day it rained, and Holden sat
still in his house considering his sorrow. On the morning
of the third day he received a telegram which said only,
"Ricketts, Myndonie. Dying. Holden relieve. Immediate."
Then he thought that before he departed he would look at
the house wherein he had been master and lord. There
was a break in the weather, and the rank earth steamed
with vapour.

He found that the rains had torn down the mud pillars
of the gateway, and the heavy wooden gate that had
guarded his life hung lazily from one hinge. There was
grass three inches high in the courtyard; Pir Khan's lodge
was empty, and the sodden thatch sagged between the
beams. A grey squirrel was in possession of the veranda,
as if the house had been untenanted for thirty years instead of three days. Ameera's mother had removed everything except some mildewed matting. The "tick-tick" of
the little scorpions as they hurried across the floor was the
only sound in the house. Ameera's room and the other
one where Tota had lived were heavy with mildew, and
the narrow staircase leading to the roof was streaked and
stained with rain-borne mud. Holden saw all these things
and came out again to meet in the road Durga Dass, his
landlord—portly, affable, clothed in white muslin, and
driving a Cee-spring buggy. He was overlooking his
property to see how the roofs stood the stress of the first
rains.

"I have heard," said he, "you will not take this place
any more, Sahib?"

"What are you going to do with it?"

"Perhaps I shall let it again."

"Then I will keep it on while I am away."

Durga Dass was silent for some time. "You shall not
take it on, Sahib," he said. "When I was a young man I

also— But today I am a member of the municipality. Ho! Ho! No. When the birds have gone, what need to keep the nest? I will have it pulled down—the timber will sell for something always. It shall be pulled down, and the municipality shall make a road across, as they desire, from the burning-ghaut to the city wall, so that no man may say where this house stood."

[First published in 1890.]

THE MARK
OF THE BEAST

❧

Your gods and my gods—do you or I know
which are the stronger?   *Native Proverb*

East of Suez, some hold, the direct control of Providence
ceases, man being there handed over to the power of the
gods and devils of Asia, and the Church of England Providence only exercising an occasional and modified super-
vision in the case of Englishmen.

This theory accounts for some of the more unnecessary
horrors of life in India; it may be stretched to explain my
story.

My friend Strickland of the police, who knows as much
of natives of India as is good for any man, can bear
witness to the facts of the case. Dumoise, our doctor, also
saw what Strickland and I saw. The inference which he
drew from the evidence was entirely incorrect. He is dead
now; he died in a rather curious manner, which has been
elsewhere described.

When Fleete came to India he owned a little money
and some land in the Himalayas, near a place called
Dharmsala. Both properties had been left him by an

61

uncle, and he came out to finance them. He was a big, heavy, genial, and inoffensive man. His knowledge of natives was, of course, limited, and he complained of the difficulties of the language.

He rode in from his place in the hills to spend New Year in the station, and he stayed with Strickland. On New Year's Eve there was a big dinner at the club, and the night was excusably wet. When men foregather from the uttermost ends of the empire, they have a right to be riotous. The frontier had sent down a contingent o' Catch-'em-Alive-O's who had not seen twenty white faces for a year, and were used to ride fifteen miles to dinner at the next fort at the risk of a Khyberee bullet where their drinks should lie. They profited by their new security, for they tried to play pool with a curled-up hedgehog found in the garden, and one of them carried the marker round the room in his teeth. Half a dozen planters had come in from the south and were talking "horse" to the Biggest Liar in Asia, who was trying to cap all their stories at once. Everybody was there, and there was a general closing up of ranks and taking stock of our losses in dead or disabled that had fallen during the past year. It was a very wet night, and I remember that we sang "Auld Lang Syne" with our feet in the Polo Championship Cup and our heads among the stars, and swore that we were all dear friends. Then some of us went away and annexed Burma, and some tried to open up the Sudan and were opened up by Fuzzies in that cruel scrub outside Suakin, and some found stars and medals, and some were married, which was bad, and some did other things which were worse, and the others of us stayed in our chains and strove to make money on insufficient experiences.

Fleete began the night with sherry and bitters, drank champagne steadily up to dessert, then raw, rasping Capri with all the strength of whisky, took Benedictine with his coffee, four or five whiskies and sodas to improve his pool strokes, beer and bones at half past two, winding up with old brandy. Consequently, when he came out at half past three in the morning into fourteen degrees of frost, he was very angry with his horse for coughing, and tried to leap-frog into the saddle. The horse broke away and went to

his stables, so Strickland and I formed a Guard of Dis-
honour to take Fleete home.

Our road lay through the bazaar, close to a little
temple of Hanuman, the monkey-god, who is a leading
divinity worthy of respect. All gods have good points, just
as have all priests. Personally, I attach much importance
to Hanuman, and am kind to his people—the great grey.
apes of the hills. One never knows when one may want a
friend.

There was a light in the temple, and as we passed we
could hear voices of men chanting hymns. In a native
temple the priests rise at all hours of the night to do
honour to their god. Before we could stop him Fleete
dashed up the steps, patted two priests on the back, and
was gravely grinding the ashes of his cigar-butt into the
forehead of the red stone image of Hanuman. Strickland
tried to drag him out, but he sat down and said solemnly,
"Shee that? Mark of the b-beasht! *I* made it. Ishn't it
fine?"

In half a minute the temple was alive and noisy, and
Strickland, who knew what came of polluting gods, said
that things might occur. He, by virtue of his official position, long residence in the country, and weakness for going among the natives, was known to the priests, and he
felt unhappy. Fleete sat on the ground and refused to
move. He said that "good old Hanuman" made a very
soft pillow.

Then, without any warning, a silver man came out of a
recess behind the image of the god. He was perfectly
naked in that bitter, bitter cold, and his body shone like
frosted silver, for he was what the Bible calls a "leper as
white as snow." Also he had no face, because he was a
leper of some years' standing, and his disease was heavy
upon him. We two stooped to haul Fleete up, and the
temple was filling and filling with folk who seemed to
spring from the earth, when the silver man ran in under
our arms, making a noise exactly like the mewing of an
otter, caught Fleete round the body, and dropped his head
on Fleete's breast before we could wrench him away.
Then he retired to a corner and sat mewing while the
crowd blocked all the doors.

The priests were very angry until the silver man touched Fleete. That nuzzling seemed to sober them.

At the end of a few minutes' silence one of the priests came to Strickland and said in perfect English, "Take your friend away. He has done with Hanuman, but Hanuman has not done with him." The crowd gave room and we carried Fleete into the road.

Strickland was very angry. He said that we might all three have been knifed and that Fleete should thank his stars that he had escaped without injury.

Fleete thanked no one. He said that he wanted to go to bed. He was gorgeously drunk.

We moved on, Strickland silent and wrathful, until Fleete was taken with violent shivering fits and sweating. He said that the smells of the bazaar were overpowering, and he wondered why slaughter-houses were permitted so near English residences. "Can't you smell the blood?" said Fleete.

We put him to bed at last, just as the dawn was breaking, and Strickland invited me to have another whisky and soda. While we were drinking he talked of the trouble in the temple and admitted that it baffled him completely. Strickland hates being mystified by natives, because his business in life is to overmatch them with their own weapons. He has not yet succeeded in doing this, but in fifteen or twenty years he will have made some small progress.

"They should have mauled us," he said, "instead of mewing at us. I wonder what they meant. I don't like it one little bit."

I said that the Managing Committee of the temple would in all probability bring a criminal action against us for insulting their religion. There was a section of the Indian Penal Code which exactly met Fleete's offence. Strickland said he only hoped and prayed that they would do this. Before I left I looked into Fleete's room and saw him lying on his right side, scratching his left breast. Then I went to bed, cold, depressed, and unhappy, at seven o'clock in the morning.

At one o'clock I rode over to Strickland's house to inquire after Fleete's head. I imagined that it would be a sore one. Fleete was breakfasting and seemed unwell. His

temper was gone, for he was abusing the cook for not sup-
plying him with an underdone chop. A man who can eat
raw meat after a wet night is a curiosity. I told Fleete this,
and he laughed.

"You breed queer mosquitoes in these parts," he said.
"I've been bitten to pieces, but only in one place."

"Let's have a look at the bite," said Strickland. "It may
have gone down since this morning."

While the chops were being cooked, Fleete opened his
shirt and showed us, just over his left breast, a mark, the
perfect double of the black rosettes—the five or six irregular blotches arranged in a circle—on a leopard's hide.
Strickland looked and said, "It was only pink this morning. It's grown black now."

Fleete ran to a glass.

"By Jove!" he said. "This is nasty. What is it?"

We could not answer. Here the chops came in, all red
and juicy, and Fleete bolted three in a most offensive
manner. He ate on his right grinders only, and threw his
head over his right shoulder as he snapped the meat.
When he had finished, it struck him that he had been behaving strangely, for he said apologetically, "I don't think
I ever felt so hungry in my life. I've bolted like an
ostrich."

After breakfast Strickland said to me, "Don't go. Stay
here, and stay for the night."

Seeing that my house was not three miles from Strickland's, this request was absurd. But Strickland insisted,
and was going to say something when Fleete interrupted
by declaring in a shamefaced way that he felt hungry
again. Strickland sent a man to my house to fetch over
my bedding and a horse, and we three went down to
Strickland's stables to pass the hours until it was time to
go out for a ride. The man who has a weakness for horses
never wearies of inspecting them, and when two men are
killing time in this way they gather knowledge and lies the
one from the other.

There were five horses in the stables, and I shall never
forget the scene as we tried to look them over. They
seemed to have gone mad. They reared and screamed and
nearly tore up their pickets; they sweated and shivered
and lathered and were distraught with fear. Strickland's

horses used to know him as well as his dogs, which made the matter more curious. We left the stable for fear of the brutes throwing themselves in their panic. Then Strickland turned back and called me. The horses were still frightened, but they let us "gentle" and make much of them, and put their heads in our bosoms.

"They aren't afraid of *us*," said Strickland. "D'you know, I'd give three months' pay if Outrage here could talk."

But Outrage was dumb and could only cuddle up to his master and blow out his nostrils, as is the custom of horses when they wish to explain things but can't. Fleete came up when we were in the stalls, and as soon as the horses saw him their fright broke out afresh. It was all that we could do to escape from the place unkicked. Strickland said, "They don't seem to love you, Fleete."

"Nonsense," said Fleete; "my mare will follow me like a dog." He went to her; she was in a loose-box; but as he slipped the bars she plunged, knocked him down, and broke away into the garden. I laughed, but Strickland was not amused. He took his moustache in both fists and pulled at it till it nearly came out. Fleete, instead of going off to chase his property, yawned, saying that he felt sleepy. He went to the house to lie down, which was a foolish way of spending New Year's Day.

Strickland sat with me in the stables and asked if I had noticed anything peculiar in Fleete's manner. I said that he ate his food like a beast but that this might have been the result of living alone in the hills out of the reach of society as refined and elevating as ours, for instance. Strickland was not amused. I do not think that he listened to me, for his next sentence referred to the mark on Fleete's breast, and I said that it might have been caused by blister-flies or that it was possibly a birthmark newly born and now visible for the first time. We both agreed that it was unpleasant to look at, and Strickland found occasion to say that I was a fool.

"I can't tell you what I think now," said he, "because you would call me a madman; but you must stay with me for the next few days if you can. I want you to watch Fleete, but don't tell me what you think till I have made up my mind."

"But I am dining out tonight," I said.

"So am I," said Strickland, "and so is Fleete. At least if he doesn't change his mind."

We walked about the garden smoking but saying nothing—because we were friends, and talking spoils good tobacco—till our pipes were out. Then we went to wake up Fleete. He was wide awake and fidgeting about his room.

"I say, I want some more chops," he said. "Can I get them?"

We laughed and said, "Go and change. The ponies will be round in a minute."

"All right," said Fleete. "I'll go when I get the chops—underdone ones, mind."

He seemed to be quite in earnest. It was four o'clock, and we had had breakfast at one; still, for a long time he demanded those underdone chops. Then he changed into riding clothes and went out into the veranda. His pony—the mare had not been caught—would not let him come near. All three horses were unmanageable—mad with fear—and finally Fleete said that he would stay at home and get something to eat. Strickland and I rode out wondering. As we passed the temple of Hanuman, the silver man came out and mewed at us.

"He is not one of the regular priests of the temple," said Strickland. "I think I should peculiarly like to lay my hands on him."

There was no spring in our gallop on the race-course that evening. The horses were stale and moved as though they had been ridden out.

"The fright after breakfast has been too much for them," said Strickland.

That was the only remark he made through the remainder of the ride. Once or twice I think he swore to himself, but that did not count.

We came back in the dark at seven o'clock and saw that there were no lights in the bungalow. "Careless ruffians my servants are!" said Strickland.

My horse reared at something on the carriage-drive, and Fleete stood up under its nose.

"What are you doing, grovelling about the garden?" said Strickland.

But both horses bolted and nearly threw us. We

dismounted by the stables and returned to Fleete, who was on his hands and knees under the orange-bushes.

"What the devil's wrong with you?" said Strickland.

"Nothing, nothing in the world," said Fleete, speaking very quickly and thickly. "I've been gardening—botanizing, you know. The smell of the earth is delightful. I think I'm going for a walk—a long walk—all night."

Then I saw that there was something excessively out of order somewhere, and I said to Strickland, "I am not dining out."

"Bless you!" said Strickland. "Here, Fleete, get up. You'll catch fever there. Come in to dinner and let's have the lamps lit. We'll all dine at home."

Fleete stood up unwillingly and said, "No lamps—no lamps. It's much nicer here. Let's dine outside and have some more chops—lots of 'em, and underdone—bloody ones with gristle."

Now, a December evening in northern India is bitterly cold, and Fleete's suggestion was that of a maniac.

"Come in," said Strickland sternly. "Come in at once."

Fleete came, and when the lamps were brought, we saw that he was literally plastered with dirt from head to foot. He must have been rolling in the garden. He shrank from the light and went to his room. His eyes were horrible to look at. There was a green light behind them, not in them, if you understand, and the man's lower lip hung down.

Strickland said, "There is going to be trouble—big trouble—tonight. Don't you change your riding things."

We waited and waited for Fleete's reappearance, and ordered dinner in the meantime. We could hear him moving about his own room, but there was no light there. Presently from the room came the long-drawn howl of a wolf.

People write and talk lightly of blood running cold and hair standing up and things of that kind. Both sensations are too horrible to be trifled with. My heart stopped as though a knife had been driven through it, and Strickland turned as white as the tablecloth.

The howl was repeated and was answered by another howl far across the fields.

That set the gilded roof on the horror. Strickland

dashed into Fleete's room. I followed, and we saw Fleete getting out of the window. He made beast noises in the back of his throat. He could not answer us when we shouted at him. He spat.

I don't quite remember what followed, but I think that Strickland must have stunned him with the long bootjack, or else I should never have been able to sit on his chest. Fleete could not speak, he could only snarl, and his snarls were those of a wolf, not of a man. The human spirit must have been giving way all day and have died out with the twilight. We were dealing with a beast that had once been Fleete.

The affair was beyond any human and rational experience. I tried to say "hydrophobia," but the word wouldn't come, because I knew that I was lying.

We bound this beast with leather thongs of the punkah rope, and tied its thumbs and big toes together, and gagged it with a shoe-horn, which makes a very efficient gag if you know how to arrange it. Then we carried it into the dining-room and sent a man to Dumoise, the doctor, telling him to come over at once. After we had dispatched the messenger and were drawing breath, Strickland said, "It's no good. This isn't any doctor's work." I also knew that he spoke the truth.

The beast's head was free, and it threw it about from side to side. Anyone entering the room would have believed that we were curing a wolf's pelt. That was the most loathsome accessory of all.

Strickland sat with his chin in the heel of his fist, watching the beast as it wriggled on the ground, but saying nothing. The shirt had been torn open in the scuffle and showed the black rosette mark on the left breast. It stood out like a blister.

In the silence of the watching we heard something without mewing like a she-otter. We both rose to our feet, and I answer for myself, not Strickland, felt sick—actually and physically sick. We told each other, as did the men in *Pinafore,* that it was the cat.

Dumoise arrived, and I never saw a little man so unprofessionally shocked. He said that it was a heart-rending case of hydrophobia and that nothing could be done. At least any palliative measures would only prolong the agony. The beast was foaming at the mouth. Fleete, as we told Dumoise, had been bitten by dogs once or twice. Any man who keeps half a dozen terriers must expect a nip now and again. Dumoise could offer no help. He could only certify that Fleete was dying of hydrophobia. The beast was then howling, for it had managed to spit out the shoe-horn. Dumoise said that he would be ready to certify to the cause of death and that the end was certain. He was a good little man, and he offered to remain with us, but Strickland refused the kindness. He did not wish to poison Dumoise's New Year. He would only ask him not to give the real cause of Fleete's death to the public.

So Dumoise left, deeply agitated; and as soon as the noise of the cart-wheels had died away, Strickland told me, in a whisper, his suspicions. They were so wildly improbable that he dared not say them out aloud; and I, who entertained all Strickland's beliefs, was so ashamed of owning to them that I pretended to disbelieve.

"Even if the silver man had bewitched Fleete for polluting the image of Hanuman, the punishment could not have fallen so quickly."

As I was whispering this the cry outside the house rose again, and the beast fell into a fresh paroxysm of struggling till we were afraid that the thongs that held it would give way.

"Watch!" said Strickland. "If this happens six times I shall take the law into my own hands. I order you to help me."

He went into his room and came out in a few minutes with the barrels of an old shotgun, a piece of fishing-line, some thick cord, and his heavy wooden bedstead. I reported that the convulsions had followed the cry by two seconds in each case, and the beast seemed perceptibly weaker.

Strickland muttered, "But he can't take away the life! He can't take away the life!"

I said, though I knew that I was arguing against myself, "It may be a cat. It must be a cat. If the silver man is responsible, why does he dare to come here?"

Strickland arranged the wood on the hearth, put the gun barrels into the glow of the fire, spread the twine on the table, and broke a walking-stick in two. There was one yard of fishing-line, gut, lapped with wire, such as is used for *mahseer*-fishing, and he tied the two ends together in a loop.

Then he said, "How can we catch him? He must be taken alive and unhurt."

I said that we must trust in Providence and go out softly with polo-sticks into the shrubbery at the front of the house. The man or animal that made the cry was evidently moving round the house as regularly as a night-watchman. We could wait in the bushes till he came by and knock him over.

Strickland accepted this suggestion, and we slipped out from a bathroom window into the front veranda and then across the carriage-drive into the bushes.

In the moonlight we could see the leper coming round the corner of the house. He was perfectly naked, and from time to time he mewed and stopped to dance with his shadow. It was an unattractive sight, and thinking of poor Fleete, brought to such degradation by so foul a creature, I put away all my doubts and resolved to help Strickland from the heated gun barrels to the loop of twine—from the loins to the head and back again—with all tortures that might be needful.

The leper halted in the front porch for a moment and we jumped out on him with the sticks. He was wonderfully strong, and we were afraid that he might escape or be fatally injured before we caught him. We had an idea that lepers were frail creatures, but this proved to be incorrect. Strickland knocked his legs from under him, and I put my foot on his neck. He mewed hideously, and even through my riding-boots I could feel that his flesh was not the flesh of a clean man.

He struck at us with his hand and feet-stumps. We looped the lash of a dog-whip round him, under the armpits, and dragged him backwards into the hall and so into the dining-room, where the beast lay. There we tied him with trunk-straps. He made no attempt to escape, but mewed.

When we confronted him with the beast the scene was beyond description. The beast doubled backwards into a bow, as though he had been poisoned with strychnine, and moaned in the most pitiable fashion. Several other things happened also, but they cannot be put down here.

"I think I was right," said Strickland. "Now we will ask him to cure this case."

But the leper only mewed. Strickland wrapped a towel round his hand and took the gun barrels out of the fire. I put the half of the broken walking-stick through the loop of fishing-line and buckled the leper comfortably to Strickland's bedstead. I understood then how men and women and little children can endure to see a witch burnt alive; for the beast was moaning on the floor, and though the silver man had no face, you could see horrible feelings passing through the slab that took its place, exactly as waves of heat play across red-hot iron—gun barrels for instance.

Strickland shaded his eyes with his hands for a moment, and we got to work. This part is not to be printed.

The dawn was beginning to break when the leper spoke. His mewings had not been satisfactory up to that point. The beast had fainted from exhaustion, and the house was very still. We unstrapped the leper and told him to take away the evil spirit. He crawled to the beast and laid his hand upon the left breast. That was all. Then he fell face down and whined, drawing in his breath as he did so.

We watched the face of the beast and saw the soul of Fleete coming back into the eyes. Then a sweat broke out on the forehead, and the eyes—they were human eyes—closed. We waited for an hour, but Fleete still slept. We carried him to his room and bade the leper go, giving him the bedstead, and the sheet on the bedstead to cover his nakedness, the gloves and the towels with which we had touched him, and the whip that had been hooked round his body. He put the sheet about him and went out into the early morning without speaking or mewing.

Strickland wiped his face and sat down. A night-gong, far away in the city, made seven o'clock.

"Exactly four and twenty hours!" said Strickland. "And I've done enough to ensure my dismissal from the service, besides permanent quarters in a lunatic asylum. Do you believe that we are awake?"

The red-hot gun barrel had fallen on the floor and was singeing the carpet. The smell was entirely real.

That morning at eleven we two together went to wake up Fleete. We looked and saw that the black leopard-rosette on his chest had disappeared. He was very drowsy and tired, but as soon as he saw us he said, "Oh! Confound you fellows. Happy New Year to you. Never mix your liquors. I'm nearly dead."

"Thanks for your kindness, but you're overtime," said Strickland. "Today is the morning of the second. You've slept the clock round with a vengeance."

The door opened, and little Dumoise put his head in. He had come on foot, and fancied that we were laying our Fleete.

"I've brought a nurse," said Dumoise. "I suppose that she can come in for—what is necessary."

"By all means," said Fleete cheerily, sitting up in bed. "Bring on your nurses."

Dumoise was dumb. Strickland led him out and explained that there must have been a mistake in the diagnosis. Dumoise remained dumb and left the house hastily. He considered that his professional reputation had been injured and was inclined to make a personal matter of the recovery. Strickland went out too. When he came back he said that he had been to call on the temple of Hanuman to offer redress for the pollution of the god, and had been solemnly assured that no white man had ever touched the idol and that he was an incarnation of all the virtues laboring under a delusion. "What do you think?" said Strickland.

I said, "There are more things—"

But Strickland hates that quotation. He says that I have worn it threadbare.

One other curious thing happened which frightened me as much as anything in all the night's work. When Fleete was dressed he came into the dining-room and sniffed. He had a quaint trick of moving his nose when he sniffed. "Horrid doggy smell here," said he. "You should really keep those terriers of yours in better order. Try sulphur, Strick."

But Strickland did not answer. He caught hold of the back of a chair and without warning went into an amazing fit of hysterics. It is terrible to see a strong man overtaken with hysteria. Then it struck me that we had fought for Fleete's soul with the silver man in that room and had disgraced ourselves as Englishmen forever, and I laughed and gasped and gurgled just as shamefully as Strickland, while Fleete thought that we had both gone mad. We never told him what we had done.

Some years later, when Strickland had married and was a church-going member of society for his wife's sake, we reviewed the incident dispassionately, and Strickland suggested that I should put it before the public.

I cannot myself see that this step is likely to clear up the mystery, because in the first place no one will believe a rather unpleasant story, and in the second, it is well known to every right-minded man that the gods of the heathen are stone and brass, and any attempt to deal with them otherwise is justly condemned.

[First published in 1890.]

"THEY"

One view called me to another, one hilltop to its fellow, half across the county, and since I could answer at no more trouble than the snapping forward of a lever, I let the county flow under my wheels. The orchid-studded flats of the East gave way to the thyme, ilex, and grey grass of the downs; these again to the rich cornland and fig-trees of the lower coast, where you carry the beat of the tide on your left hand for fifteen level miles; and when at last I turned inland through a huddle of rounded hills and woods I had run myself clean out of my known marks. Beyond that precise hamlet which stands godmother to the capital of the United States, I found hidden villages where bees, the only things awake, boomed in eighty-foot lindens that overhung grey Norman churches; miraculous brooks diving under stone bridges built for heavier traffic than would ever vex them again; tithe-barns larger than their churches; and an old smithy that cried out aloud how it had once been a hall of the Knights of the Temple. Gypsies I found on a common where the gorse, bracken, and heath fought it out together up a mile of Roman road; and a little further on I disturbed a red fox rolling dog-fashion in the naked sunlight.

As the wooded hills closed about me I stood up in the

car to take the bearings of that great down whose ringed head is a landmark for fifty miles across the low countries. I judged that the lie of the country would bring me across some westward-running road that went to his feet, but I did not allow for the confusing veils of the woods. A quick turn plunged me first into a green cutting brimful of liquid sunshine, next into a gloomy tunnel where last year's dead leaves whispered and scuffled about my tyres. The strong hazel stuff meeting overhead had not been cut for a couple of generations at least, nor had any axe helped the moss-cankered oak and beech to spring above them. Here the road changed frankly into a carpeted ride on whose brown velvet spent primrose-clumps showed like jade, and a few sickly, white-stalked blue-bells nodded together. As the slope favoured, I shut off the power and slid over the whirled leaves, expecting every moment to meet a keeper; but I only heard a jay, far off, arguing against the silence under the twilight of the trees.

Still the track descended. I was on the point of reversing and working my way back on the second speed ere I ended in some swamp when I saw sunshine through the tangle ahead and lifted the brake.

It was down again at once. As the light beat across my face my fore-wheels took the turf of a great still lawn from which sprang horsemen ten feet high with levelled lances, monstrous peacocks, and sleek round-headed maids of honour—blue, black, and glistening—all of clipped yew. Across the lawn—the marshalled woods beseiged it on three sides—stood an ancient house of lichened and weather-worn stone, with mullioned windows and roofs of rose-red tile. It was flanked by semicircular walls, also rose-red, that closed the lawn on the fourth side, and at their feet a box hedge grew man-high. There were doves on the roof about the slim brick chimneys, and I caught a glimpse of an octagonal dove-house behind the screening wall.

Here, then, I stayed, a horseman's green spear laid at my breast, held by the exceeding beauty of that jewel in that setting.

"If I am not packed off for a trespasser, or if this knight does not ride a wallop at me," thought I, "Shakespeare and Queen Elizabeth at least must come out of that half-open garden door and ask me to tea."

A child appeared at an upper window, and I thought the little thing waved a friendly hand. But it was to call a companion, for presently another bright head showed. Then I heard a laugh among the yew-peacocks, and turning to make sure (till then I had been watching the house only), I saw the silver of a fountain behind a hedge thrown up against the sun. The doves on the roof cooed to the cooing water; but between the two notes I caught the utterly happy chuckle of a child absorbed in some light mischief.

The garden door—heavy oak sunk deep in the thickness of the wall—opened further; a woman in a big garden hat set her foot slowly on the time-hollowed stone step and as slowly walked across the turf. I was forming some apology when she lifted up her head and I saw that she was blind.

"I heard you," she said. "Isn't that a motor-car?"

"I'm afraid I've made a mistake in my road. I should have turned off up above. I never dreamed—" I began.

"But I'm very glad. Fancy a motor-car coming into the garden! It will be such a treat—" She turned and made as though looking about her, "You—you haven't seen anyone, have you—perhaps?"

"No one to speak to, but the children seemed interested at a distance."

"Which?"

"I saw a couple up at the window just now, and I think I heard a little chap in the grounds."

"Oh, lucky you!" she cried, and her face brightened. "I hear them, of course, but that's all. You've seen them and heard them?"

"Yes," I answered. "And if I know anything of children, one of them's having a beautiful time by the fountain yonder. Escaped, I should imagine."

"You're fond of children?"

I gave her one or two reasons why I did not altogether hate them.

"Of course, of course," she said. "Then you understand. Then you won't think it foolish if I ask you to take your car through the gardens once or twice—quite slowly.

I'm sure they'd like to see it. They see so little, poor things. One tries to make their life pleasant, but—" She threw out her hands towards the woods. "We're so out of the world here."

"That will be splendid," I said. "But I can't cut up your grass."

She faced to the right. "Wait a minute," she said. "We're at the south gate, aren't we? Behind those peacocks there's a flagged path. We call it the Peacocks' Walk. You can't see it from here, they tell me, but if you squeeze along by the edge of the wood you can turn at the first peacock and get onto the flags."

It was sacrilege to wake that dreaming house-front with the clatter of machinery, but I swung the car to clear the turf, brushed along the edge of the wood, and turned in on the broad stone path where the fountain basin lay like one star sapphire.

"May I come too?" she cried. "No, please don't help me. They'll like it better if they see me."

She felt her way lightly to the front of the car, and with one foot on the step she called, 'Children, oh, children! Look and see what's going to happen!"

The voice would have drawn lost souls from the Pit, for the yearning that underlay its sweetness, and I was not surprised to hear an answering shout behind the yews. It must have been the child by the fountain, but he fled at our approach, leaving a little toy boat in the water. I saw the glint of his blue blouse among the still horsemen.

Very disposedly we paraded the length of the walk, and at her request backed again. This time the child had got the better of his panic, but stood far off and doubting.

"The little fellow's watching us," I said. "I wonder if he'd like a ride."

"They're very shy still. Very shy. But, oh, lucky you to be able to see them! Let's listen."

I stopped the machine at once, and the humid stillness, heavy with the scent of box, cloaked us deep. Shears I could hear where some gardener was clipping, a mumble of bees and broken voices that might have been the doves.

"Oh, unkind!" she said weariedly.

"Perhaps they're only shy of the motor. The little maid at the window looks tremendously interested."

"Yes?" She raised her head. "It was wrong of me to say that. They are really fond of me. It's the only thing that makes life worth living—when they're fond of you—isn't it? I daren't think what the place would be without them. By the way, is it beautiful?"

"I think it is the most beautiful place I have ever seen."

"So they all tell me. I can feel it, of course, but that isn't quite the same thing."

"Then have you never—" I began, but stopped abashed.

"Not since I can remember. It happened when I was only a few months old, they tell me. And yet I must remember something, else how could I dream about colours? I see light in my dreams, and colours, but I never see *them*. I only hear them, just as I do when I'm awake."

"It's difficult to see faces in dreams. Some people can, but most of us haven't the gift," I went on, looking up at the window where the child stood all but hidden.

"I've heard that too," she said. "And they tell me that one never sees a dead person's face in a dream. Is that true?"

"I believe it is—now I come to think of it."

"But how is it with yourself—yourself?" The blind eyes turned towards me.

"I have never seen the faces of my dead in any dream," I answered.

"Then it must be as bad as being blind."

The sun had dipped behind the woods, and the long shades were possessing the insolent horsemen one by one. I saw the light die from off the top of a glossy-leaved lance and all the brave hard green turn to soft black. The house, accepting another day at end, as it had accepted an hundred thousand gone, seemed to settle deeper into its rest among the shadows.

"Have you ever wanted to?" she said after the silence.

"Very much sometimes," I replied. The child had left the window as the shadows closed upon it.

"Ah! So've I, but I don't suppose it's allowed. Where d'you live?"

"Quite the other side of the county, sixty miles and more, and I must be going back. I've come without my big lamp."

"But it's not dark yet. I can feel it."

"I'm afraid it will be by the time I get home. Could you lend me someone to set me on my road at first? I've utterly lost myself."

"I'll send Madden with you to the cross-roads. We are so out of the world, I don't wonder you were lost! I'll guide you round to the front of the house; but you will go slowly, won't you, till you're out of the grounds? It isn't foolish, do you think?"

"I promise you I'll go like this," I said, and let the car start herself down the flagged path.

We skirted the left wing of the house, whose elaborately cast lead guttering alone was worth a day's journey; passed under a great rose-grown gate in the red wall, and so round to the high front of the house, which in beauty and stateliness as much excelled the back as that all others I had seen.

"Is it so very beautiful?" she said wistfully when she heard my raptures. "And you like the lead figures too? There's the old azalea garden behind. They say that this place must have been made for children. Will you help me out, please? I should like to come with you as far as the cross-roads, but I mustn't leave them. Is that you, Madden? I want you to show this gentleman the way to the cross-roads. He has lost his way, but—he has seen them."

A butler appeared noiselessly at the miracle of old oak that must be called the front door, and slipped aside to put on his hat. She stood looking at me with open blue eyes in which no sight lay, and I saw for the first time that she was beautiful.

"Remember," she said quietly, "if you are fond of them you will come again," and disappeared within the house.

The butler in the car said nothing till we were nearly at the lodge gates, where, catching a glimpse of a blue blouse in a shrubbery, I swerved amply lest the devil that leads little boys to play should drag me into child-murder.

"Excuse me," he asked of a sudden, "but why did you do that, sir?"

"The child yonder."

"Our young gentleman in blue?"

"Of course."

"He runs about a good deal. Did you see him by the fountain, sir?"

"Oh, yes, several times. Do we turn here?"

"Yes, sir. And did you 'appen to see them upstairs. too?"

"At the upper window? Yes."

"Was that before the mistress come out to speak to you, sir?"

"A little before that. Why d'you want to know?"

He paused a little. "Only to make sure that—that they had seen the car, sir, because with children running about, though I'm sure you're driving particularly careful, there might be an accident. That was all, sir. Here are the cross-roads. You can't miss your way from now on. Thank you, sir, but that isn't *our* custom, not with——"

"I beg your pardon," I said, and thrust away the British silver.

"Oh, it's quite right with the rest of 'em as a rule. Good-bye, sir."

He retired into the armour-plated conning tower of his caste and walked away. Evidently a butler solicitous for the honour of his house, and interested, probably through a maid, in the nursery.

Once beyond the signposts at the cross-roads I looked back, but the crumpled hills interlaced so jealously that I could not see where the house had lain. When I asked its name at a cottage along the road, the fat woman who sold sweetmeats there gave me to understand that people with motor-cars had small right to live—much less to "go about talking like carriage-folk." They were not a pleasant-mannered community.

When I retraced my route on the map that evening I was little wiser. Hawkin's Old Farm appeared to be the survey title of the place, and the old county gazetteer, generally so ample, did not allude to it. The big house of those parts was Hodnington Hall, Georgian with early Victorian embellishments, as an atrocious steel engraving attested. I carried my difficulty to a neighbour—a deep-rooted tree of that soil—and he gave me a name of a family which conveyed no meaning.

A month or so later I went again, or it may have been that my car took the road of her own volition. She over-ran the fruitless downs, threaded every turn of the maze of lanes below the hills, drew through the high-walled woods, impenetrable in their full leaf, came out at the cross-roads where the butler had left me, and a little fur-ther on developed an internal trouble which forced me to turn her in on a grass way-waste that cut into a summer-silent hazel wood. So far as I could make sure by the sun and a six-inch ordnance map, this should be the road flank of that wood which I had first explored from the heights above. I made a mighty serious business of my re-pairs and a glittering shop of my repair kit, spanners, pump, and the like, which I spread out orderly upon a rug. It was a trap to catch all childhood, for on such a day, I argued, the children would not be far off. When I paused in my work I listened, but the wood was so full of the noises of summer (though the birds had mated) that I could not at first distinguish these from the tread of small cautious feet stealing across the dead leaves. I rang my bell in an alluring manner, but the feet fled, and I re-pented, for to a child a sudden noise is very real terror. I must have been at work half an hour when I heard in the wood the voice of the blind woman crying, "Children, oh, children, where are you?" and the stillness made slow to close on the perfection of that cry. She came towards me, half feeling her way between the tree-boles, and though a child, it seemed, clung to her skirt, it swerved into the leafage like a rabbit as she drew nearer.

"Is that you," she said, "from the other side of the county?"

"Yes, it's me from the other side of the county."

"Then why didn't you come through the upper woods? They were there just now."

"They were here a few minutes ago. I expect they knew my car had broken down and came to see the fun."

"Nothing serious, I hope? How do cars break down?"

"In fifty different ways. Only mine has chosen the fifty-first."

She laughed merrily at the tiny joke, cooed with delicious laughter, and pushed her hat back.

"Let me hear," she said.

"Wait a moment," I cried, "and I'll get you a cushion."

She set a foot on the rug all covered with spare parts, and stooped above it eagerly. "What delightful things!" The hands through which she saw glanced in the chequered sunlight. "A box here—another box! Why, you've arranged them like playing shop!"

"I confess now that I put it out to attract them. I don't need half those things really."

"How nice of you! I heard your bell in the upper wood. You say they were here before that?"

"I'm sure of it. Why are they so shy? That little fellow in blue who was with you just now ought to have got over his fright. He's been watching me like a Red Indian."

"It must have been your bell," she said. "I heard one of them go past me in trouble when I was coming down. They're shy—so shy even with me." She turned her face over her shoulder and cried again, "Children! Oh, children! Look and see!"

"They must have gone off together on their own affairs," I suggested, for there was a murmur behind us of lowered voices broken by the sudden squeaking giggles of childhood. I returned to my tinkerings and she leaned forward, her chin on her hand, listening interestedly.

"How many are they?" I said at last. The work was finished, but I saw no reason to go.

Her forehead puckered a little in thought. "I don't quite know," she said simply. "Sometimes more, sometimes less. They come and stay with me because I love them, you see."

"That must be very jolly," I said, replacing a drawer; and as I spoke, I heard the inanity of my answer.

"You—you aren't laughing at me," she cried. "I—I haven't any of my own. I never married. People laugh at me sometimes about them because—because—"

"Because they're savages," I returned. "It's nothing to fret for. That sort laugh at everything that isn't in their own fat lives."

"I don't know. How should I? I only don't like being laughed at about *them*. It hurts; and when one can't see— I don't want to seem silly"—her chin quivered like a child's as she spoke—"but we blindies have only one skin, I think. Everything outside hits straight at our souls. It's different with you. You've such good defences in your eyes—looking out—before anyone can really pain you in your soul. People forget that with us."

I was silent, reviewing that inexhaustible matter—the more than inherited (since it is also carefully taught) brutality of the Christian peoples, beside which the mere heathendom of the West Coast Nigger is clean and restrained. It led me a long distance into myself.

"Don't do that!" she said of a sudden, putting her hands before her eyes.

"What?"

She made a gesture with her hand.

"That! It's—it's all purple and black. Don't! That colour hurts."

"But how in the world do you know about colours?" I exclaimed, for here was a revelation indeed.

"Colours as colours?" she asked.

"No. *Those* colours which you saw just now."

"You know as well as I do," she laughed, "else you wouldn't have asked that question. They aren't in the world at all. They're in *you*—when you went so angry."

"D'you mean a dull purplish patch, like port wine mixed with ink?" I said.

"I've never seen ink or port wine, but the colours aren't mixed. They are separate—all separate."

"Do you mean black streaks and jags across the purple?"

She nodded. "Yes, if they are like this," and zigzagged her finger again, "but it's more red than purple—that bad colour."

"And what are the colours at the top of the—whatever you see?"

Slowly she leaned forward and traced on the rug the figure of the Egg itself.

"I see them so," she said, pointing with a grass stem, "white, green, yellow, red, purple, and when people are angry or bad, black across the red—as you were just now."

"Who told you anything about it—in the beginning?" I demanded.

"About the colours? No one. I used to ask what colours were when I was little—in table-covers and curtains and carpets, you see—because some colours hurt me and some made me happy. People told me; and when I got older, that was how I saw people." Again she traced the outline of the Egg which it is given to very few of us to see.

"All by yourself?" I repeated.

"All by myself. There wasn't anyone else. I only found out afterwards that other people did not see the colours."

She leaned against the tree-bole plaiting and unplaiting chance-plucked grass stems. The children in the wood had drawn nearer. I could see them with the tail of my eye frolicking like squirrels.

"Now I am sure you will never laugh at me," she went on after a long silence. "Nor at *them*."

"Goodness! No!" I cried, jolted out of my train of thought. "A man who laughs at a child—unless the child is laughing too—is a heathen!"

"I didn't mean that of course. You'd never laugh *at* children, but I thought—I used to think—that perhaps you might laugh *about* them. So now I beg your pardon. What are you going to laugh at?"

I had made no sound, but she knew.

"At the notion of your begging my pardon. If you had done your duty as a pillar of the state and a landed proprietress, you ought to have summoned me for trespass when I barged through your woods the other day. It was disgraceful of me—inexcusable."

She looked at me, her head against the tree trunk, long and steadfastly, this woman who could see the naked soul.

"How curious," she half whispered. "How very curious."

"Why, what have I done?"

"You don't understand, and yet you understood about the colours. Don't you understand?"

She spoke with a passion that nothing had justified, and I faced her bewilderedly as she rose. The children had gathered themselves in a roundel behind a bramble bush. One sleek head bent over something smaller, and the set

of the little shoulders told me that fingers were on lips.
They too had some child's tremendous secret. I alone was
hopelessly astray there in the broad sunlight.

"No," I said, and shook my head as though the dead
eyes could note. "Whatever it is, I don't understand yet.
Perhaps I shall later, if you'll let me come again."

"You will come again," she answered. "You will surely
come again and walk in the wood."

"Perhaps the children will know me well enough by
that time to let me play with them—as a favour. You
know what children are like."

"It isn't a matter of favour but of right," she replied,
and while I wondered what she meant, a dishevelled
woman plunged round the bend of the road, loose-haired,
purple, almost lowing with agony as she ran. It was my
rude, fat friend of the sweetmeat shop. The blind woman
heard and stepped forward. "What is it, Mrs.
Madehurst?" she asked.

The woman flung her apron over her head and literally
grovelled in the dust, crying that her grandchild was sick
to death, that the local doctor was away fishing, that
Jenny, the mother, was at her wits' end, and so forth,
with repetitions and bellowings.

"Where's the next nearest doctor?" I asked between
paroxysms.

"Madden will tell you. Go round to the house and take
him with you. I'll attend to this. Be quick!" She half supported the fat woman into the shade. In two minutes I
was blowing all the horns of Jericho under the front of
the House Beautiful, and Madden, in the pantry, rose to
the crisis like a butler and a man.

A quarter of an hour at illegal speeds caught us a doctor five miles away. Within the half hour we had decanted
him, much interested in motors, at the door of the sweetmeat shop, and drew up the road to await the verdict.

"Useful things, cars," said Madden, all man and no
butler. "If I'd had one when mine took sick she wouldn't
have died."

"How was it?" I asked.

"Croup. Mrs. Madden was away. No one knew what to
do. I drove eight miles in a tax cart for the doctor. She

was choked when we came back. This car'd ha' saved her. She'd have been close on ten now."

"I'm sorry," I said. "I thought you were rather fond of children from what you told me going to the cross-roads the other day."

"Have you seen 'em again, sir—this mornin'?"

"Yes, but they're well broke to cars. I couldn't get any of them within twenty yards of it."

He looked at me carefully as a scout considers a stranger—not as a menial should lift his eyes to his divinely appointed superior.

"I wonder why," he said just above the breath that he drew.

We waited on. A light wind from the sea wandered up and down the long lines of the woods, and the wayside grasses, whitened already with summer dust, rose and bowed in sallow waves.

A woman, wiping the suds off her arms, came out of the cottage next the sweetmeat shop.

"I've been listenin' in de back yard," she said cheerily. "He says Arthur's unaccountable bad. Did ye hear him shruck just now? Unaccountable bad. I reckon 'twill come Jenny's turn to walk in de wood nex' week along, Mr. Madden."

"Excuse me, sir, but your lap-robe is slipping," said Madden deferentially. The woman started, dropped a curtsy, and hurried away.

"What does she mean by 'walking in the wood'?" I asked.

"It must be some saying they use hereabouts. I'm from Norfolk myself," said Madden. "They're an independent lot in this county. She took you for a chauffeur, sir."

I saw the doctor come out of the cottage followed by a draggle-tailed wench who clung to his arm as though he could make treaty for her with Death. "Dat sort," she wailed, "dey're just as much to us dat has 'em as if dey was lawful born. Just as much—just as much! An' God— he'd be just as pleased if you saved 'un, doctor. Don't take it from me. Miss Florence will tell ye de very same. Don't leave 'im, doctor!"

"I know. I know," said the man, "but he'll be quiet for a while now. We'll get the nurse and the medicine as fast as we can." He signalled me to come forward with the car, and I strove not to be privy to what followed; but I saw the girl's face, blotched and frozen with grief, and I felt the hand without a ring clutching at my knees when we moved away.

The doctor was a man of some humour, for I remember he claimed my car under the Oath of Aesculapius and used it and me without mercy. First we convoyed Mrs. Madehurst and the blind woman to wait by the sick-bed till the nurse should come. Next we invaded a neat county town for prescriptions (the doctor said the trouble was cerebro-spinal meningitis), and when the County Institute, banked and flanked with scared market cattle, reported itself out of nurses, for the moment we literally flung ourselves loose upon the county. We conferred with the owners of great houses—magnates at the ends of overarching avenues whose big-boned womenfolk strode away from their tea-tables to listen to the imperious doctor. At last a white-haired lady sitting under a cedar of Lebanon and surrounded by a court of magnificent borzois—all hostile to motors—gave the doctor, who received them as from a princess, written orders which we bore many miles at top speed, through a park, to a French nunnery, where we took over in exchange a pallid-faced and trembling Sister. She knelt at the bottom of the tonneau telling her beads without pause till, by short-cuts of the doctor's invention, we had her to the sweet-meat shop once more. It was a long afternoon crowded with mad episodes that rose and dissolved like the dust of our wheels, cross-sections of remote and incomprehensible lives through which we raced at right angles; and I went home in the dusk, wearied out, to dream of the clashing horns of cattle, round-eyed nuns walking in a garden of graves, pleasant tea-parties beneath shaded trees, the carbolic-scented, grey-painted corridors of the County Institute, the steps of shy children in the wood, and the hands that clung to my knees as the motor began to move.

I had intended to return in a day or two, but it pleased Fate to hold me from that side of the county on many pretexts till the elder and the wild rose had fruited. There came at last a brilliant day, swept clear from the southwest, that brought the hills within hand's reach—a day of unstable airs and high filmy clouds. Through no merit of my own I was free, and set the car for the third time on that known road. As I reached the crest of the downs I felt the soft air change, saw it glaze under the sun, and looking down at the sea, in that instant beheld the blue of the Channel turn through polished silver and dulled steel to dingy pewter. A laden collier hugging the coast steered outward for deeper water, and across copper-coloured haze I saw sails rise one by one on the anchored fishing-fleet. In a deep dene behind me an eddy of sudden wind drummed through sheltered oaks and spun aloft the first dry sample of autumn leaves. When I reached the beach road the sea-fog fumed over the brickfields, and the tide was telling all the groins of the gale beyond Ushant. In less than an hour summer England vanished in chill grey. We were again the shut island of the North, all the ships of the world bellowing at our perilous gates; and between their outcries ran the piping of bewildered gulls. My cap dripped moisture, the folds of the rug held it in pools or sluiced it away in runnels, and the salt-rine stuck to my lips.

Inland the smell of autumn loaded the thickened fog among the trees, and the drip became a continuous shower. Yet the late flowers—mallow of the wayside, scabious of the field, and dahlia of the garden—showed gay in the mist, and beyond the sea's breath there was little sign of decay in the leaf. Yet in the villages the house doors were all open, and bare-legged, bare-headed children sat at ease on the damp doorsteps to shout "pip-pip" at the stranger.

I made bold to call at the sweetmeat shop, where Mrs. Madehurst met me with a fat woman's hospitable tears. Jenny's child, she said, had died two days after the nun had come. It was, she felt, best out of the way, even though insurance offices, for reasons which she did not pretend to follow, would not willingly insure such stray lives. "Not but what Jenny didn't tend to Arthur as though he'd come all proper at de end of de first year—like Jenny herself." Thanks to Miss Florence, the child had been buried with a pomp which, in Mrs. Madehurst's opinion, more than covered the small irregularity of its birth. She described the coffin, within and without, the glass hearse, and the evergreen lining of the grave.

"But how's the mother?" I asked.

"Jenny! Oh, she'll get over it. I've felt dat way with one or two o' my own. She'll get over. She's walkin' in de wood now."

"In this weather?"

Mrs. Madehurst looked at me with narrowed eyes across the counter.

"I dunno but it opens de 'eart like. Yes, it opens de 'eart. Dat's where losin' and bearin' comes so alike in de long run, we do say."

Now, the wisdom of the old wives is greater than that of all the Fathers, and this last oracle sent me thinking so extendedly as I went up the road that I nearly ran over a woman and a child at the wooded corner by the lodge gates of the House Beautiful.

"Awful weather!" I cried as I slowed dead for the turn.

"Not so bad," she answered placidly out of the fog. "Mine's used to 'un. You'll find yours indoors, I reckon."

Indoors Madden received me with professional courtesy and kind inquiries for the health of the motor, which he would put under cover.

I waited in a still, nut-brown hall, pleasant with late flowers and warm with a delicious wood fire—a place of good influence and great peace. (Men and women may sometimes, after great effort, achieve a creditable lie, but the house, which is their temple, cannot say anything save the truth of those who have lived in it.) A child's cart and a doll lay on the black-and-white floor, where a rug had been kicked back. I felt that the children had only just hurried away—to hide themselves, most like—in the many turns of the great adzed staircase that climbed state-lily out of the hall, or to crouch and gaze behind the lions and roses of the carvern gallery above. Then I heard her voice above me, singing as the blind sing, from the soul:

In the pleasant orchard-closes,

And all my early summer came back at the call.

In the pleasant orchard-closes,
God bless all our gains say we—

But may God bless all our losses,
Better suits with our degree.

She dropped the marring fifth line, and repeated:

Better suits with our degree!

I saw her lean over the gallery, her linked hands white as pearl against the oak.

"Is that you—from the other side of the county?" she called.

"Yes, me—from the other side of the county," I answered, laughing.

"What a long time before you had to come here again." She ran down the stairs, one hand lightly touching the broad rail. "It's two months and four days. Summer's gone!"

"I meant to come before, but Fate prevented."

"I knew it. Please do something to that fire. They won't let me play with it, but I can feel it's behaving badly. Hit it!"

I looked on either side of the deep fire-place and found but a half-charred hedge-stake, with which I punched a black log into flame.

"It never goes out, day or night," she said, as though explaining. "In case anyone comes in with cold toes, you see."

"It's even lovelier inside than it was out," I murmured. The red light poured itself along the age-polished dusky panels till the Tudor roses and lions of the gallery took colour and motion. An old eagle-topped convex mirror gathered the picture into its mysterious heart, distorting afresh the distorted shadows and curving the gallery lines into the curves of a ship. The day was shutting down in half a gale as the fog turned to stringy scud. Through the uncurtained mullions of the broad window I could see valiant horsemen of the lawn rear and recover against the wind that taunted them with legions of dead leaves.

"Yes, it must be beautiful," she said. "Would you like to go over it? There's still light enough upstairs."

I followed her up the unflinching, wagon-wide staircase

to the gallery, whence opened the thin, fluted Elizabethan doors.

"Feel how they put the latch low down for the sake of the children." She swung a light door inward.

"By the way, where are they?" I asked. "I haven't even heard them today."

She did not answer at once. Then, "I can only hear them," she replied softly. "This is one of their rooms— everything ready, you see."

She pointed into a heavily timbered room. There were little low gate-tables and children's chairs. A doll's house, its hooked front half open, faced a great dappled rock-ing-horse, from whose padded saddle it was but a child's scramble to the broad window-seat overlooking the lawn. A toy gun lay in a corner beside a gilt wooden cannon.

"Surely they've only just gone," I whispered. In the failing light a door creaked cautiously. I heard the rustle of a frock and the patter of feet—quick feet through a room beyond.

"I heard that," she cried triumphantly. "Did you? Children, oh, children, where are you?"

The voice filled the walls that held it lovingly to the last perfect note, but there came no answering shout such as I had heard in the garden. We hurried on from room to oak-floored room, up a step here, down three steps there, among a maze of passages, always mocked by our quarry. One might as well have tried to work an unstopped war-ren with a single ferret. There were bolt-holes innumer-able—recesses in walls, embrasures of deep slitten win-dows now darkened, whence they could start up behind us; and abandoned fire-places, six feet deep in the masonry, as well as the tangle of communicating doors. Above all, they had the twilight for their helper in our game. I had caught one or two joyous chuckles of evasion and once or twice had seen the silhouette of a child's frock against some darkening window at the end of a pas-sage; but we returned empty-handed to the gallery just as a middle-aged woman was setting a lamp in its niche.

"No, I haven't seen her either this evening, Miss Florence," I heard her say, "but that Turpin, he says he wants to see you about his shed."

"Oh, Mr. Turpin must want to see me very badly. Tell him to come to the hall, Mrs. Madden."

I looked down into the hall whose only light was the dulled fire, and deep in the shadow I saw them at last. They must have slipped down while we were in the passages, and now thought themselves perfectly hidden behind an old gilt leather screen. By child's law, my fruitless chase was as good as an introduction, but since I had taken so much trouble I resolved to force them to come forward later by the simple trick, which children detest, of pretending not to notice them. They lay close, in a little huddle, no more than shadows except when a quick flame betrayed an outline.

"And now we'll have some tea," she said. "I believe I ought to have offered it you at first, but one doesn't arrive at manners, somehow, when one lives alone and is considered—h'm—peculiar." Then with very pretty scorn: "Would you like a lamp to see to eat by?"

"The firelight's much pleasanter, I think." We descended into that delicious gloom and Madden brought tea.

I took my chair in the direction of the screen, ready to surprise or be surprised as the game should go, and at her permission, since a hearth is always sacred, bent forward to play with the fire.

"Where do you get these beautiful short faggots from?" I asked idly. "Why, they are tallies!"

"Of course," she said. "As I can't read or write I'm driven back on the early English tally for my accounts. Give me one and I'll tell you what it meant."

I passed her an unburnt hazel tally, about a foot long, and she ran her thumb down the nicks.

"This is the milk record for the home farm for the month of April last year, in gallons," said she. "I don't know what I should have done without tallies. An old forester of mine taught me the system. It's out of date now for everyone else, but my tenants respect it. One of them's coming now to see me. Oh, it doesn't matter. He has no business here out of office hours. He's a greedy, ignorant man—very greedy, or he wouldn't come here after dark."

"Have you much land, then?"

"Only a couple of hundred acres in hand, thank goodness. The other six hundred are nearly all let to folk who knew my folk before me, but this Turpin is quite a new man—and a highway robber."

"But are you sure I shan't be—"

"Certainly not. You have the right. He hasn't any children."

"Ah, the children!" I said, and slid my low chair back till it nearly touched the screen that hid them. "I wonder whether they'll come out for me."

There was a murmur of voices—Madden's and a deeper note—at the low, dark side door, and a ginger-headed, canvas-gaitered giant of the unmistakable tenant-farmer type stumbled or was pushed in.

"Come to the fire, Mr. Turpin," she said.

"If—if you please, Miss, I'll—I'll be quite as well by the door." He clung to the latch as he spoke, like a frightened child. Of a sudden I realized that he was in the grip of some almost overpowering fear.

"Well?"

"About that new shed for the young stock—that was all. These first autumn storms settin' in— But I'll come again, miss." His teeth did not chatter much more than the door-latch.

"I think not," she answered levelly. "The new shed—m'm. What did my agent write you on the fifteenth?"

"I—fancied p'r'aps that if I came to see you—ma—man to man like, miss—but—"

His eyes rolled into every corner of the room, wide with horror. He half opened the door through which he had entered, but I noticed it shut again—from without, and firmly.

"He wrote what I told him," she went on. "You are overstocked already. Dunnett's Farm never carried more than fifty bullocks, even in Mr. Wright's time. And *he* used cake. You've sixty-seven and you don't cake. You've broken the lease in that respect. You're dragging the heart out of the farm."

"I'm—I'm getting some minerals—superphosphates—next week. I've as good as ordered a truck-load already. I'll go down to the station tomorrow about 'em. Then I can come and see you man to man like, miss, in the day-light. That gentleman's not going away, is he?" He almost shrieked.

I had only slid the chair a little further back, reaching behind me to tap on the leather of the screen, but he jumped like a rat.

"No. Please attend to me, Mr. Turpin." She turned in her chair and faced him with his back to the door. It was an old and sordid little piece of scheming that she forced from him—his plea for the new cowshed at his landlady's expense, that he might with the covered manure pay his next year's rent out of the valuation after, as she made clear, he had bled the enriched pastures to the bone. I could not but admire the intensity of his greed, when I saw him out-facing for its sake whatever terror it was that ran wet on his forehead.

I ceased to tap the leather—was indeed calculating the cost of the shed—when I felt my relaxed hand taken and turned softly between the soft hands of a child. So at last I had triumphed. In a moment I would turn and acquaint myself with those quick-footed wanderers.

The little brushing kiss fell in the centre of my palm, as a gift on which the fingers were, once, expected to close, as the all-faithful half-reproachful signal of a waiting child not used to neglect even when grown-ups were busiest—a fragment of the mute code devised very long ago.

Then I knew. And it was as though I had known from the first day when I looked across the lawn at the high window.

I heard the door shut. The woman turned to me in silence, and I felt that she knew.

What time passed after this I cannot say. I was roused by the fall of a log, and mechanically rose to put it back. Then I returned to my place in the chair very close to the screen.

"Now you understand," she whispered across the packed shadows.

"Yes, I understand—now. Thank you."

"I—I only hear them." She bowed her head in her hands. "I have no right, you know—no other right. I have neither borne nor lost—neither borne nor lost!"

"Be very glad then," said I, for my soul was torn open within me.

"Forgive me!"

She was still, and I went back to my sorrow and my joy.

"It was because I loved them so," she said at last, brokenly. "*That* was why it was, even from the first—even before I knew that they—they were all I should ever have. And I loved them so!"

She stretched out her arms to the shadows and the shadows within the shadow.

"They came because I loved them, because I needed them. I—I must have made them come. Was that wrong, think you?"

"No—no."

"I—I grant you that the boys and—and all that sort of thing were nonsense, but—but I used to so hate empty rooms myself when I was little." She pointed to the gallery. "And the passages all empty. And how could I ever bear the garden door shut? Suppose——"

"Don't! For pity's sake, don't!" I cried. The twilight had brought a cold rain with gusty squalls that plucked at the leaded windows.

"And the same thing with keeping the fire in all night. *I* don't think it so foolish—do you?"

I looked at the broad brick hearth, saw, through tears I believe, that there was no unpassable iron on or near it, and bowed my head.

"I did all that and lots of other things—just to make believe. Then they came. I heard them, but I didn't know that they were not mine by right till Mrs. Madden told me——"

"The butler's wife? What?"

"One of them—I heard—she saw—and knew. Hers! *Not* for me. I didn't know at first. Perhaps I was jealous. Afterwards I began to understand that it was only because I loved them, not because—— Oh, you *must* bear or lose," she said piteously. "There is no other way; and yet they love me. They must! Don't they?"

There was no sound in the room except the lapping voices of the fire, but we two listened intently, and she at least took comfort from what she heard. She recovered herself and half rose. I sat still in my chair by the screen.

"Don't think me a wretch to whine about myself like

this, but—but I'm all in the dark, you know, and *you* can see."

In truth I could see, and my vision confirmed me in my resolve, though that was like the very parting of spirit and flesh. Yet a little longer I would stay since it was the last time.

"You think it is wrong, then?" she cried sharply, though I had said nothing.

"Not for you. A thousand times no. For you it is right. I am grateful to you beyond words. For me it would be wrong. For me only."

"Why?" she said, but passed her hand before her face as she had done at our second meeting in the wood. "Oh, I see," she went on simply as a child. "For you it would be wrong." Then with a little indrawn laugh. "And, d'you remember, I called you lucky—once—at first. You who must never come here again!"

She left me to sit a little longer by the screen, and I heard the sound of her feet die out along the gallery above.

[First published in 1904.]

THE BRUSHWOOD BOY

Girls and boys, come out to play:
The moon is shining as bright as day!
Leave your supper and leave your sleep,
And come with your playfellows out in the street!
Up the ladder and down the wall—

A child of three sat up in his crib and screamed at the top of his voice, his fists clinched and his eyes full of terror. At first no one heard, for his nursery was in the west wing, and the nurse was talking to a gardener among the laurels. Then the housekeeper passed that way and hurried to soothe him. He was her special pet, and she disapproved of the nurse.

"What was it, then? What was it, then? There's nothing to frighten him, Georgie dear."

"It was—it was a policeman! He was on the Down—I saw him! He came in. Jane *said* he would."

"Policemen don't come into houses, dearie. Turn over, and take my hand."

"I saw him—on the Down. He came here. Where is your hand, Harper?"

The housekeeper waited till the sobs changed to the regular breathing of sleep before she stole out.

"Jane, what nonsense have you been telling Master Georgie about policemen?"

"I haven't told him anything."

"You have. He's been dreaming about them."

"We met Tisdall on Dowhead when we were in the donkey-cart this morning. P'r'aps that's what put it into his head."

"Oh! Now you aren't going to frighten the child into fits with your silly tales, and the master know nothing about it. If ever I catch you again, etc."

A child of six was telling himself stories as he lay in bed. It was a new power, and he kept it a secret. A month before, it had occurred to him to carry on a nursery tale left unfinished by his mother, and he was delighted to find the tale as it came out of his own head just as surprising as though he were listening to it "all new from the beginning." There was a prince in that tale, and he killed dragons, but only for one night. Ever afterwards Georgie dubbed himself prince, pasha, giant-killer, and all the rest (you see, he could not tell anyone, for fear of being laughed at), and his tales faded gradually into dreamland, where adventures were so many that he could not recall the half of them. They all began in the same way, or, as Georgie explained to the shadows of the night-light, there was "the same starting-off place"—a pile of brushwood stacked somewhere near a beach; and round this pile Georgie found himself running races with little boys and girls. These ended, ships ran high up the dry land and opened into cardboard boxes; or gilt-and-green iron railings that surrounded beautiful gardens turned all soft and could be walked through and overthrown so long as he remembered it was only a dream. He could never hold that knowledge more than a few seconds ere things became real, and instead of pushing down houses full of grown-up people (a just revenge), he sat miserably upon gigantic doorsteps trying to sing the multiplication table up to four times six.

The princess of his tales was a person of wonderful

beauty (she came from the old illustrated edition of Grimm, now out of print), and as she always applauded Georgie's valour among the dragons and buffaloes, he gave her the two finest names he had ever heard in his life—Annie and Louise, pronounced "Annie*an*louise." When the dreams swamped the stories, she would change into one of the little girls round the brushwood pile, still keeping her title and crown. She saw Georgie drown once in a dream-sea by the beach (it was the day after he had been taken to bathe in a real sea by his nurse); and he said as he sank: "Poor Annie*an*louise! She'll be sorry for me now!" But Annie*an*louise, walking slowly on the beach, called, " 'Ha! Ha!' said the duck, laughing," which to a waking mind might not seem to bear on the situation. It consoled Georgie at once, and must have been some kind of spell, for it raised the bottom of the deep, and he waded out with a twelve-inch flower-pot on each foot. As he was strictly forbidden to meddle with flower-pots in real life, he felt triumphantly wicked.

The movements of the grown-ups, whom Georgie tolerated but did not pretend to understand, removed his world, when he was seven years old, to a place called Oxford-on-a-visit. Here were huge buildings surrounded by vast prairies, with streets of infinite length, and, above all, something called the buttery, which Georgie was dying to see because he knew it must be greasy and therefore delightful. He perceived how correct were his judgments when his nurse led him through a stone arch into the presence of an enormously fat man, who asked him if he would like some bread and cheese. Georgie was used to eat all round the clock, so he took what buttery gave him and would have taken some brown liquid called audit-ale but that his nurse led him away to an afternoon performance of a thing called *Pepper's Ghost*. This was intensely thrilling. People's heads came off and flew all over the stage, and skeletons danced bone by bone, while Mr. Pepper himself, beyond a question a man of the worst, waved his arms and flapped a long gown, and in a deep bass voice (Georgie had never heard a man sing before) told of his sorrows unspeakable. Some grown-up or other tried to explain that the illusion was made with mirrors and that there was no need to be frightened. Georgie did not know what illusions were, but he did know that a mirror was the looking-glass with the ivory handle on his mother's dressing-table. Therefore the grown-up was "just saying things" after the distressing custom of grown-ups, and Georgie cast about for amusement between scenes. Next to him sat a little girl dressed all in black, her hair combed off her forehead exactly like the girl in the book called *Alice in Wonderland,* which had been given him on his last birthday. The little girl looked at Georgie, and Georgie looked at her. There seemed to be no need of any further introduction.

"I've got a cut on my thumb," said he. It was the first work of his first real knife, a savage triangular hack, and he esteemed it a most valuable possession.

"I'm tho thorry!" she lisped. "Let me look—pleathe."

"There's a di-ack-lum plaster on, but it's all raw under," Georgie answered, complying.

"Dothen't it hurt?" Her grey eyes were full of pity and interest.

"Awf'ly. Perhaps it will give me lockjaw."

"It lookth very horrid. I'm *tho* thorry!" She put a fore-finger to his hand and held her head sidewise for a better view.

Here the nurse turned and shook him severely. "You mustn't talk to strange little girls, Master Georgie."

"She isn't strange. She's very nice. I like her, an' I've showed her my new cut."

"The idea! You change places with me."

She moved him over and shut out the little girl from his view, while the grown-up behind renewed the futile explanations.

"I am *not* afraid, truly," said the boy, wriggling in despair; "but why don't you go to sleep in the afternoons, same as Provost of Oriel?"

Georgie had been introduced to a grown-up of that name, who slept in his presence without apology. Georgie understood that he was the most important grown-up in Oxford; hence he strove to gild his rebuke with flatteries. This grown-up did not seem to like it, but he collapsed,

and Georgie lay back in his seat, silent and enraptured.
Mr. Pepper was singing again, and the deep, ringing voice,
the red fire, and the misty, waving gown all seemed to be
mixed up with the little girl who had been so kind about
his cut. When the performance was ended she nodded to
Georgie, and Georgie nodded in return. He spoke no
more than was necessary till bedtime, but meditated on
new colours and sounds and lights and music and things
as far as he understood them, the deep-mouthed agony of
Mr. Pepper mingling with the little girl's lisp. That night
he made a new tale, from which he shamelessly removed
the Rapunzel-Rapunzel-let-down-your-hair princess, gold
crown, Grimm edition, and all, and put a new Annie*an*-
louise in her place. So it was perfectly right and natural
that when he came to the brushwood pile he should find
her waiting for him, her hair combed off her forehead
more like Alice in Wonderland than ever, and the races
and adventures began.

Ten years at an English public-school do not encourage
dreaming. Georgie won his growth and chest measure-
ment, and a few other things which did not appear in the
bills, under a system of cricket, football, and paper-
chases, from four to five days a week, which provided for
three lawful cuts of a ground-ash if any boy absented
himself from these entertainments. He became a rumple-
collared, dusty-hatted fag of the Lower Third and a light
half-back at Little Side football, was pushed and prodded
through the slack backwaters of the Lower Fourth, where
the raffle of a school generally accumulates, won his Second Fifteen cap at football, enjoyed the dignity of a study
with two companions in it, and began to look forward to
office as a sub-prefect. At last he blossomed into full glory
as head of the school; ex-officio captain of the games; head
of his house, where he and his lieutenants preserved discipline and decency among seventy boys from twelve to
seventeen; general arbiter in the quarrels that spring up
among the touchy Sixth—and intimate friend and ally of
the head himself. When he stepped forth in the black jersey, white knickers and black stockings of the First Fifteen, the new match ball under his arm, and his old and

frayed cap at the back of his head, the small fry of the lower forms stood apart and worshipped, and the "new caps" of the team talked to him ostentatiously, that the world might see. And so, in summer, when he came back to the pavilion after a slow but eminently safe game, it mattered not whether he had made nothing or, as once happened, a hundred and three, the school shouted just the same, and women-folk who had come to look at the match looked at Cottar—Cottar, *major*. "That's Cottar!" Above all, he was responsible for that thing called the tone of the school, and few realize with what passionate devotion a certain type of boy throws himself into this work. Home was a far-away country, full of ponies and fishing and shooting, and men-visitors who interfered with one's plans; but school was the real world, where things of vital importance happened, and crises arose that must be dealt with promptly and quietly. Not for nothing was it written, "Let the consuls look to it that the Republic takes no harm," and Georgie was glad to be back in authority when the holidays ended. Behind him, but not too near, was the wise and temperate head, now suggesting the wisdom of the serpent, now counselling the mildness of the dove; leading him on to see, more by half hints than by any direct word, how boys and men are all of a piece and how he who can handle the one will assuredly in time control the other.

For the rest, the school was not encouraged to dwell on its emotions, but rather to keep in hard condition, to avoid false quantities, and to enter the army direct, without the help of the expensive London crammer, under whose roof young blood learns too much. Cottar, *major*, went the way of hundreds before him. The head gave him six months' final polish, taught him what kind of answers best please a certain kind of examiners, and handed him over to the properly constituted authorities, who passed him into Sandhurst. Here he had sense enough to see that he was in the Lower Third once more, and behaved with respect towards his seniors, till they in turn respected him. and he was promoted to the rank of corporal and sat in authority over mixed peoples with all the vices of men and boys combined. His reward was another string of athletic cups, a good-conduct sword, and at last, her Majesty's commission as a subaltern in a first-class line regiment. He did not know that he bore with him from school and college a character worth much fine gold, but was pleased to find his mess so kindly. He had plenty of money of his own; his training had set the public-school mask upon his face and had taught him how many were the "things no fellow can do." By virtue of the same training he kept his pores open and his mouth shut.

The regular working of the empire shifted his world to India, where he tasted utter loneliness in subaltern's quarters—one room and one bullock-trunk—and, with his mess, learned the new life from the beginning. But there were horses in the land—ponies at reasonable price; there was polo for such as could afford it; there were the disreputable remnants of a pack of hounds; and Cottar worried his way along without too much despair. It dawned on him that a regiment in India was nearer the chance of active service than he had conceived and that a man might as well study his profession. A major of the new school backed this idea with enthusiasm, and he and Cottar accumulated a library of military works and read and argued and disputed far into the nights. But the adjutant said the old thing. "Get to know your men, young un, and they'll follow you anywhere. That's all you want—know your men." Cottar thought he knew them fairly well at cricket and the regimental sports, but he never realized the true inwardness of them till he was sent off with a detachment of twenty to sit down in a mud fort near a rushing river which was spanned by a bridge of boats. When the floods came they went forth and hunted strayed pontoons along the banks. Otherwise there was nothing to do, and the men got drunk, gambled, and quarrelled. They were a sickly crew, for a junior subaltern is by custom saddled with the worst men. Cottar endured their rioting as long as he could, and then sent down country for a dozen pairs of boxing-gloves.

"I wouldn't blame you for fightin'," said he, "if you only knew how to use your hands; but you don't. Take these things, and I'll show you." The men appreciated his efforts. Now, instead of blaspheming and swearing at a comrade and threatening to shoot him, they could take him apart, and soothe themselves to exhaustion. As one explained whom Cottar found with a shut eye and a diamond-shaped mouth spitting blood through an embrasure, "We tried it with the gloves, sir, for twenty minutes, and *that* done us no good, sir. Then we took off the gloves and tried it that was for another twenty minutes, same as you showed us, sir, an' that done us a world o' good. 'Twasn't fightin', sir; there was a bet on."

Cottar dared not laugh, but he invited his men to other sports, such as racing across country in shirt and trousers after a trail of torn paper, and to single-stick in the evenings, till the native population, who had a lust for sport in every form, wished to know whether the white men understood wrestling. They sent in an ambassador, who took the soldiers by the neck and threw them about the dust; and the entire command were all for this new game. They spent money on learning new falls and holds, which was better than buying other doubtful commodities; and the peasantry grinned five deep round the tournaments.

That detachment, who had gone up in bullock-carts, returned to headquarters at an average rate of thirty miles a day, fair heel-and-toe, no sick, no prisoners, and no courts-martial pending. They scattered themselves among their friends, singing the praises of their lieutenant and looking for causes of offence.

"How did you do it, young un?" the adjutant asked.

"Oh, I sweated the beef off 'em, and then I sweated some muscle on to 'em. It was rather a lark."

"If that's your way of lookin' at it, we can give you all the larks you want. Young Davies isn't feelin' quite fit, and he's next for detachment duty. Care to go for him?"

"Sure he wouldn't mind? I don't want to shove myself forward, you know."

"You needn't bother on Davies' account. We'll give you the sweepin's of the corps, and you can see what you can make of 'em."

"All right," said Cottar. "It's better fun than loafin' about cantonments."

"Rummy thing," said the adjutant after Cottar had returned to his wilderness with twenty other devils worse

than the first. "If Cottar only knew it, half the women in
the station would give their eyes—confound 'em!—to
have the young un in tow."

"That accounts for Mrs. Elery sayin' I was workin' my
nice new boy too hard," said a wing commander.

"Oh, yes; and 'Why doesn't he come to the bandstand
in the evenings?' and 'Can't I get him to make up a four
at tennis with the Hammon girls?' " the adjutant snorted.
"Look at young Davies makin' an ass of himself over
mutton-dressed-as-lamb old enough to be his mother!"

"No one can accuse young Cottar of runnin' after
women, white *or* black," the major replied thoughtfully.
"But, then, that's the kind that generally goes the worst
mucker in the end."

"Not Cottar. I've only run across one of his muster before—a fellow called Ingles, in South Africa. He was just
the same hard-trained, athletic-sports build of animal. Always kept himself in the pink of condition. Didn't do him
much good, though. Shot at Wesselstroom the week before Majuba. Wonder how the young un will lick his detachment into shape."

Cottar turned up six weeks later, on foot, with his pu-
pils. He never told his experiences, but the men spoke en-
thusiastically, and fragments of it leaked back to the
colonel through sergeants, batmen, and the like.

There was great jealousy between the first and second
detachments, but the men united in adoring Cottar, and
their way of showing it was by sparing him all the trouble
that men know how to make for an unloved officer. He
sought popularity as little as he had sought it at school,
and therefore it came to him. He favoured no one, not
even when the company sloven pulled the company
cricket-match out of the fire with an unexpected forty-
three at the last moment. There was very little getting
round him, for he seemed to know by instinct exactly
when and where to head off a malingerer; but he did not
forget that the difference between a dazed and sulky
junior of the upper school and a bewildered, browbeaten
lump of a private fresh from the depot was very small
indeed. The sergeants, seeing these things, told him
secrets generally hid from young officers. His words were

quoted as barrack authority on bets in canteen and at tea;
and the veriest shrew of the corps, bursting with charges
against other women who had used the cooking-ranges
out of turn, forbore to speak when Cottar, as the regulations ordained, asked of a morning if there were "any
complaints."

"I'm full o' complaints," said Mrs. Corporal Morrison,.
"an' I'd kill O'Halloran's fat sow of a wife any day, but ye
know how it is. 'E puts 'is head just inside the door, an'
looks down 'is blessed nose so bashful, an' 'e whispers,
'Any complaints?' Ye can't complain after that. *I* want to
kiss him. Some day I think I will. Heigh-ho! She'll be a
lucky woman that gets Young Innocence. See 'im now,
girls. Do ye blame me?"

Cottar was cantering across to polo, and he looked a
very satisfactory figure of a man as he gave easily to the
first excited bucks of his pony and slipped over a low mud
wall to the practice-ground. There were more than Mrs.
Corporal Morrison who felt as she did. But Cottar was
busy for eleven hours of the day. He did not care to have
his tennis spoiled by petticoats in the court; and after one
long afternoon at a garden-party, he explained to his major that this sort of thing was "futile piffle," and the major
laughed. Theirs was not a married mess, except for the
colonel's wife, and Cottar stood in awe of the good lady.
She said "my regiment," and the world knows what that
means. Nonetheless, when they wanted her to give away
the prizes after a shooting-match and she refused because
one of the prize-winners was married to a girl who had
made a jest of her behind her broad back, the mess
ordered Cottar to "tackle her" in his best calling-kit. This
he did, simply and laboriously, and she gave way altogether.

"She only wanted to know the facts of the case," he explained. "I just told her, and she saw at once."

"Ye-es," said the adjutant. "I expect that's what she
did. Comin' to the Fusiliers' dance tonight, Galahad?"

"No, thanks. I've got a fight on with the major." The
virtuous apprentice sat up till midnight in the major's
quarters, with a stop-watch and a pair of compasses,
shifting little painted lead blocks about a four-inch map.

Then he turned in and slept the sleep of innocence, which is full of healthy dreams. One peculiarity of his dreams he noticed at the beginning of his second hot weather. Two or three times a month they duplicated or ran in series. He would find himself sliding into dreamland by the same road—a road that ran along a beach near a pile of brushwood. To the right lay the sea, sometimes at full tide, sometimes withdrawn to the very horizon; but he knew it for the same sea. By that road he would travel over a swell of rising ground covered with short, withered grass, into valleys of wonder and unreason. Beyond the ridge, which was crowned with some sort of street-lamp, anything was possible; but up to the lamp it seemed to him that he knew the road as well as he knew the parade-ground. He learned to look forward to the place, for once there, he was sure of a good night's rest, and Indian hot weather can be rather trying. First, shadowy under closing eyelids, would come the outline of the brushwood pile; next the white sand of the beach-road, almost overhanging the black, changeful sea; then the turn inland and uphill to the single light. When he was unrestful for any reason, he would tell himself how he was sure to get there—sure to get there—if he shut his eyes and surrendered to the drift of things. But one night after a foolishly hard hour's polo (the thermometer was ninety-four degrees in his quarters at ten o'clock), sleep stood away from him altogether, though he did his best to find the well-known road, the point where true sleep began. At last he saw the brushwood pile and hurried along to the ridge, for behind him he felt was the wide-awake, sultry world. He reached the lamp in safety, tingling with drowsiness, when a policeman—a common country policeman—sprang up before him and touched him on the shoulder ere he could dive into the dim valley below. He was filled with terror—the hopeless terror of dreams—for the policeman said in the awful, distinct voice of dream-people. "I am Policeman Day coming back from the City of Sleep. You come with me." Georgie knew it was true—that just beyond him in the valley lay the lights of the City of Sleep, where he would have been sheltered, and that his policeman-thing had full power and authority to head him back to miserable wakefulness. He found himself looking at the moonlight on the wall, dripping with fright; and he never overcame that horror, though he met the policeman several times that hot weather, and his coming was the forerunner of a bad night.

But other dreams—perfectly absurd ones—filled him with an incommunicable delight. All those that he remembered began by the brushwood pile. For instance, he found a small clockwork steamer (he had noticed it many nights before) lying by the sea-road, and stepped into it, whereupon it moved with surpassing swiftness over an absolutely level sea. This was glorious, for he felt he was exploring great matters; and it stopped by a lily carved in stone, which, most naturally, floated on the water. Seeing the lily was labelled "Hong Kong," Georgie said: "Of course. This is precisely what I expected Hong Kong would be like. How magnificent!" Thousands of miles farther on it halted at yet another stone lily, labelled "Java"; and this, again, delighted him hugely, because he knew that now he was at the world's end. But the little boat ran on and on till it lay in a deep fresh-water lock, the sides of which were carven marble, green with moss. Lily-pads lay on the water, and reeds arched above. Someone moved among the reeds, someone whom Georgie knew he had travelled to this world's end to reach. Therefore everything was entirely well with him. He was unspeakably happy and vaulted over the ship's side to find this person. When his feet touched that still water, it changed, with the rustle of unrolling maps, to nothing less than a sixth quarter of the globe, beyond the most remote imagining of man—a place where islands were coloured yellow and blue, their lettering strung across their faces. They gave on unknown seas, and Georgie's urgent desire was to return swiftly across this floating atlas to known bearings. He told himself repeatedly that it was no good to hurry; but still he hurried desperately, and the islands slipped and slid under his feet, the straits yawned and widened, till he found himself utterly lost in the world's fourth dimension, with no hope of return. Yet only a little distance away he could see the old world with the rivers and mountain-chains marked according to the Sandhurst rules of map-making. Then that person for whom he had come to the Lily Lock (that was its name) ran up across unexplored territories and showed him a way. They fled hand in hand till they reached a road that spanned ravines and ran along the edge of precipices and was tunnelled through mountains. "This goes to our brushwood pile," said his companion; and all his trouble was at an end. He took a pony, because he understood that this was the Thirty Mile Ride and he must ride swiftly, and raced through the clattering tunnels and round the curves, always downhill, till he heard the sea to his left and saw it raging under a full moon against sandy cliffs. It was heavy going, but he recognized the nature of the country, the dark-purple downs inland, and the bents that whistled in the wind. The road was eaten away in places, and the sea lashed at him—black, foamless tongues of smooth and glossy rollers; but he was sure that there was less danger from the sea than from "Them," whoever "They" were, inland to his right. He knew too that he would be safe if he could reach the down with the lamp on it. This came as he expected: he saw the one light a mile ahead along the beach, dismounted, turned to the right, walked quietly over to the brushwood pile, found the little steamer had returned to the beach whence he had unmoored it, and—must have fallen asleep, for he could remember no more. "I'm gettin' the hang of the geography of that place," he said to himself as he shaved next morning. "I must have made some sort of circle. Let's see. The Thirty Mile Ride (now how the deuce did I know it was called the Thirty Mile Ride?) joins the sea-road beyond the first down where the lamp is. And that atlas-country lies at the back of the Thirty Mile Ride, somewhere out to the right beyond the hills and tunnels. Rummy things, dreams. Wonder what makes mine fit into each other so?"

He continued on his solid way through the recurring duties of the seasons. The regiment was shifted to another station, and he enjoyed road-marching for two months, with a good deal of mixed shooting thrown in, and when they reached their new cantonments he became a member of the local Tent Club, and chased the mighty boar on

horseback with a short stabbing-spear. There he met the
mahseer of the Poonch, beside whom the tarpon is as a
herring, and he who lands him can say that he is a fisher-
man. This was as new and as fascinating as the big-game
shooting that fell to his portion, when he had himself pho-
tographed for the mother's benefit sitting on the flank of
his first tiger.

Then the adjutant was promoted, and Cottar rejoiced
with him, for he admired the adjutant greatly and marvelled who might be big enough to fill his place; so that
he nearly collapsed when the mantle fell on his own
shoulders, and the colonel said a few sweet things that
made him blush. An adjutant's position does not differ
materially from that of head of the school, and Cottar
stood in the same relation to the colonel as he had to his
old head in England. Only, tempers wear out in hot
weather, and things were said and done that tried him
sorely, and he made glorious blunders, from which the
regimental sergeant-major pulled him with a loyal soul
and a shut mouth. Slovens and incompetents raged
against him; the weak-minded strove to lure him from the
ways of justice; the small-minded—yea, men whom Cottar believed would never do "things no fellow can do"—
imputed motives mean and circuitous to actions that he
had not spent a thought upon; and he tasted injustice, and
it made him very sick. But his consolation came on
parade, when he looked down the full companies, and reflected how few were in hospital or cells, and wondered
when the time would come to try the machine of his love
and labour.

But they needed and expected the whole of a man's
working-day, and maybe three or four hours of the night.
Curiously enough, he never dreamed about the regiment
as he was popularly supposed to. The mind, set free from
the day's doings, generally ceased working altogether, or,
if it moved at all, carried him along the old beach-road to
the downs, the lamp-post, and once in a while to terrible
Policeman Day. The second time that he returned to
the world's lost continent (this was a dream that repeated itself again and again, with variations, on the same
ground) he knew that if he only sat still the person from

the Lily Lock would help him, and he was not disappointed. Sometimes he was trapped in mines of vast depth hollowed out of the heart of the world, where men in torment chanted echoing songs; and he heard this person coming along through the galleries, and everything was made safe and delightful. They met again in low-roofed Indian railway-carriages that halted in a garden surrounded by gilt-and-green railings, where a mob of stony white people, all unfriendly, sat at breakfast-tables covered with roses, and separated Georgie from his companion, while underground voices sang deep-voiced songs. Georgie was filled with enormous despair till they two met again. They foregathered in the middle of an endless hot tropic night and crept into a huge house that stood, he knew, somewhere north of the railway station, where the people ate among the roses. It was surrounded with gardens, all moist and dripping; and in one room, reached through leagues of white-washed passages, a sick thing lay in bed. Now the least noise, Georgie knew, would unchain some waiting horror, and his companion knew it too; but when their eyes met across the bed, Georgie was disgusted to see that she was a child—a little girl in strapped shoes, with her black hair combed back from her forehead.

"What disgraceful folly!" he thought. "Now she could do nothing whatever if its head came off."

Then the thing coughed, and the ceiling shattered down in plaster on the mosquito-netting, and "They" rushed in from all quarters. He dragged the child through the stifling garden, voices chanting behind them, and they rode the Thirty Mile Ride under whip and spur along the sandy beach by the booming sea till they came to the downs, the lamp-post, and the brushwood pile, which was safety. Very often dreams would break up about them in this fashion, and they would be separated, to endure awful adventures alone. But the most amusing times were when he and she had a clear understanding that it was all make-believe and walked through mile-wide roaring rivers without even taking off their shoes, or set light to populous cities to see how they would burn, and were rude as any children to the vague shadows met in their rambles. Later in the night they were sure to suffer for this, either at the hands of the Railway People eating among the roses, or in the tropic uplands at the far end of the Thirty Mile Ride. Together, this did not much affright them; but often Georgie would hear her shrill cry of "Boy! Boy!" half a world away, and hurry to her rescue before "They" maltreated her.

He and she explored the dark-purple downs as far. inland from the brushwood pile as they dared, but that was always a dangerous matter. The interior was filled with "Them," and "They" went about singing in the hollows, and Georgie and she felt safer on or near the sea-board. So thoroughly had he come to know the place of his dreams that even waking he accepted it as a real country, and made a rough sketch of it. He kept his own. counsel, of course, but the permanence of the land puzzled him. His ordinary dreams were as formless and as fleeting as any healthy dreams could be, but once at the brushwood pile he moved within known limits and could see where he was going. There were months at a time when nothing notable crossed his sleep. Then the dreams would come in a batch of five or six, and next morning the map that he kept in his writing-case would be written up to date, for Georgie was a most methodical person. There was, indeed, a danger—his seniors said so—of his developing into a regular "Auntie Fuss" of an adjutant, and when an officer once takes to old-maidism there is more hope for the virgin of seventy than for him.

But fate sent the change that was needed, in the shape of a little winter campaign on the border, which, after the manner of little campaigns, flashed out into a very ugly war; and Cottar's regiment was chosen among the first.

"Now," said a major, "this'll shake the cobwebs out of us all—especially you, Galahad; and we can see what your hen-with-one-chick attitude has done for the regiment."

Cottar nearly wept with joy as the campaign went forward. They were fit—physically fit beyond the other troops; they were good children in camp, wet or dry, fed or unfed; and they followed their officers with the quick suppleness and trained obedience of a first-class football fifteen. They were cut off from their apology for a base, and cheerfully cut their way back to it again; they crowned and cleaned out hills full of the enemy with the precision of well-broken dogs of chase; and in the hour of retreat, when, hampered with the sick and wounded of the column, they were persecuted down eleven miles of water-less valley, they, serving as rear-guard, covered them-selves with a great glory in the eyes of fellow profes-sionals. Any regiment can advance, but few know how to retreat with a sting in the tail. Then they turned to make roads, most often under fire, and dismantled some incon-venient mud redoubts. They were the last corps to be withdrawn when the rubbish of the campaign was all swept up; and after a month in standing camp, which tries morals severely, they departed to their own place in column of fours, singing:

> 'E's goin' to do without 'em—
>   Don't want 'em anymore;
> 'E's goin' to do without 'em,
>   As 'e's often done before.
> 'E's goin' to be a martyr
> On a 'ighly novel plan,
> An' all the boys and girls will say,
>   "Ow! what a nice young man—man—man!
>   Ow! what a nice young man!"

There came out a *Gazette* in which Cottar found that he had been behaving with "courage and coolness and discretion" in all his capacities; that he had assisted the wounded under fire, and blown in a gate, also under fire. Net result, his captaincy and a brevet majority, coupled with the Distinguished Service Order.

As to his wounded, he explained that they were both heavy men, whom he could lift more easily than anyone else. "Otherwise, of course, I should have sent out one of my men; and, of course, about that gate business, we were safe the minute we were well under the walls." But this did not prevent his men from cheering him furiously whenever they saw him, or the mess from giving him a dinner on the eve of his departure to England. (A year's leave was among the things he had "snaffled out of the campaign," to use his own words.) The doctor, who had taken quite as much as was good for him, quoted poetry

about "a good blade carving the casques of men," and so
on, and everybody told Cottar that he was an excellent
person; but when he rose to make his maiden speech they
shouted so that he was understood to say, "It isn't any
use tryin' to speak with you chaps rottin' me like this.
Let's have some pool."

It is not unpleasant to spend eight and twenty days in
an easy-going steamer on warm waters in the company of
a woman who lets you see that you are head and shoulders superior to the rest of the world, even though that
woman may be, and most often is, ten counted years your
senior. P.&O. boats are not lighted with the disgustful par-
ticularity of Atlantic liners. There is more phosphores-
cence at the bows and greater silence and darkness by the
hand-steering gear aft.

Awful things might have happened to Georgie but for
the little fact that he had never studied the first principles
of the game he was expected to play. So when Mrs. Zuleika, at Aden, told him how motherly an interest she felt
in his welfare, medals, brevet, and all, Georgie took her at
the foot of the letter and promptly talked of his own
mother, three hundred miles nearer each day, of his
home, and so forth, all the way up the Red Sea. It was
much easier than he had supposed to converse with a
woman for an hour at a time. Then Mrs. Zuleika, turning
from parental affections, spoke of love in the abstract as a
thing not unworthy of study, and in discreet twilights after
dinner demanded confidences. Georgie would have been
delighted to supply them, but he had none, and did not
know it was his duty to manufacture them. Mrs. Zuleika
expressed surprise and unbelief and asked those questions
which deep asks of deep. She learned all that was necessary to conviction, and being very much a woman,
resumed (Georgie never knew that she had abandoned)
the motherly attitude.

"Do you know," she said, somewhere in the Mediter-
ranean, "I think you're the very dearest boy I have ever
met in my life, and I'd like you to remember me a little.
You will when you are older, but I want you to remember
me now. You'll make some girl very happy."

"Oh! Hope so," said Georgie gravely; "but there's heaps of time for marryin' an' all that sort of thing, aren't there?"

"That depends. Here are your bean-bags for the Ladies Competition. I think I'm growing too old to care for these *tamashas*."

They were getting up sports, and Georgie was on the committee. He never noticed how perfectly the bags were sewn, but another woman did, and smiled—once. He liked Mrs. Zuleika greatly. She was a bit old, of course, but uncommonly nice. There was no nonsense about her.

A few nights after they passed Gibraltar his dream returned to him. She who waited by the brushwood pile was no longer a little girl, but a woman with black hair that grew into a "widow's peak," combed back from her forehead. He knew her for the child in black, the companion of the last six years, and as it had been in the time of the meetings on the lost continent, he was filled with delight unspeakable. "They," for some dreamland reason, were friendly or had gone away that night, and the two flitted together over all their country, from the brushwood pile up the Thirty Mile Ride, till they saw the house of the sick thing, a pin-point in the distance to the left; stamped through the railway waiting-room where the roses lay on the spread breakfast-tables; and returned, by the ford and the city they had once burned for sport, to the great swells of the downs under the lamp-post. Wherever they moved a strong singing followed them underground, but this night there was no panic. All the land was empty except for themselves, and at the last (they were sitting by the lamp-post hand in hand) she turned and kissed him. He woke with a start, staring at the waving curtain of the cabin door; he could almost have sworn that the kiss was real.

Next morning the ship was rolling in a Biscay sea, and people were not happy; but as Georgie came to breakfast, shaven, tubbed, and smelling of soap, several turned to look at him because of the light in his eyes and the splendour of his countenance.

"Well, you look beastly fit," snapped a neighbour. "Anyone left you a legacy in the middle of the bay?"

Georgie reached for the curry with a seraphic grin. "I suppose it's the gettin' so near home, and all that. I do feel rather festive this mornin'. Rolls a bit, doesn't she?"

Mrs. Zuleika stayed in her cabin till the end of the voyage, when she left without bidding him farewell, and wept passionately on the dock-head for pure joy of meeting her children, who, she had often said, were so like their father.

Georgie headed for his own country, wild with delight of his first long furlough after the lean seasons. Nothing was changed in that orderly life, from the coachman who met him at the station to the white peacock that stormed at the carriage from the stone wall above the shaven lawns. The house took toll of him with due regard to precedence—first the mother, then the father, then the housekeeper, who wept and praised God, then the butler, and so on down to the under-keeper, who had been dog-boy in Georgie's youth and called him "Master Georgie" and was reproved by the groom, who had taught Georgie to ride.

"Not a thing changed," he sighed contentedly when the three of them sat down to dinner in the late sunlight, while the rabbits crept out upon the lawn below the cedars and the big trout in the ponds by the home paddock rose for their evening meal.

"*Our* changes are all over, dear," cooed the mother; "and now I am getting used to your size and your tan (you're very brown, Georgie), I see you haven't changed in the least. You're exactly like the pater."

The father beamed on this man after his own heart—"youngest major in the army, and should have had the V. C., sir"—and the butler listened with his professional mask off when Master Georgie spoke of war as it is waged today and his father cross-questioned.

They went out on the terrace to smoke among the roses, and the shadow of the old house lay long across the wonderful English foliage, which is the only living green in the world.

"Perfect! By Jove, it's perfect!" Georgie was looking at the round-bosomed woods beyond the home paddock, where the white pheasant boxes were ranged; and the golden air was full of a hundred sacred scents and sounds. Georgie felt his father's arm tighten in his.

"It's not half bad; but *hodie mihi, cras tibi,* isn't it? I suppose you'll be turning up some fine day with a girl under your arm, if you haven't one now, eh?"

"You can make your mind easy, sir. I haven't one."

"Not in all these years?" said the mother.

"I hadn't time, Mummy. They keep a man pretty busy these days in the service, and most of our mess are unmarried too."

"But you must have met hundreds in society—at balls and so on?"

"I'm like the Tenth, Mummy: I don't dance."

"Don't dance! What have you been doing with yourself, then—backing other men's bills?" said the father.

"Oh, yes; I've done a little of that too; but you see, as things are now, a man has all his work cut out for him to keep abreast of his profession, and my days are always too full to let me lark about half the night."

"Hmm!"—suspiciously.

"It's never too late to learn. We ought to give some kind of housewarming for the people about, now you've come back. Unless you want to go straight up to town, dear?"

"No. I don't want anything better than this. Let's sit still and enjoy ourselves. I suppose there will be something for me to ride if I look for it?"

"Seeing I've been kept down to the old brown pair for the last six weeks because all the others were being got ready for Master Georgie, I should say there might be," the father chuckled. "They're reminding me in a hundred ways that I must take the second place now."

"Brutes!"

"The pater doesn't mean it, dear; but everyone has been trying to make your homecoming a success; and you do like it, don't you?"

"Perfect! Perfect! There's no place like England—when you've done your work."

"That's the proper way to look at it, my son."

And so up and down the flagged walk till their shadows grew long in the moonlight, and the mother went indoors and played such songs as a small boy once clamoured for, and the squat silver candlesticks were brought in, and Georgie climbed to the two rooms in the west wing that had been his nursery and his playroom in the beginning. Then who should come to tuck him up for the night but the mother? And she sat down on the bed, and they talked for a long hour, as mother and son should, if there is to be any future for the empire. With a simple woman's deep guile she asked questions and suggested answers that should have waked some sign in the face on the pillow, and there was neither quiver of eyelid nor quickening of breath, neither evasion nor delay in reply. So she blessed him and kissed him on the mouth, which is not always a mother's property, and said something to her husband later, at which he laughed profane and incredulous laughs.

All the establishment waited on Georgie next morning, from the tallest six-year-old, "with a mouth like a kid glove, Master Georgie," to the under-keeper strolling carelessly along the horizon, Georgie's pet rod in his hand, and "There's a four-pounder risin' below the lasher. You don't 'ave 'em in Injia, Mast—Major Georgie." It was all beautiful beyond telling, even though the mother insisted on taking him out in the landau (the leather had the hot Sunday smell of his youth) and showing him off to her friends at all the houses for six miles round; and the pater bore him up to town and a lunch at the club, where he introduced him, quite carelessly, to not less than thirty ancient warriors whose sons were not the youngest majors in the army and had not the D. S. O. After that it was Georgie's turn; and remembering his friends, he filled up the house with that kind of officer who live in cheap lodgings at Southsea or Montpelier Square, Brompton— good men all, but not well off. The mother perceived that they needed girls to play with; and as there was no scarcity of girls, the house hummed like a dovecote in spring. They tore up the place for amateur theatricals; they disappeared in the gardens when they ought to have been rehearsing; they swept off every available horse and vehicle, especially the governess-cart and the fat pony; they fell into the trout-ponds; they picnicked and they tennised;

and they sat on gates in the twilight, two by two, and
Georgie found that he was not in the least necessary to
their entertainment.

"My word!" said he when he saw the last of their dear
backs. "They told me they've enjoyed 'emselves, but they
haven't done half the things they said they would."

"I know they've enjoyed themselves—immensely," said
the mother. "You're a public benefactor, dear."

"Now we can be quiet again, can't we?"

"Oh, quite. I've a very dear friend of mine that I want
you to know. She couldn't come with the house so full,
because she's an invalid, and she was away when you first
came. She's a Mrs. Lacy."

"Lacy! I don't remember the name about here."

"No; they came after you went to India—from Oxford.
Her husband died there, and she lost some money, I believe. They bought The Firs on the Bassett Road. She's a
very sweet woman, and we're very fond of them both."

"She's a widow, didn't you say?"

"She has a daughter. Surely I said so, dear?"

"Does she fall into trout-ponds, and gas and giggle, and
'Oh, Major Cottah!' and all that sort of thing?"

"No, indeed. She's a very quiet girl, and very musical.
She always came over here with her music-books—
composing, you know; and she generally works all day, so
you won't——"

"Talking about Miriam?" said the pater, coming up.
The mother edged towards him within elbow reach. There
was no finesse about Georgie's father. "Oh, Miriam's a
dear girl. Plays beautifully. Rides beautifully too. She's a
regular pet of the household. Used to call me——" The
elbow went home, and ignorant but obedient always, the
pater shut himself off.

"What used she to call you, sir?"

"All sorts of pet names. I'm very fond of Miriam."

"Sounds Jewish—Miriam."

"Jew! You'll be calling yourself a Jew next. She's one
of the Herefordshire Lacys. When her aunt dies——"
Again the elbow.

"Oh, you won't see anything of her, Georgie. She's
busy with her music or her mother all day. Besides, you're

going up to town tomorrow, aren't you? I thought you said something about an Institute meeting?" The mother spoke.

"Go up to town *now!* What nonsense!" Once more the pater was shut off.

"I had some idea of it, but I'm not quite sure," said the son of the house. Why did the mother try to get him away because a musical girl and her invalid parent were expected? He did not approve of unknown females calling his father pet names. He would observe these pushing persons who had been only seven years in the county.

All of which the delighted mother read in his countenance, herself keeping an air of sweet disinterestedness.

"They'll be here this evening for dinner. I'm sending the carriage over for them, and they won't stay more than a week."

"Perhaps I shall go up to town. I don't quite know yet." Georgie moved away irresolutely. There was a lecture at the United Services Institute on the supply of ammunition in the field, and the one man whose theories most irritated Major Cottar would deliver it. A heated discussion was sure to follow, and perhaps he might find himself moved to speak. He took his rod that afternoon and went down to thrash it out among the trout.

"Good sport, dear!" said the mother from the terrace.

" 'Fraid it won't be, Mummy. All those men from town, and the girls particularly, have put every trout off his feed for weeks. There isn't one of 'em that cares for fishin'—really. Fancy stampin' and shoutin' on the bank, and tellin' every fish for half a mile exactly what you're goin' to do, and then chuckin' a brute of a fly at him! By Jove, it would scare *me* if I was a trout!"

But things were not as bad as he had expected. The black gnat was on the water, and the water was strictly preserved. A three-quarter-pounder at the second cast set him for the campaign, and he worked downstream, crouching behind the reed and meadow-street, creeping between a horn-beam hedge and a foot-wide strip of bank where he could see the trout but where they could not distinguish him from the background, lying almost on his stomach to switch the blue-upright sidewise through the checkered shadows of a gravelly ripple under overarching trees. But he had known every inch of the water since he was four feet high. The aged and astute between sunk roots, with the large and fat that lay in the frothy scum below some strong rush of water, sucking as lazily as carp, came to trouble in their turn at the hand that imitated so delicately the flicker and wimple of an egg-dropping fly. Consequently Georgie found himself five miles from home when he ought to have been dressing for dinner. The housekeeper had taken good care that her boy should not go empty, and before he changed to the white moth he sat down to excellent claret with sandwiches of potted egg and things that adoring women make and men never notice. Then back, to surprise the otter grubbing for fresh-water mussels, the rabbits on the edge of the beechwoods foraging in the clover, and the policeman-like white owl stooping to the little fieldmice, till the moon was strong, and he took his rod apart, and went home through well-remembered gaps in the hedges. He fetched a compass round the house, for though he might have broken every law of the establishment every hour, the law of his boyhood was unbreakable; after fishing you went in by the south garden back door, cleaned up in the outer scullery, and did not present yourself to your elders and your betters till you had washed and changed.

"Half past ten, by Jove! Well, we'll make the sport an excuse. They wouldn't want to see me the first evening at any rate. Gone to bed, probably." He skirted by the open French windows of the drawing-room. "No, they haven't. They look very comfy in there."

He could see his father in his own particular chair, the mother in hers, and the back of a girl at the piano by the big potpourri-jar. The gardens looked half divine in the moonlight, and he turned down through the roses to finish his pipe.

A prelude ended, and there floated out a voice of the kind that in his childhood he used to call "creamy"—a full, true contralto; and this is the song that he heard, every syllable of it:

Over the edge of the purple down,
  Where the single lamplight gleams,
Know ye the road to the Merciful Town
  That is hard by the Sea of Dreams—
Where the poor may lay their wrongs away,
  And the sick may forget to weep?
But we—pity us! Oh, pity us!
  We wakeful; ah, pity us!—
We must go back with Policeman Day—
  Back from the City of Sleep!·

Weary they turn from the scroll and crown,
  Fetter and prayer and plough—
They that go up to the Merciful Town,
  For her gates are closing now.
It is their right in the Baths of Night
  Body and soul to steep:
But we—pity us! Ah, pity us!
  We wakeful; oh, pity us!—
We must go back with Policeman Day—
  Back from the City of Sleep!

Over the edge of the purple down,
  Ere the tender dreams begin,
Look—we may look—at the Merciful Town,
  But we may not enter in!
Outcasts all, from her guarded wall
  Back to our watch we creep;
We—pity us! Ah, pity us!
  We wakeful; oh, pity us!—
We that go back with Policeman Day—
  Back from the City of Sleep!

At the last echo he was aware that his mouth was dry and unknown pulses were beating in the roof of it. The housekeeper, who would have it that he must have fallen in and caught a chill, was waiting to catch him on the stairs, and since he neither saw nor answered her, carried a wild tale abroad that brought his mother knocking at the door.

"Anything happened, dear? Harper said she thought you weren't——"

"No; it's nothing. I'm all right, Mummy. *Please* don't bother."

He did not recognize his own voice, but that was a small matter beside what he was considering. Obviously, most obviously, the whole coincidence was crazy lunacy. He proved it to the satisfaction of Major George Cottar, who was going up to town tomorrow to hear a lecture on the supply of ammunition in the field; and having so proved it, the soul and brain and heart and body of Georgie cried joyously: "That's the Lily Lock girl—the lost continent girl—the Thirty Mile Ride girl—the Brushwood girl! *I* know her!"

He waked, stiff and cramped in his chair, to reconsider the situation by sunlight, when it did not appear normal. But a man must eat, and he went to breakfast, his heart between his teeth, holding himself severely in hand.

"Late, as usual," said the mother. "My boy, Miss Lacy."

A tall girl in black raised her eyes to his, and Georgie's life training deserted him—just as soon as he realized that she did not know. He stared coolly and critically. There was the abundant black hair, growing in a widow's peak, turned back from the forehead, with that peculiar ripple over the right ear; there were the grey eyes set a little close together, the short upper lip, resolute chin, and the known poise of the head. There was also the small well-cut mouth that had kissed him.

"Georgie—*dear!*" said the mother amazedly, for Miriam was flushing under the stare.

"I—I beg your pardon!" he gulped. "I don't know whether the mother has told you, but I'm rather an idiot at times, specially before I've had any breakfast. It's—it's a family failing."

He turned to explore among the hot-water dishes on the sideboard, rejoicing that she did not know—she did not know.

His conversation for the rest of the meal was mildly insane, though the mother thought she had never seen her boy look half so handsome. How could any girl, least of all one of Miriam's discernment, forbear to fall down and worship? But deeply Miriam was displeased. She had never been stared at in that fashion before, and promptly retired into her shell when Georgie announced that he had changed his mind about going to town and would stay to play with Miss Lacy if she had nothing better to do.

"Oh, but don't let me throw you out. I'm at work. I've things to do all the morning."

"What possessed Georgie to behave so oddly?" the mother sighed to herself. "Miriam's a bundle of feelings—like her mother."

"You compose, don't you? Must be a fine thing to be able to do that. ["Pig—oh, pig!" thought Miriam.] I think I heard you singin' when I came in last night after fishin'. All about a Sea of Dreams, wasn't it? [Miriam shuddered to the core of the soul that afflicted her.] Awfully pretty song. How d'you think of such things?"

"You only composed the music, dear, didn't you?"

"The words too. I'm sure of it," said Georgie with a sparkling eye. No; she did not know.

"Yeth; I wrote the words too." Miriam spoke slowly, for she knew she lisped when she was nervous.

"Now how *could* you tell, Georgie?" said the mother, as delighted as though the youngest major in the army were ten years old, showing off before company.

"I was sure of it, somehow. Oh, there are heaps of things about me, Mummy, that you don't understand. Looks as if it were goin' to be a hot day—for England. Would you care for a ride this afternoon, Miss Lacy? We can start out after tea, if you'd like it."

Miriam could not in decency refuse, but any woman might see she was not filled with delight.

"That will be very nice, if you take the Bassett Road. It will save me sending Martin down to the village," said the mother, filling in gaps.

Like all good managers, the mother had her one weakness—a mania for little strategies that should economize horses and vehicles. Her men-folk complained that she turned them into common carriers, and there was a legend in the family that she had once said to the pater on the morning of a meet: "If you *should* kill near Bassett, dear, and if it isn't too late, would you mind just popping over and matching me this?"

"I knew that was coming. You'd never miss a chance, Mother. If it's a fish or a trunk I won't." Georgie laughed.

"It's only a duck. They can do it up very neatly at Mallett's," said the mother simply. "You won't mind, will you? We'll have a scratch dinner at nine, because it's so hot."

The long summer day dragged itself out for centuries; but at last there was tea on the lawn, and Miriam appeared.

She was in the saddle before he could offer to help, with the clean spring of the child who mounted the pony for the Thirty Mile Ride. The day held mercilessly, though Georgie got down thrice to look for imaginary stones in Rufus' foot. One cannot say even simple things in broad light, and this that Georgie meditated was not simple. So he spoke seldom, and Miriam was divided between relief and scorn. It annoyed her that the great hulking thing should know she had written the words of the song overnight, for though a maiden may sing her most secret fancies aloud, she does not care to have them trampled over by the male Philistine. They rode into the little red-brick street of Bassett, and Georgie made untold fuss over the disposition of that duck. It must go in just such a package, and be fastened to the saddle in just such a manner, though eight o'clock had struck and they were miles from dinner.

"We must be quick!" said Miriam, bored and angry.

"There's no great hurry; but we can cut over Dowhead Down, and let 'em out on the grass. That will save us half an hour."

The horses capered on the short, sweet-smelling turf, and the delaying shadows gathered in the valley as they cantered over the great dun down that overhangs Bassett and the western coaching-road. Insensibly the pace quickened without thought of mole-hills, Rufus, gentleman that he was, waiting on Miriam's Dandy till they should have cleared the rise. Then down the two-mile slope they raced together, the wind whistling in their ears, to the steady throb of eight hooves and the light click-click of the shifting bits.

"Oh, that was glorious!" Miriam cried, reining in. "Dandy and I are old friends, but I don't think we've ever gone better together."

"No; but you've gone quicker, once or twice."

"Really! When?"

Georgie moistened his lips. "Don't you remember the Thirty Mile Ride—with me—when 'They' were after us—on the beach-road, with the sea to the left—going towards the lamp-post on the downs?"

The girl gasped. "What—what do you mean?" she said hysterically.

"The Thirty Mile Ride, and—all the rest of it."

"You mean— I didn't sing anything about the Thirty Mile Ride. I know I didn't. I have never told a living soul."

"You told about Policeman Day, and the lamp at the top of the downs, and the City of Sleep. It all joins on, you know—it's the same country—and it was easy enough to see where you had been."

"Good God! It joins on—of course it does; but—I have been—you have been— Oh, let's walk, please, or I shall fall off!"

Georgie ranged alongside and laid a hand that shook below her bridle-hand, pulling Dandy into a walk. Miriam was sobbing as he had seen a man sob under the touch of the bullet.

"It's all right—it's all right," he whispered feebly. "Only—only it's true, you know."

"True! Am I mad?"

"Not unless I'm mad as well. *Do* try to think a minute quietly. How could anyone conceivably know anything about the Thirty Mile Ride having anything to do with you unless he had been there?"

"But where? But *where?* Tell me!"

"There—wherever it may be—in our country, I suppose. Do you remember the first time you rode it—the Thirty Mile Ride, I mean? You must."

"It was all dreams—all dreams!"

"Yes, but tell, please; because I know."

"Let me think. I—we were on no account to make any noise—on no account to make any noise." She was staring between Dandy's ears with eyes that did not see, and a suffocating heart.

"Because '*It*' was dying in the big house?" Georgie went on, reining in again.

"There was a garden with green-and-gilt railings—all hot. Do *you* remember?"

"I ought to. I was sitting on the other side of the bed before 'It' coughed and 'They' came in."

"You!" The deep voice was unnaturally full and strong, and the girl's wide-opened eyes burned in the dusk as she stared him through and through. "Then you're the boy—my Brushwood boy—and I've known you all my life!"

She fell forward on Dandy's neck. Georgie forced himself out of the weakness that was overmastering his limbs, and slid an arm round her waist. The head dropped on his shoulder, and he found himself with parched lips saying things that up till then he believed existed only in painted works of fiction. Mercifully the horses were quiet. She made no attempt to draw herself away when she recovered, but lay still, whispering, "Of course you're the boy, and I didn't know—I didn't know."

"I knew last night, and when I saw you at breakfast——"

"Oh, *that* was why! I wondered at the time. You would, of course."

"I couldn't speak before this. Keep your head where it is, dear. It's all right now—all right now, isn't it?"

"But how was it *I* didn't know—after all these years and years? I remember—oh, what lots of things I remember!"

"Tell me some. I'll look after the horses."

"I remember waiting for you when the steamer came in. Do you?"

"At the Lily Lock, between Hong Kong and Java?"

"Do *you* call it that too?"

"You told me it was when I was lost in the continent. That was you that showed me the way through the mountains?"

"When the islands slid? It must have been, because you're the only one I remember. All the others were 'Them.'"

"Awful brutes they were too."

"I remember showing you the Thirty Mile Ride the first time. You ride just as you used to—then. You *are* you!"

"That's odd. I thought that of you this afternoon. Isn't it wonderful?"

"What does it all mean? Why should you and I of the millions of people in the world have this—this thing between us? What does it mean? I'm frightened."

"This!" said Georgie. The horses quickened their pace. They thought they had heard an order. "Perhaps when we die we may find out more, but it means this now."

There was no answer. What could she say? As the world went, they had known each other rather less than eight and a half hours, but the matter was one that did not concern the world. There was a very long silence, while the breath in their nostrils drew cold and sharp as it might have been a fume of ether.

"That's the second," Georgie whispered. "You remember, don't you?"

"It's not!"—furiously. "It's not!"

"On the downs the other night—months ago. You were just as you are now, and we went over the country for miles and miles."

"It was all empty too. 'They' had gone away. Nobody frightened us. I wonder why, boy?"

"Oh, if you remember *that*, you must remember the rest. Confess!"

"I remember lots of things, but I *know* I didn't. I never have—till just now."

"You *did*, dear."

"I know I didn't because—oh, it's no use keeping anything back! Because I truthfully meant to."

"And truthfully did."

"No; meant to; but someone else came by."

"There wasn't anyone else. There never has been."

"There was—there always is. It was another woman—out there on the sea. I saw her. It was the twenty-sixth of May. I've got it written down somewhere."

"Oh, *you've* kept a record of your dreams too? That's odd about the other woman, because I happened to be on the sea just then."

"I was right. How do I know what you've done when you were awake—and I thought it was only *you!*"

"You never were more wrong in your life. What a little temper you've got! Listen to me a minute, dear." And Georgie, though he knew it not, committed black perjury. "It—it isn't the kind of thing one says to anyone, because they'd laugh; but on my word and honour, darling, I've never been kissed by a living soul outside my own people in all my life. Don't laugh, dear. I wouldn't tell anyone but you, but it's the solemn truth."

"I knew! You are you. Oh, I *knew* you'd come some-day; but I didn't know you were you in the least till you spoke."

"Then give me another."

"And you never cared or looked anywhere? Why, all the round world must have loved you from the very minute they saw you, boy."

"They kept it to themselves if they did. No; I never cared."

"And we shall be late for dinner—horribly late. Oh, how can I look at you in the light before your mother—and mine!"

"We'll play you're Miss Lacy till the proper time comes. What's the shortest limit for people to get en-gaged? S'pose we have got to go through all the fuss of an engagement, haven't we?"

"Oh, I don't want to talk about that. It's so common-place. I've thought of something that you don't know. I'm sure of it. What's my name?"

"Miri— No it isn't, by Jove! Wait half a second, and it'll come back to me. You aren't—you can't? Why, *those* old tales—before I went to school! I've never thought of 'em from that day to this. Are you the original, only An-nie*an*louise?"

"It was what you always called me ever since the be-ginning. Oh! We've turned into the avenue, and we must be an hour late."

"What does it matter? The chain goes as far back as

those days? It must, of course—of course it must. I've got
to ride round with this pestilent old bird—confound him!"

" ' "Ha! Ha!" said the duck, laughing'—do you remember *that?*"

"Yes, I do—flower-pots on my feet, and all. We've
been together all this while; and I've got to say good-bye
to you till dinner. *Sure* I'll see you at dinner-time? *Sure*
you won't sneak up to your room, darling, and leave me
all the evening? Good-bye, dear—good-bye."

"Good-bye, boy, good-bye. Mind the arch! Don't let
Rufus bolt into his stables. Good-bye. Yes, I'll come
down to dinner; but—what shall I do when I see you in
the light!"

[First published in 1895.]

.007

A locomotive is, next to a marine engine, the most sensitive thing man ever made; and No. .007, besides being sensitive, was new. The red paint was hardly dry on his spotless bumper-bar, his headlight shone like a fireman's helmet, and his cab might have been a hardwood-finish parlour. They had run him into the roundhouse after his trial—he had said good-bye to his best friend in the shops, the overhead travelling crane; the big world was just outside; and the other locos were taking stock of him. He looked at the semicircle of bold, unwinking headlights, heard the low purr and mutter of the steam mounting in the gauges—scornful hisses of contempt as a slack valve lifted a little—and would have given a month's oil for leave to crawl through his own driving-wheels into the brick ash-pit beneath him. .007 was an eight-wheeled "American" loco, slightly different from others of his type, and as he stood he was worth ten thousand dollars on the company's books. But if you had bought him at his own valuation after half an hour's waiting in the darkish, echoing round-house, you would have saved exactly nine thousand nine hundred and ninety-nine dollars and ninety-eight cents.

A heavy Mogul freight, with a short cow-catcher and a

fire-box that came down within three inches of the rail, began the impolite game, speaking to a Pittsburgh Consolidation, who was visiting.

"Where did this thing blow in from?" he asked with a dreamy puff of light steam.

"It's all I can do to keep track of our makes," was the answer, "without lookin' after *your* back numbers. Guess it's something Peter Cooper left over when he died."

.007 quivered; his steam was getting up, but he held his tongue. Even a hand-car knows what sort of locomotive it was that Peter Cooper experimented upon in the far-away thirties. It carried its coal and water in two apple-barrels and was not much bigger than a bicycle.

Then up and spoke a small, newish switching-engine, with a little step in front of his bumper-timber, and his wheels so close together that he looked like a bronco getting ready to buck.

"Something's wrong with the road when a Pennsylvania gravel-pusher tells us anything about our stock, *I* think. That kid's all right. Eustis designed him, and Eustis designed me. Ain't that good enough?"

.007 could have carried the switching-loco round the yard in his tender, but he felt grateful for even this little word of consolation.

"We don't use hand-cars on the Pennsylvania," said the Consolidation. "That—er—peanut-stand's old enough and ugly enough to speak for himself."

"He hasn't been spoken to yet. He's been spoke *at*. Hain't ye any manners on the Pennsylvania?" said the switching-loco.

"You ought to be in the yard, Poney," said the Mogul severely. "We're all long-haulers here."

"That's what you think," the little feller replied. "You'll know more 'fore the night's out. I've been down to Track 17, and the freight there—oh, Christmas!"

"I've trouble enough in my own division," said a lean, light suburban loco with very shiny brake-shoes. "My commuters wouldn't rest till they got a parlour-car. They've hitched it back of all, and it hauls worse'n a snow-plough. I'll snap her off some day sure, and then they'll blame everyone except their fool selves. They'll be askin' me to haul a vestibule next!"

"They made you in New Jersey, didn't they?" said Poney. "Thought so. Commuters and truck-wagons ain't any sweet haulin', but I tell *you* they're a heap better'n cuttin' out refrigerator-cars or oil-tanks. Why, I've hauled——"

"Haul! You?" said the Mogul contemptuously. "It's all you can do to bunt a cold-storage car up the yard. Now, I"—he paused a little to let the words sink in—"I handle the Flying Freight—e-leven cars worth just anything you please to mention. On the stroke of eleven I pull out; and I'm timed for thirty-five an hour. Costly—perishable— fragile—immediate—that's me! Suburban traffic's only but one degree better than switching. Express freight's what pays."

"Well, I ain't given to blowing, as a rule," began the Pittsburgh Consolidation.

"No? You was sent in here because you grunted on the grade," Poney interrupted.

"Where I grunt, you'd lie down, Poney; but as I was saying, I don't blow much. Notwithstandin', *if* you want to see freight that is freight moved lively, you should see me warbling through the Alleghenies with thirty-seven ore-cars behind me, and my brakemen fightin' tramps so's they can't attend to my tooter. I have to do all the holdin' back then, and though I say it, I've never had a load get away from me yet. *No*, sir. Haulin's one thing, but judgment and discretion's another. You want judgment in my business."

"Ah! But—but are you not paralysed by a sense of your overwhelming responsibilities?" said a curious, husky voice from a corner.

"Who's that?" .007 whispered to the Jersey commuter.

"Compound—experiment—N.G. She's been switchin' in the B. & A. yards for six months, when she wasn't in the shops. She's economical (*I* call it mean) in her coal, but she takes it out in repairs. Ahem! I presume you found Boston somewhat isolated, madam, after your New York season?"

"I am never so well occupied as when I am alone."

The Compound seemed to be talking from halfway up her smokestack.

"Sure," said the irreverent Poney under his breath. "They don't hanker after her any in the yard."

"But with my constitution and temperament—my work lies in Boston—I find your *outrecuidance*——"

"Outer which?" said the Mogul freight. "Simple cylinders are good enough for me."

"Perhaps I should have said *faroucherie*," hissed the Compound.

"I don't hold with any make of papier-mâché wheel," the Mogul insisted.

The Compound sighed pityingly and said no more.

"Git 'em all shapes in this world, don't ye?" said Poney. "That's Mass'chusetts all over. They half start, an' then they stick on a dead-centre an' blame it all on other folks' way o' treatin' them. Talkin' o' Boston, Comanche told me last night he had a hot-box just beyond the Newtons Friday. That was why, *he* says, the Accommodation was held up. Made out no end of a tale, Comanche did."

"If I'd heard that in the shops, with my boiler out for repairs, I'd know 'twas one o' Comanche's lies," the New Jersey commuter snapped. "Hot-box! Him! What happened was they'd put an extra car on, and he just lay down on the grade and squealed. They had to send 127 to help him through. Made it out a hot-box, did he? Time before that he said he was ditched! Looked me square in the headlight and told me that as cool as—as a water-tank in a cold wave. Hot-box! You ask 127 about Comanche's hot-box. Why, Comanche he was side-tracked, and 127—*he* was just about as mad as they make 'em on account o' being called out at ten o'clock at night—took hold and snapped her into Boston in seventeen minutes. Hot-box! Hot fraud! That's what Comanche is."

Then .007 put both drivers and his pilot into it, as the saying is, for he asked what sort of thing a hot-box might be.

"Paint my bell sky-blue!" said Poney, the switcher. "Make me a surface-railroad loco with a hard-wood skirtin'-board round my wheels. Break me up and cast me into five-cent sidewalk-fakirs' mechanical toys! Here's an eight-wheel coupled 'American' don't know what a hot-box is! Never heard of an emergency-stop either, did ye? Don't know what ye carry jack-screws for? You're too innocent to be left alone with your own tender. Oh, you— you flat-car!"

There was a roar of escaping steam before anyone could answer, and .007 nearly blistered his paint off with pure mortification.

"A hot-box," began the Compound, picking and choosing her words as though they were coal, "a hot-box is the penalty exacted from inexperience by haste. Ahem!"

"Hot-box!" said the Jersey Suburban. "It's the price you pay for going on the tear. It's years since I've had one. It's a disease that don't attack short-haulers, as a rule."

"We never have hot-boxes on the Pennsylvania," said the Consolidation. "They get 'em in New York—same as nervous prostration."

"Ah, go home on a ferry-boat," said the Mogul. "You think because you use worse grades than our road 'u'd allow, you're a kind of Allegheny angel. Now, I'll tell you what you— Here's my folk. Well, I can't stop. See you later perhaps."

He rolled forward majestically to the turn-table, and swung like a man-of-war in a tideway, till he picked up his track. "But as for you, you pea-green swivellin' coffee-pot"—this to .007—"you go out and learn something before you associate with those who've made more mileage in a week than you'll roll up in a year. Costly—perishable—fragile—immediate—that's me! S' long."

"Split my tubes if that's actin' polite to a new member o' the Brotherhood," said Poney. "There wasn't any call to trample on ye like that. But manners was left out when Moguls was made. Keep up your fire, kid, an' burn your own smoke. Guess we'll all be wanted in a minute."

Men were talking rather excitedly in the round-house. One man, in a dingy jersey, said that he hadn't any locomotives to waste on the yard. Another man, with a piece of crumpled paper in his hand, said that the yard-master said that he was to say that if the other man said anything, he (the other man) was to shut his head. Then the other man waved his arms and wanted to know if he was expected to keep locomotives in his hip pocket. Then a man in a black Prince Albert without a collar came up dripping, for it was a hot August night, and said that what *he* said went; and between the three of them the locomotives began to go too—first the Compound, then the Consolidation, then .007.

Now, deep down in his fire-box, .007 had cherished a hope that as soon as his trial was done he would be led forth with songs and shoutings and attached to a green-and-chocolate vestibuled flier, under charge of a bold and noble engineer who would pat him on his back and weep over him and call him his Arab steed. (The boys in the shops where he was built used to read wonderful stories of railroad life, and .007 expected things to happen as he had heard.)

But there did not seem to be many vestibuled fliers in the roaring, rumbling, electric-lighted yards, and his engineer only said, "Now, what sort of a fool-sort of an injector has Eustis loaded on to this rig this time?" And he put the lever over with an angry snap, crying, "Am I supposed to switch with this thing, hey?"

The collarless man mopped his head and replied that in the present state of the yard and freight and a few other things, the engineer would switch and keep on switching till the cows came home. .007 pushed out gingerly, his heart in his headlight, so nervous that the clang of his own bell almost made him jump the track. Lanterns waved, or danced up and down, before and behind him; and on every side, six tracks deep, sliding backward and forward, with clashings of couplers and squeals of hand-brakes, were cars—more cars than .007 had dreamed of. There were oil-cars, and hay-cars, and stock-cars full of lowing beasts, and ore-cars, and potato-cars with stove-pipe-ends sticking out in the middle; cold-storage and refrigerator cars dripping ice-water on the tracks; ventilated fruit- and milk-cars, flat-cars with truck-wagons full of market-stuff; flat-cars loaded with reapers and binders, all red and green and gilt under the sizzling electric lights; flat-cars piled high with strong-scented hides, pleasant hemlock-plank, and bundles of shingles, flat-cars creaking to the weight of thirty-ton castings, angle-irons, and rivet-boxes for some new bridge; and hundreds and hundreds and hundreds of box-cars loaded, locked, and chalked. Men—hot and angry—crawled among and between and under the thousand wheels; men took flying jumps through his cab when he halted for a moment; men sat on his pilot as he went forward and on his tender as he returned; and regiments of men ran along the tops of the box-cars beside him, screwing down brakes, waving their arms, and crying curious things.

He was pushed forward a foot at a time; whirled backward, his rear drivers clinking and clanking, a quarter of a mile; jerked into a switch (yard-switches are very stubby and unaccommodating); bunted into a Red D or Merchant's Transport car; and with no hint or knowledge of the weight behind him, started up anew. When his load was fairly on the move, three or four cars would be cut off and .007 would bound forward, only to be held hiccuping on the brake. Then he would wait a few minutes, watching the whirled lanterns, deafened with the clang of the bells, giddy with the vision of the sliding cars, his brake-pump panting forty to the minute, his front coupler lying sideways on his cow-catcher like a tired dog's tongue in his mouth, and the whole of him covered with half-burnt coal-dust.

" 'Tisn't so easy switching with a straight-backed tender," said his little friend of the round-house, bustling by at a trot. "But you're comin' on pretty fair. Ever seen a flyin' switch? No? Then watch me."

Poney was in charge of a dozen heady flat-cars. Suddenly he shot away from them with a sharp *"Whutt!"* A switch opened in the shadows ahead; he turned up it like a rabbit as it snapped behind him, and the long line of twelve-foot-high lumber jolted on into the arms of a full-sized road-loco, who acknowledged receipt with a dry howl.

"My man's reckoned the smartest in the yard at that trick," he said, returning. "Gives me cold shivers when another fool tries it, though. That's where my short wheel-base comes in. Like as not you'd have your tender scraped off if *you* tried it."

.007 had no ambitions that way, and said so.

"No? Of course this ain't your regular business, but say, don't you think it's interestin'? Have you seen the yard-master? Well, he's the greatest man on earth, an' don't you forget it. When are we through? Why, kid, it's always like this day *an'* night—Sundays an' weekdays. See that thirty-car freight slidin' in four, no, five tracks off? She's all mixed freight, sent here to be sorted out into straight trains. That's why we're cuttin' out the cars one by one." He gave a vigorous push to a west-bound car as he spoke, and started back with a little snort of surprise, for the car was an old friend—an M. T. K. box-car.

"Jack my drivers, but it's Homeless Kate! Why, Kate, ain't there *no* gettin' you back to your friends? There's forty chasers out for you from your road, if there's one. Who's holdin' you now?"

"Wish I knew," whimpered Homeless Kate. "I belong in Topeka, but I've been to Cedar Rapids, I've been to Winnipeg, I've been to Newport News, I've been all down the old Atlanta and West Point, an' I've been to Buffalo. Maybe I'll fetch up at Haverstraw. I've only been out ten months, but I'm homesick—I'm just achin' homesick."

"Try Chicago, Katie," said the switching-loco; and the battered old car lumbered down the track, jolting: "I want to be in Kansas when the sun-flowers bloom."

"Yard's full o' Homeless Kates an' Wanderin' Willies," he explained to .007. "I knew an old Fitchburg flat-car out seventeen months, an' one of ours was gone fifteen 'fore ever we got track of her. Dunno quite how our men fix it. Swap around, I guess. Anyway, I've done *my* duty. She's on her way to Kansas, via Chicago; but I'll lay my next boilerful she'll be held there to wait consignee's convenience and sent back to us with wheat in the fall."

Just then the Pittsburgh Consolidation passed, at the head of a dozen cars.

"I'm goin' home," he said proudly.

"Can't get all them twelve on to the flat. Break 'em in half, Dutchy!" cried Poney. But it was .007 who was backed down to the last six cars, and he nearly blew up with surprise when he found himself pushing them on to a huge ferry-boat. He had never seen deep water before, and shivered as the flat drew away and left his bogies within six inches of the black, shiny tide.

After this he was hurried to the freight-house, where he saw the yard-master, a smallish, white-faced man in shirt, trousers, and slippers, looking down upon a sea of trucks, a mob of bawling truckmen, and squadrons of backing, turning, sweating, spark-striking horses.

"That's shippers' carts loadin' on to the receivin' trucks," said the small engine reverently. "But *he* don't care. He lets 'em cuss. He's the Czar—King—Boss! He says 'Please,' and then they kneel down an' pray. There's three or four strings o' today's freight to be pulled before he can attend to *them*. When he waves his hand that way, things happen."

A string of loaded cars slid out down the track, and a string of empties took their place. Bales, crates, boxes, jars, carboys, frails, cases, and packages flew into them from the freight-house as though the cars had been magnets and they iron filings.

"Ki-yah!" shrieked little Poney. "Ain't it great?"

A purple-faced truckman shouldered his way to the yard-master and shook his fist under his nose. The yard-master never looked up from his bundle of freight-receipts. He crooked his forefinger slightly, and a tall young man in a red shirt, lounging carelessly beside him, hit the truckman under the left ear so that he dropped, quivering and clucking, on a hay-bale.

"Eleven, seven, ninety-seven, L. Y. S.; fourteen ought ought three; nineteen thirteen; one one four; seventeen ought twenty-one M. B.; *and* the ten west-bound. All straight except the two last. Cut 'em off at the junction. An' *that's* all right. Pull that string." The yard-master, with mild blue eyes, looked out over the howling truckmen at the waters in the moonlight beyond and hummed:

> All things bright and beautiful,
> All creatures great and small,
> *All* things wise and wonderful,
> The Lawd Gawd He made all!

.007 moved out the cars and delivered them to the regular road-engine. He had never felt quite so limp in his life before.

"Curious, ain't it?" said Poney, puffing, on the next track. "You an' me, if we got that man under our bumpers, we'd work him into red waste an' not know what we'd done; but—up there—with the steam hummin' in his boiler that awful quiet way—"

"*I* know," said .007. "Makes me feel as if I'd dropped my fire an' was getting cold. He is the greatest man on earth."

They were at the far north end of the yard now, under a switch-tower, looking down on the four-track way of the main traffic. The Boston Compound was to haul .007's string to some far-away northern junction over an indifferent road-bed, and she mourned aloud for the ninety-six-pound rails of the B. & A.

"You're young; you're young," she coughed. "You don't realize your responsibilities."

"Yes, he does," said Poney sharply, "but he don't lie down under 'em." Then, with a side-spurt of steam, exactly like a tough spitting: "There ain't more than fifteen thousand dollars' worth o' freight behind her anyway, and she goes on as if 'twere a hundred thousand—same as the Mogul's. Excuse me, madam, but you've the track. She's stuck on a dead-centre again—bein' specially designed not to."

The Compound crawled across the tracks on a long slant, groaning horribly at each switch and moving like a cow in a snow-drift. There was a little pause along the yard after her tail-lights had disappeared; switches locked crisply, and everyone seemed to be waiting.

"Now I'll show you something worth," said Poney. "When the Purple Emperor ain't on time, it's about time to amend the Constitution. The first stroke of twelve' is——"

"Boom!" went the clock in the big yard-tower, and far away .007 heard a full, vibrating *"Yah! Yah! Yah!"* A headlight twinkled on the horizon like a star, grew an overpowering blaze, and whooped up the humming track to the roaring music of a happy giant's song:

With a michnai—ghignai—shtingal! Yah! Yah! Yah!
Ein—zwei—drei—Mutter! Yah! Yah! Yah!
    She climb upon der shteeple,
    Und she frighten all der people.
Singin' michnai—ghignai—shtingal! Yah! Yah!"

The last defiant "Yah! Yah!" was delivered a mile and a half beyond the passenger-depot; but .007 had caught one glimpse of the superb six-wheeled-coupled racing-locomotive who hauled the pride and glory of the road—the gilt-edged Purple Emperor, the millionaires' south-bound express, laying the miles over his shoulder as a man peels a shaving from a soft board. The rest was a blur of maroon enamel, a bar of white light from the electrics in the cars. and a flicker of nickel-plated hand-rail on the rear platform.

"Ooh!" said .007.

"Seventy-five miles an hour these five miles. Baths, I've heard; barber's shops; ticker; and a library and the rest to match. Yes, sir; seventy-five an hour! But he'll talk to you in the round-house just as democratic as I would. And I—cuss my wheel-base!—I'd kick clean off the track at half his gait. He's the master of our Lodge. Cleans up at our house. I'll introduce you someday. He's worth knowin'! There ain't many can sing that song either."

.007 was too full of emotions to answer. He did not hear a raging of telephone-bells in the switch-tower, nor the man, as he leaned out and called to .007's engineer, "Got any steam?"

" 'Nough to run her a hundred mile out o' this, if I could," said the engineer, who belonged to the open road and hated switching.

"Then get. The Flying Freight's ditched forty mile out, with fifty rod o' track ploughed up. No; no one's hurt, but both tracks are blocked. Lucky the wreckin'-car an' derrick are this end of the yard. Crew'll be along in a minute. Hurry! You've the track."

"Well, I could jest kick my little sawed-off self," said Poney as .007 was backed, with a bang, onto a grim and grimy car like a caboose, but full of tools—a flat-car and a derrick behind it. "Some folks are one thing, and some are another; but *you're* in luck, kid. They push a wrecking-car. Now, don't get rattled. Your wheel-base will keep you on the track, and there ain't any curves worth mentionin'. Oh, say! Comanche told me there's one section o' saw-edged track that's liable to jounce ye a little. Fifteen an' a half out, *after* the grade at Jackson's crossin'. You'll know it by a farmhouse an' a windmill an' five maples in the dooryard. Windmill's west o' the maples. An' there's an eighty-foot iron bridge in the middle o' that section with no guard-rails. See you later. Luck!"

Before he knew well what had happened, .007 was flying up the track into the dumb, dark world. Then fears of the night beset him. He remembered all he had ever heard of landslides, rain-piled boulders, blown trees, and strayed cattle, all that the Boston Compound had ever said of responsibility, and a great deal more that came out of his own head. With a very quavering voice he whistled for his first grade-crossing (an event in the life of a locomotive), and his nerves were in no way restored by the sight of a frantic horse and a white-faced man in a buggy less than a yard from his right shoulder. Then he was sure he would jump the track, felt his flanges mounting the rail at every curve, knew that his first grade would make him lie down even as Comanche had done at the Newtons. He whirled down the grade to Jackson's crossing, saw the windmill west of the maples, felt the badly laid rails spring under him, and sweated big drops all over his boiler. At each jarring bump he believed an axle had smashed, and he took the eighty-foot bridge without the guard-rail like a hunted cat on the top of a fence. Then a wet leaf stuck against the glass of his headlight and threw a flying shadow on the track, so that he thought it was some little dancing animal that would feel soft if he ran over it; and anything soft underfoot frightens a locomotive as it does an elephant. But the men behind seemed quite calm. The wrecking-crew were climbing carelessly from the caboose to the tender, even jesting with the engineer, for he heard a shuffling of feet among the coal, and the snatch of a song, something like this:

Oh, the Empire State must learn to wait,
And the Cannon-ball go hang!
When the West-bound's ditched and the tool-car's hitched,
And it's 'way for the Breakdown Gang (Tara-ra!)
'Way for the Breakdown Gang!

"Say! Eustis knew what he was doin' when he designed this rig. She's a hummer. New, too."

"Snff! Phew! She *is* new. That ain't paint. That's—"

A burning pain shot through .007's right rear driver—a crippling, stinging pain.

"This," said .007 as he flew, "is a hot-box. Now I know what it means. I shall go to pieces, I guess. My first road-run too!"

"Het a bit, ain't she?" the fireman ventured to suggest to the engineer.

"She'll hold for all we want of her. We're 'most there. Guess you chaps back had better climb into your car," said the engineer, his hand on the brake-lever. "I've seen men snapped off—"

But the crew fled back with laughter. They had no wish to be jerked onto the track. The engineer half turned his wrist, and .007 found his drivers pinned firm.

"Now it's come!" said .007 as he yelled aloud and slid like a sleigh. For the moment he fancied that he would jerk bodily from off his underpinning.

"That must be the emergency stop that Poney guyed me about," he gasped as soon as he could think. "Hot-box—emergency stop. They both hurt, but now I can talk back in the round-house."

He was halted, all hissing hot, a few feet in the rear of what doctors would call a compound-comminuted car. His engineer was kneeling down among his drivers, but he did not call .007 his Arab steed, nor cry over him as the engineers did in the newspapers. He just bad-worded .007 and pulled yards of charred cotton waste from about the axles and hoped he might someday catch the idiot who had packed it. Nobody else attended to him, for Evans, the Mogul's engineer, a little cut about the head but very angry, was exhibiting by lantern-light the mangled corpse of a slim blue pig.

" 'Tweren't even a decent-sized hog," he said. " 'Twere a shote."

"Dangerousest beasts they are," said one of the crew. "Get under the pilot an' sort o' twiddle ye off the track, don't they?"

"Don't they?" roared Evans, who was a red-headed Welshman. "You talk as if I was ditched by a hog every fool day o' the week. *I* ain't friends with all the cussed half-fed shotes in the state o' New York. No, indeed! Yes, this is him—an' look what he's done!"

It was not a bad night's work for one stray piglet. The Flying Freight seemed to have flown in every direction, for the Mogul had mounted the rails and run diagonally a few hundred feet from right to left, taking with him such cars as cared to follow. Some did not. They broke their couplers and lay down, while rear cars frolicked over them. In that game they had ploughed up and removed and twisted a good deal of the left-hand track. The Mogul himself had waddled into a cornfield, and there he knelt, fantastic wreaths of green twisted round his crank-pins, his pilot covered with solid clods of field on which corn nodded drunkenly, his fire put out with dirt (Evans had done that as soon as he recovered his senses), and his broken headlight half full of half-burnt moths. His tender had thrown coal all over him, and he looked like a disreputable buffalo who had tried to wallow in a general store. For there lay scattered over the landscape, from the burst cars, typewriters, sewing-machines, bicycles in crates, a consignment of silver-plated imported harness, French dresses and gloves, a dozen finely moulded hard-wood mantels, a fifteen-foot naphtha-launch with a solid brass bedstead crumpled around her bows, a case of telescopes and microscopes, two coffins, a case of very best candies, some gilt-edged dairy produce, butter and eggs in an ome- ;
lette, a broken box of expensive toys, and a few hundred other luxuries. A camp of tramps hurried up from nowhere and generously volunteered to help the crew. So the brakemen, armed with coupler-pins, walked up and down on one side, and the freight conductor and the fire-man patrolled the other with their hands in their hip pockets. A long-bearded man came out of a house beyond

the cornfield and told Evans that if the accident had happened a little later in the year, all his corn would have been burned, and accused Evans of carelessness. Then he ran away, for Evans was at his heels shrieking, " 'Twas his hog done it—his hog done it! Let me kill him! Let me kill him!" Then the wrecking-crew laughed, and the farmer put his head out of a window and said that Evans was no gentleman.

But .007 was very sober. He had never seen a wreck before, and it frightened him. The crew still laughed, but they worked at the same time; and .007 forgot horror in amazement at the way they handled the Mogul freight. They dug round him with spades, they put ties in front of his wheels and jack-screws under him, they embraced him with the derrick-chain and tickled him with crowbars, while .007 was hitched on to wrecked cars and backed away till the knot broke or the cars rolled clear of the track. By dawn thirty or forty men were at work, replacing and ramming down the ties, gauging the rails and spiking them. By daylight all cars who could move had gone on in charge of another loco; the track was freed for traffic; and .007 had hauled the old Mogul over a small pavement of ties, inch by inch, till his flanges bit the rail once more and he settled down with a clank. But his spirit was broken, and his nerve was gone.

" 'Tweren't even a hog," he repeated dolefully; " '*twere* a shote; and you—*you* of all of 'em—had to help me on."

"But how in the whole long road did it happen?" asked .007, sizzling with curiosity.

"Happen! It didn't happen! It just come! I sailed right on top of him around that last curve—thought he was a skunk. Yes; he was all as little as that. He hadn't more'n squealed once 'fore I felt my bogies lift (he'd rolled right under the pilot), and I couldn't catch the track again to save me. Swivelled clean off, I was. Then I felt him sling himself along, all greasy, under my left leadin' driver, and, oh, Boilers! that mounted the rail. I heard my flanges zippin' along the ties, an' the next I knew I was playin' 'Sally, Sally Waters' in the corn, my tender shuckin' coal through my cab, an' old man Evans lyin' still an' bleedin' in front o' me. Shook? There ain't a stay or a bolt or a rivet in me that ain't sprung to glory somewhere."

"Umm!" said .007. "What d'you reckon you weigh?"

"Without these lumps o' dirt I'm all of a hundred thousand pound."

"And the shote?"

"Eighty. Call him a hundred pound at the outside. He's worth about four 'n' a half dollars. Ain't it awful? Ain't it enough to give you nervous prostration? Ain't it paralysin'? Why, I come just around that curve—" And the Mogul told the tale again, for he was very badly shaken.

"Well, it's all in the day's run, I guess," said .007 soothingly; "an'—an' a cornfield's pretty soft fallin'."

"If it had been a sixty-foot bridge, an' I could ha' slid off into deep water an' blown up an' killed both men, same as others have done, I wouldn't ha' cared; but to be ditched by a shote—an' you to help me out—in a cornfield—an' an old hayseed in his nightgown cussin' me like as if I was a sick truck-horse! Oh, it's awful! Don't call me Mogul! I'm a sewin'-machine. They'll guy my sandbox off in the yard."

And .007, his hot-box cooled and his experience vastly enlarged, hauled the Mogul freight slowly to the roundhouse.

"Hello, old man! Been out all night, hain't ye?" said the irrepressible Poney, who had just come off duty. "Well, I must say you look it. Costly—perishable—fragile—immediate—that's you! Go to the shops, take them vine-leaves out o' your hair, an' git 'em to play the hose on you."

"Leave him alone, Poney," said .007 severely as he was swung on the turntable, "or I'll———"

"Didn't know the old granger was any special friend o' yours, kid. He wasn't overcivil to you last time I saw him."

"I know it, but I've seen a wreck since then, and it has about scared the paint off me. I'm not going to guy anyone as long as I steam—not when they're new to the business an' anxious to learn. And I'm not goin' to guy the old Mogul either, though I did find him wreathed

around with roastin'-ears. 'Twas a little bit of a shote—
not a hog—just a shote, Poney—no bigger'n a lump of
anthracite—I saw it—that made all the mess. Anybody
can be ditched, I guess."

"Found that out already, have you? Well, that's a good
beginnin'." It was the Purple Emperor, with his high,
tight, plate-glass cab and green-velvet cushion, waiting to
be cleaned for his next day's fly.

"Let me make you two gen'lemen acquainted," said
Poney. "This is our Purple Emperor, kid, whom you were
admirin' and, I may say, envyin' last night. This is a new
brother, worshipful sir, with most of his mileage ahead of
him; but so far as a serving-brother can, I'll answer for
him."

"Happy to meet you," said the Purple Emperor with a
glance round the crowded round-house. "I guess there are
enough of us here to form a full meetin'. Ahem! By virtue of the authority vested in me as head of the road, I
hereby declare and pronounce No. .007 a full and accepted brother of the Amalgamated Brotherhood of Locomotives, and as such entitled to all shop, switch, track,
tank, and round-house privileges throughout my jurisdic-
tion, in the degree of Superior Flier, it bein' well known
and credibly reported to me that our brother has covered
forty-one miles in thirty-nine minutes and a half on an er-
rand of mercy to the afflicted. At a convenient time, I myself will communicate to you the song and signal of this
degree whereby you may be recognized in the darkest
night. Take your stall, newly entered brother among locomotives!"

Now, in the darkest night, even as the Purple Emperor
said, if you will stand on the bridge across the freight-
yard looking down upon the four-track way at 2:30 A.M.,
neither before nor after, when the White Moth, that takes
the overflow from the Purple Emperor, tears south with
her seven vestibuled cream-white cars, you will hear, as
the yard-clock makes the half hour, a far-away sound like
the bass of a violoncello, and then, a hundred feet to each
word:

With a michnai—ghignai—shtingal! Yah! Yah! Yah!
Ein—zwei—drei—Mutter! Yah! Yah! Yah!
    She climb upon der shteeple,
    Und she frighten all der people,
Singin' michnai—ghignai—shtingal! Yah! Yah!

That is .007 covering his one hundred and fifty-six miles in two hundred and twenty-one minutes.

[First published in 1897.]

GEORGIE PORGIE

Georgie Porgie, pudding and pie,
Kissed the girls and made them cry.
When the girls came out to play
Georgie Porgie ran away.

If you will admit that a man has no right to enter his
drawing-room early in the morning, when the housemaid
is setting things right and clearing away the dust, you will
concede that civilized people who eat out of china and
own card-cases have no right to apply their standard of
right and wrong to an unsettled land. When the place is
made fit for their reception by those men who are told off
to the work, they can come up, bringing in their trunks
their own society and the Decalogue and all the other ap-
paratus. Where the queen's law does not carry, it is irra-
tional to expect an observance of other and weaker rules.
The men who run ahead of the cars of Decency and Pro-
priety and make the jungle ways straight cannot be judged
in the same manner as the stay-at-home folk of the ranks
of the regular *Tchin*.

Not many months ago the queen's law stopped a few
miles north of Thayetmyo on the Irrawaddy. There was
no very strong Public Opinion up to that limit, but it existed to keep men in order. When the government said that
the queen's law must carry up to Bhamo and the Chinese
border, the order was given, and some men whose desire
was to be ever a little in advance of the rush of Respect-
ability flocked forward with the troops. These were the

men who could never pass examinations, and would have been too pronounced in their ideas for the administration of bureau-worked provinces. The supreme government stepped in as soon as might be, with codes and regulations, and all but reduced New Burma to the dead Indian level; but there was a short time during which strong men were necessary and ploughed a field for themselves.

Among the forerunners of Civilization was Georgie Porgie, reckoned by all who knew him a strong man. He held an appointment in Lower Burma when the order came to break the frontier, and his friends called him Georgie Porgie because of the singularly Burmese-like manner in which he sang a song whose first line is something like the words "Georgie Porgie." Most men who have been in Burma will know the song. It means: "Puff, puff, puff, puff, great steamboat!" Georgie sang it to his banjo, and his friends shouted with delight, so that you could hear them far away in the teak-forest.

When he went to Upper Burma he had no special regard for God or man, but he knew how to make himself respected and to carry out the mixed military-civil duties that fell to most men's share in those months. He did his office-work and entertained now and again the detachments of fever-shaken soldiers who blundered through his part of the world in search of a flying party of dacoits. Sometimes he turned out and dressed down dacoits on his own account, for the country was still smouldering and would blaze when least expected. He enjoyed these charivaris, but the dacoits were not so amused. All the officials who came in contact with him departed with the idea that Georgie Porgie was a valuable person, well able to take care of himself, and on that belief he was left to his own devices.

At the end of a few months he wearied of his solitude and cast about for company and refinement. The queen's law had hardly begun to be felt in the country, and Public Opinion, which is more powerful than the queen's law, had yet to come. Also, there was a custom in the country which allowed a white man to take to himself a wife of the Daughters of Heth upon due payment. The marriage was not quite so binding as is the *nikkah* ceremony among Muhammadans, but the wife was very pleasant.

When all our troops are back from Burma there will be a proverb in their mouths, "As thrifty as a Burmese wife," and pretty English ladies will wonder what in the world it means.

The headman of the village next to Georgie Porgie's post had a fair daughter who had seen Georgie Porgie and loved him from afar. When news went abroad that the Englishman with the heavy hand who lived in the stockade was looking for a housekeeper, the headman came in and explained that for five hundred rupees down he would entrust his daughter to Georgie Porgie's keeping, to be maintained in all honour, respect, and comfort, with pretty dresses, according to the custom of the country. This thing was done, and Georgie Porgie never repented it.

He found his rough-and-tumble house put straight and down by one half, and himself petted and made much of by his new acquisition, who sat at the head of his table and sang songs to him and ordered his madrasi servants about, and was in every way as sweet and merry and honest and winning a little woman as the most exacting of bachelors could have desired. No race, men say who know, produces such good wives and heads of households as the Burmese. When the next detachment tramped by on the war-path, the subaltern in command found at Georgie Porgie's table a hostess to be deferential to, a woman to be treated in every way as one occupying an assured position. When he gathered his men together next dawn and replunged into the jungle, he thought regretfully of the nice little dinner and the pretty face and envied Georgie Porgie from the bottom of his heart. Yet *he* was engaged to a girl at home, and that is how some men are constructed.

The Burmese girl's name was not a pretty one, but as she was promptly christened Georgina by Georgie Porgie, the blemish did not matter. Georgie Porgie thought well of the petting and the general comfort and vowed that he had never spent five hundred rupees to a better end.

After three months of domestic life, a great idea struck him. Matrimony—English matrimony—could not be such a bad thing after all. If he were so thoroughly comfortable at the back of beyond with this Burmese girl who smoked cheroots, how much more comfortable would he be with a sweet English maiden who would not smoke cheroots and would play upon a piano instead of a banjo? Also he had a desire to return to his kind, to hear a band once more, and to feel how it felt to wear a dress-suit again. Decidedly, matrimony would be a very good thing. He thought the matter out at length of evenings, while Georgina sang to him or asked him why he was so silent and whether she had done anything to offend him. As he thought he smoked, and as he smoked he looked at Georgina and in his fancy turned her into a fair, thrifty, amusing, merry little English girl, with hair coming low down on her forehead, and perhaps a cigarette between her lips. Certainly not a big, thick, Burma cheroot of the brand that Georgina smoked. He would wed a girl with Georgina's eyes and most of her ways. But not all. She could be improved upon. Then he blew thick smoke-wreaths through his nostrils and stretched himself. He would taste marriage. Georgina had helped him to save money, and there were six months' leave due to him.

"See here, little woman," he said, "we must put by more money for these next three months. I want it." That was a direct slur on Georgina's housekeeping, for she prided herself on her thrift; but since her God wanted money she would do her best.

"You want money?" she said with a little laugh. "I *have* money. Look!" She ran to her own room and fetched out a small bag of rupees. "Of all that you give me, I keep back some. See! One hundred and seven rupees. Can you want more money than that? Take it. It is my pleasure if you use it." She spread out the money on the table and pushed it towards him with her quick little pale-yellow fingers.

Georgie Porgie never referred to economy in the household again.

Three months later, after the dispatch and receipt of several mysterious letters which Georgina could not understand, and hated for that reason, Georgie Porgie said that he was going away and she must return to her father's house and stay there.

Georgina wept. She would go with her God from the

world's end to the world's end. Why should she leave him? She loved him.

"I am only going to Rangoon," said Georgie Porgie. "I shall be back in a month, but it is safer to stay with your father. I will leave you two hundred rupees."

"If you go for a month, what need of two hundred? Fifty are more than enough. There is some evil here. Do not go, or at least let me go with you."

Georgie Porgie does not like to remember that scene even at this date. In the end he got rid of Georgina by a compromise of seventy-five rupees. She would not take more. Then he went by steamer and rail to Rangoon.

The mysterious letters had granted him six months' leave. The actual flight and an idea that he might have been treacherous hurt severely at the time, but as soon as the big steamer was well out into the blue, things were easier, and Georgina's face, and the queer little stockaded house, and the memory of the rushes of shouting dacoits by night, the cry and struggle of the *first* man that he had ever killed with his own hand, and a hundred other more intimate things faded and faded out of Georgie Porgie's heart, and the vision of approaching England took its place. The Steamer was full of men on leave, all rampantly jovial souls who had shaken off the dust and sweat of Upper Burma and were as merry as schoolboys. They helped Georgie Porgie to forget.

Then came England with its luxuries and decencies and comforts, and Georgie Porgie walked in a pleasant dream upon pavements of which he had nearly forgotten the ring, wondering why men in their senses ever left town. He accepted his keen delight in his furlough as the reward of his services. Providence further arranged for him another and greater delight—all the pleasures of a quiet English wooing, quite different from the brazen businesses of the East, when half the community stand back and bet on the result and the other half wonder what Mrs. So-and-So will say to it.

It was a pleasant girl and a perfect summer, and a big country-house near Petworth where there are acres and acres of purple heather and high-grassed water-meadows to wander through. Georgie Porgie felt that he had at last found something worth the living for, and naturally assumed that the next thing to do was to ask the girl to share his life in India. She, in her ignorance, was willing to go. On this occasion there was no bartering with a village headman. There was a fine middle-class wedding in the country, with a stout papa and a weeping mama, and a best man in purple and fine linen, and six snub-nosed girls from the Sunday-school to throw roses on the path between the tombstones up to the church door. The local paper described the affair at great length, even down to giving the hymns in full. But that was because the *Direction* were starving for want of material.

Then came a honeymoon at Arundel, and the mama wept copiously before she allowed her one daughter to sail away to India under the care of Georgie Porgie the bridegroom. Beyond any question, Georgie Porgie was immensely fond of his wife, and she was devoted to him as the best and greatest man in the world. When he reported himself at Bombay he felt justified in demanding a good station for his wife's sake; and because he had made a little mark in Burma and was beginning to be appreciated, they allowed him nearly all that he asked for and posted him to a station which we will call Sutrain. It stood upon several hills, and was styled officially a "sanitarium," for the good reason that the drainage was utterly neglected. Here Georgie Porgie settled down, and found married life come very naturally to him. He did not rave, as do many bridegrooms, over the strangeness and delight of seeing his own true love sitting down to breakfast with him every morning "as though it were the most natural thing in the world." "He had been there before," as the Americans say, and checking the merits of his own present grace by those of Georgina, he was more and more inclined to think that he had done well.

But there was no peace or comfort across the Bay of Bengal, under the teak-trees where Georgina lived with her father, waiting for Georgie Porgie to return. The headman was old, and remembered the war of fifty-one. He had been to Rangoon and knew something of the ways of the *Kullahs*. Sitting in front of his door in the evenings, he taught Georgina a dry philosophy which did not console her in the least.

The trouble was that she loved Georgie Porgie just as

much as the French girl in the English history books loved the priest whose head was broken by the king's bullies. One day she disappeared from the village, with all the rupees that Georgie Porgie had given her, and a very small smattering of English—also gained from Georgie Porgie.

The headman was angry at first, but lit a fresh cheroot and said something uncomplimentary about the sex in general. Georgina had started on a search for Georgie Porgie, who might be in Rangoon, or across the Black Water, or dead for aught that she knew. Chance favoured her. An old Sikh policeman told her that Georgie Porgie had crossed the Black Water. She took a steerage passage from Rangoon and went to Calcutta, keeping the secret of her search to herself.

In India every trace of her was lost for six weeks, and no one knows what trouble of heart she must have undergone.

She reappeared four hundred miles north of Calcutta, steadily heading northwards, very worn and haggard, but very fixed in her determination to find Georgie Porgie. She could not understand the langauge of the people, but India is infinitely charitable, and the womenfolk along the Grand Trunk gave her food. Something made her believe that Georgie Porgie was to be found at the end of that pitiless road. She may have been a sepoy who knew him in Burma, but of this no one can be certain. At last she found a regiment on the line of march and met there one of the many subalterns whom Georgie Porgie had invited to dinner in the far-off old days of the dacoit-hunting. There was a certain amount of amusement among the tents when Georgina threw herself at the man's feet and began to cry. There was no amusement when her story was told, but a collection was made, and that was more to the point. One of the subalterns knew of Georgie Porgie's whereabouts, but not of his marriage. So he told Georgina and she went her way joyfully to the north in a railway carriage, where there was rest for tired feet and shade for a dusty little head. The marches from the train through the hills into Sutrain were trying, but Georgina had money, and families journeying in bullock-carts gave her help. It was an almost miraculous journey, and Georgina felt sure that the good spirits of Burma were looking after her. The hill-road to Sutrain is a chilly stretch, and Georgina caught a bad cold. Still there was Georgie Porgie at the end of all the trouble to take her up in his arms and pet her, as he used to do in the old days when the stockade was shut for the night and he had approved of the evening meal. Georgina went forward as fast as she could, and her good spirits did her one last favour.

An Englishman stopped her in the twilight, just at the turn of the road into Sutrain, saying, "Good Heavens! What are you doing here?"

He was Gillis, the man who had been Georgie Porgie's assistant in Upper Burma and who occupied the next post to Georgie Porgie's in the jungle. Georgie Porgie had applied to have him to work with at Sutrain because he liked him.

"I have come," said Georgina simply. "It was such a long way, and I have been months in coming. Where is his house?"

Gillis gasped. He had seen enough of Georgina in the old times to know that explanations would be useless. You cannot explain things to the Oriental. You must show.

"I'll take you there," said Gillis, and he led Georgina off the road, up the cliff, by a little pathway, to the back of a house set on a platform cut into the hillside.

The lamps were just lit, but the curtains were not drawn. "Now look," said Gillis, stopping in front of the drawing-room window. Georgina looked and saw Georgie Porgie and the bride.

She put her hand up to her hair, which had come out of its top-knot and was straggling about her face. She tried to set her ragged dress in order, but the dress was past pulling straight, and she coughed a queer little cough, for she really had taken a very bad cold. Gillis looked too, but while Georgina only looked at the bride once, turning her eyes always on Georgie Porgie, Gillis looked at the bride all the time.

"What are you going to do?" said Gillis, who held Georgina by the wrist in case of any unexpected rush into the lamplight. "Will you go in and tell that Englishwoman that you lived with her husband?"

"No," said Georgina faintly. "Let me go. I am going away. I swear that I am going away." She twisted herself free and ran off into the dark.

"Poor little beast!" said Gillis, dropping onto the main road. "I'd ha' given her something to get back to Burma with. What a narrow shave, though! And that angel would never have forgiven it."

This seems to prove that the devotion of Gillis was not entirely due to his affection for Georgie Porgie.

The bride and the bridegroom came out into the veranda after dinner in order that the smoke of Georgie Porgie's cheroots might not hang in the new drawing-room curtains.

"What is that noise down there?" said the bride. Both listened.

"Oh," said Georgie Porgie, "I suppose some brute of a hillman has been beating his wife."

"Beating—his—wife! How ghastly!" said the bride. "Fancy *your* beating *me!*" She slipped an arm round her husband's waist, and leaning her head against his shoulder, looked out across the cloud-filled valley in deep content and security.

But it was Georgina crying, all by herself, down the hillside, among the stones of the water-course where the washermen wash the clothes.

[First published in 1888.]

THE STRANGE RIDE
OF MORROWBIE JUKES

∽❧∾

> Alive or dead—there is no other way.
> *Native Proverb*

There is no invention about this tale. Jukes by accident stumbled upon a village that is well known to exist, though he is the only Englishman who has been there. A somewhat similar institution used to flourish on the outskirts of Calcutta, and there is a story that if you go into the heart of Bikanir, which is in the heart of the great Indian desert, you shall come across not a village but a town where the dead who did not die but may not live have established their headquarters. And since it is perfectly true that in the same desert is a wonderful city where all the rich money-lenders retreat after they have made their fortunes (fortunes so vast that the owners cannot trust even the strong hand of the government to protect them, but take refuge in the waterless sands), and drive sumptuous Cee-spring barouches, and buy beautiful girls, and decorate their palaces with gold and ivory and Minton tiles and mother-o'-pearl, I do not see why Jukes's tale should not be true. He is a civil engineer, with a head for plans and distances and things of that kind, and he certainly would not take the trouble to invent imaginary traps. He could earn more by doing his legitimate work. He never varies the tale in the telling, and grows very hot and indignant when he thinks of the disrespectful treatment he received. He wrote this quite straightforwardly at first, but he has touched it up in places and introduced moral reflections; thus:

In the beginning it all arose from a slight attack of fever. My work necessitated my being in camp for some months between Pakpattan and Mubarakpur—a desolate sandy stretch of country, as everyone who has had the misfortune to go there may know. My coolies were neither more nor less exasperating than other gangs, and my work demanded sufficient attention to keep me from moping, had I been inclined to so unmanly a weakness.

On the 23rd December, 1884, I felt a little feverish. There was a full moon at the time, and in consequence, every dog near my tent was baying it. The brutes assembled in twos and threes and drove me frantic. A few days previously I had shot one loud-mouthed singer and suspended his carcass *in terrorem* about fifty yards from my tent door, but his friends fell upon, fought for, and ultimately devoured the body, and as it seemed to me, sang their hymns of thanksgiving afterwards with renewed energy.

The light-headedness which accompanies fever acts differently on different men. My irritation gave way after a short time to a fixed determination to slaughter one huge black-and-white beast who had been foremost in song and first in flight throughout the evening. Thanks to a shaking hand and a giddy head, I had already missed him twice with both barrels of my shotgun, when it struck me that my best plan would be to ride him down in the open and finish him off with a hog-spear. This, of course, was merely the semi-delirious notion of a fever patient, but I remember that it struck me at the time as being eminently practical and feasible.

I therefore ordered my groom to saddle Pornic and bring him round quietly to the rear of my tent. When the pony was ready, I stood at his head prepared to mount and dash out as soon as the dog should again lift up his voice. Pornic, by the way, had not been out of his pickets for a couple of days; the night air was crisp and chilly; and I was armed with a specially long and sharp pair of persuaders with which I had been rousing a sluggish cob that afternoon. You will easily believe, then, that when he was let go he went quickly. In one moment, for the brute bolted as straight as a die, the tent was left far behind, and we were flying over the smooth sandy soil at racing speed. In another we had passed the wretched dog, and I had almost forgotten why it was that I had taken horse and hog-spear.

The delirium of fever and the excitement of rapid motion through the air must have taken away the remnant of my senses. I have a faint recollection of standing upright in my stirrups, and of brandishing my hog-spear at the great white moon that looked down so calmly on my mad gallop, and of shouting challenges to the camel-thorn-bushes as they whizzed past. Once or twice, I believe, I swayed forward on Pornic's neck, and literally hung on by my spurs—as the marks next morning showed.

The wretched beast went forward like a thing possessed, over what seemed to be a limitless expanse of moonlit sand. Next, I remember, the ground rose suddenly in front of us, and as we topped the ascent I saw the waters of the Sutlej shining like a silver bar below. Then Pornic blundered heavily on his nose, and we rolled together down some unseen slope.

I must have lost consciousness, for when I recovered I was lying on my stomach in a heap of soft white sand, and the dawn was beginning to break dimly over the edge of the slope down which I had fallen. As the light grew stronger I saw I was at the bottom of a horseshoe-shaped crater of sand opening on one side directly on to the shoals of the Sutlej. My fever had altogether left me, and with the exception of a slight dizziness in the head, I felt no bad effects from the fall overnight.

Pornic, who was standing a few yards away, was naturally a good deal exhausted but had not hurt himself in the least. His saddle, a favourite polo one, was much knocked about and had been twisted under his belly. It took me some time to put him to rights, and in the meantime I had ample opportunities of observing the spot into which I had so foolishly dropped.

At the risk of being considered tedious, I must describe it at length, inasmuch as an accurate mental picture of its peculiarities will be of material assistance in enabling the reader to understand what follows.

Imagine then, as I have said before, a horseshoe-shaped crater of sand with steeply graded sand walls about thirty-five feet high. (The slope, I fancy, must have been about sixty-five degrees.) This crater enclosed a level piece of ground about fifty yards long by thirty at its broadest part, with a rude well in the centre. Round the bottom of the crater, about three feet from the level of the ground proper, ran a series of eighty-three semicircular, ovoid, square, and multilateral holes, all about three feet at the mouth. Each hole on inspection showed that it was carefully shored internally with driftwood and bamboos, and over the mouth a wooden drip-board projected, like the peak of a jockey's cap, for two feet. No sign of life was visible in these tunnels, but a most sickening stench pervaded the entire amphitheatre—a stench fouler than any which my wanderings in Indian villages have introduced me to.

Having remounted Pornic, who was as anxious as I to get back to camp, I rode round the base of the horseshoe to find some place whence an exit would be practicable. The inhabitants, whoever they might be, had not thought fit to put in an appearance, so I was left to my own devices. My first attempt to "rush" Pornic up the steep sand-banks showed me that I had fallen into a trap exactly on the same model as that which the ant-lion sets for its prey. At each step the shifting sand poured down from above in tons and rattled on the drip-boards of the holes like small shot. A couple of ineffectual charges sent us both rolling down to the bottom, half choked with the torrents of sand; and I was constrained to turn my attention to the river-bank.

Here everything seemed easy enough. The sand-hills ran down to the river edge, it is true, but there were plenty of shoals and shallows across which I could gallop Pornic and find my way back to terra firma by turning sharply to the right or the left. As I led Pornic over the sands I was startled by the faint pop of a rifle across the river; and at the same moment a bullet dropped with a sharp *"whit"* close to Pornic's head.

There was no mistaking the nature of the missile—a regulation Martini-Henry "picket." About five hundred yards away a country-boat was anchored in midstream; and a jet of smoke drifting away from its bows in the still morning air showed me whence the delicate attention had come. Was ever a respectable gentleman in such an impasse? The treacherous sand slope allowed no escape from a spot which I had visited most involuntarily, and a promenade on the river frontage was the signal for a bombardment from some insane native in a boat. I'm afraid that I lost my temper very much indeed.

Another bullet reminded me that I had better save my breath to cool my porridge, and I retreated hastily up the sands and back to the horseshoe, where I saw that the noise of the rifle had drawn sixty-five human beings from the badger-holes which I had up till that point supposed to be untenanted. I found myself in the midst of a crowd of spectators—about forty men, twenty women, and one child, who could not have been more than five years old. They were all scantily clothed in that salmon-coloured cloth which one associates with Hindu mendicants, and at first sight gave me the impression of a band of loathsome fakirs. The filth and repulsiveness of the assembly were beyond all description, and I shuddered to think what their life in the badger-holes must be.

Even in these days, when local self-government has destroyed the greater part of a native's respect for a Sahib, I have been accustomed to a certain amount of civility from my inferiors, and on approaching the crowd naturally expected that there would be some recognition of my presence. As a matter of fact, there was, but it was by no means what I had looked for.

The ragged crew actually laughed at me—such laughter I hope I may never hear again. They cackled, yelled, whistled, and howled as I walked into their midst, some of them literally throwing themselves down on the ground in convulsions of unholy mirth. In a moment I had let go Pornic's head, and irritated beyond expression at the morning's adventure, commenced cuffing those nearest to me with all the force I could. The wretches dropped under my blows like ninepins, and the laughter gave place to wails for mercy, while those yet untouched clasped me round the knees, imploring me in all sorts of uncouth tongues to spare them.

In the tumult, and just when I was feeling very much ashamed of myself for having thus easily given way to my temper, a thin, high voice murmured in English from behind my shoulder, "Sahib! Sahib! Do you not know me? Sahib, it is Gunga Dass, the telegraph-master."

I spun round quickly and faced the speaker.

Gunga Dass (I have, of course, no hesitation in mentioning the man's real name) I had known four years before as a Deccanee Brahmin lent by the Punjab government to one of the Khalsia States. He was in charge of a branch telegraph-office there, and when I had last met him was a jovial, full-stomached, portly government servant with a marvellous capacity for making bad puns in English—a peculiarity which made me remember him long after I had forgotten his services to me in his official capacity. It is seldom that a Hindu makes English puns.

Now, however, the man was changed beyond all recognition. Caste-mark, stomach, slate-coloured continuations, and unctuous speech were all gone. I looked at a withered skeleton, turbanless and almost naked, with long matted hair and deep-set codfish eyes. But for a crescent-shaped scar on the left cheek—the result of an accident for which I was responsible—I should never have known him. But it was indubitably Gunga Dass, and—for this I was thankful—an English-speaking native who might at least tell me the meaning of all that I had gone through that day.

The crowd retreated to some distance as I turned towards the miserable figure and ordered him to show me some method of escaping from the crater. He held a freshly plucked crow in his hand, and in reply to my question climbed slowly on a platform of sand which ran in front of the holes, and commenced lighting a fire there in silence. Dried bents, sand-poppies, and driftwood burn quickly, and I derived much consolation from the fact that he lit them with an ordinary sulphur match. When they were in a bright glow, and the crow was neatly spitted in front thereof, Gunga Dass began without a word of preamble: "There are only two kinds of men, sar. The alive and the dead. When you are dead you are dead, but when you. are alive you live." (Here the crow demanded his attention for an instant as it twirled before the fire in danger of being burnt to a cinder.) "If you die at home and do not die when you come to the ghat to be burnt, you come here."

The nature of the reeking village was made plain now, and all that I had known or read of the grotesque and the horrible paled before the fact just communicated by the ex-Brahmin. Sixteen years ago, when I first landed in Bombay, I had been told by a wandering Armenian of the existence, somewhere in India, of a place to which such Hindus as had the misfortune to recover from trance or catalepsy were conveyed and kept, and I recollect laughing heartily at what I was then pleased to consider a traveller's tale. Sitting at the bottom of the sand-trap, the memory of Watson's Hotel, with its winging punkahs, white-robed servants, and the sallow-faced Armenian, rose up in my mind as vividly as a photograph, and I burst into a loud fit of laughter. The contrast was too absurd!

Gunga Dass, as he bent over the unclean bird, watched me curiously. Hindus seldom laugh, and his surroundings were not such as to move him that way. He removed the crow solemnly from the wooden spit and as solemnly devoured it. Then he continued his story, which I give in his own words:

"In epidemics of the cholera you are carried to be burnt almost before you are dead. When you come to the riverside, the cold air perhaps makes you alive, and then, if you are only little alive, mud is put on your nose and mouth and you die conclusively. If you are rather more alive, more mud is put; but if you are too lively they let you go and take you away. I was too lively, and made protestation with anger against the indignities that they endeavoured to press upon me. In those days I was Brahmin and proud man. Now I am dead man and eat"— here he eyed the well-gnawed breast-bone with the first sign of emotion that I had seen in him since we met— "crows, and—other things. They took me from my sheets when they saw that I was too lively and gave me medicines for one week, and I survived successfully. Then they sent me by rail from my place to Okara Station, with a man to take care of me; and at Okara Station we met two other men, and they conducted we three on camels, in the night, from Okara Station to this place, and they propelled me from the top to the bottom, and the other two succeeded, and I have been here ever since, two and a half years. Once I was Brahmin and proud man, and now I eat crows."

"There is no way of getting out?"

"None of what kind at all. When I first came I made experiments frequently, and all the others also, but we have always succumbed to the sand which is precipitated upon our heads."

"But surely," I broke in at this point, "the river-front is open, and it is worthwhile dodging the bullets; while at night——"

I had already matured a rough plan of escape which a natural instinct of selfishness forbade me sharing with Gunga Dass. He, however, divined my unspoken thought almost as soon as it was formed, and to my intense astonishment, gave vent to a long, low chuckle of derision—the laughter, be it understood, of a superior or at least of an equal.

"You will not"—he had dropped the "sir" after his first sentence—"make any escape that way. But you can try. I have tried. Once only."

The sensation of nameless terror which I had in vain attempted to strive against overmastered me completely. My long fast—it was now close upon ten o'clock, and I had eaten nothing since tiffin on the previous day—combined with the violent agitation of the ride had exhausted me, and I verily believe that for a few minutes I acted as one mad. I hurled myself against the sand-slope. I ran round the base of the crater blaspheming and praying by turns. I crawled out among the sedges of the river-front, only to be driven back each time in an agony of nervous dread by the rifle-bullets which cut up the sand round me—for I dared not face the death of a mad dog among that hideous crowd—and so fell, spent and raving, at the kerb of the well. No one had taken the slightest notice of an exhibition which makes me blush hotly even when I think of it now.

Two or three men trod on my panting body as they drew water, but they were evidently used to this sort of thing and had no time to waste upon me. Gunga Dass, indeed, when he had banked the embers of his fire with sand, was at some pains to throw half a cupful of fetid water over my head, an attention for which I could have fallen on my knees and thanked him, but he was laughing all the while in the same mirthless, wheezy key that greeted me on my first attempt to force the shoals. And so, in a half-fainting state, I lay till noon. Then, being only a man after all, I felt hungry, and said as much to Gunga Dass, whom I had begun to regard as my natural protector. Following the impulse of the outer world when dealing with natives, I put my hand into my pocket and drew out four annas. The absurdity of the gift struck me at once, and I was about to replace the money.

Gunga Dass, however, cried: "Give me the money, all you have, or I will get help, and we will kill you!"

A Briton's first impulse, I believe, is to guard the contents of his pockets, but a moment's thought showed me the folly of differing with the one man who had it in his power to make me comfortable, and with whose help it was possible that I might eventually escape from the crater. I gave him all the money in my possession, Rs. 9-8-5—nine rupees, eight annas, and five pie—for I always keep small change as *bakshish* when I am in camp. Gunga Dass clutched the coins and hid them at once in his ragged loin-cloth, looking round to assure himself that no one had observed us.

"*Now* I will give you something to eat," said he.

What pleasure my money could have given him I am unable to say, but inasmuch as it did please him, I was not sorry that I had parted with it so readily, for I had no doubt that he would have had me killed if I had refused. One does not protest against the doings of a den of wild beasts, and my companions were lower than any beasts. While I ate what Gunga Dass had provided, a coarse *chapatti* and a cupful of the foul well-water, the people showed not the faintest sign of curiosity—that curiosity which is so rampant, as a rule, in an Indian village.

I could even fancy that they despised me. At all events, they treated me with the most chilling indifference, and Gunga Dass was nearly as bad. I plied him with questions about the terrible village, and received extremely unsatisfactory answers. So far as I could gather, it had been in existence from time immemorial—whence I concluded that it was at least a century old—and during that time no one had ever been known to escape from it. (I had to control myself here with both hands lest the blind terror should lay hold of me a second time and drive me raving round the crater.) Gunga Dass took a malicious pleasure in emphasizing this point and in watching me wince. Nothing that I could do would induce him to tell me who the mysterious "They" were.

"It is so ordered," he would reply, "and I do not yet know anyone who has disobeyed the orders."

"Only wait till my servant finds that I am missing," I retorted, "and I promise you that this place shall be cleared off the face of the earth, and I'll give you a lesson in civility too, my friend."

"Your servants would be torn in pieces before they came near this place; and besides, you are dead, my dear friend. It is not your fault, of course, but nonetheless you are dead *and* buried."

At irregular intervals supplies of food, I was told, were dropped down from the land side into the amphitheatre, and the inhabitants fought for them like wild beasts. When a man felt his death coming on he retreated to his lair and died there. The body was sometimes dragged out of the hole and thrown onto the sand, or allowed to rot where it lay.

The phrase "thrown onto the sand" caught my attention, and I asked Gunga Dass whether this sort of thing was not likely to breed a pestilence.

"That," said he with another of his wheezy chuckles, "you may see for yourself subsequently. You will have much time to make observations."

Whereat, to his great delight, I winced once more and hastily continued the conversation: "And how do you live here from day to day? What do you do?" The question elicited exactly the same answer as before, coupled with the information that "this place is like your European heaven; there is neither marrying nor giving in marriage."

Gunga Dass had been educated at a mission school, and as he himself admitted, had he only changed his religion "like a wise man," might have avoided the living grave which was now his portion. But as long as I was with him I fancy he was happy.

Here was a Sahib, a representative of the dominant race, helpless as a child and completely at the mercy of his native neighbours. In a deliberate, lazy way he set himself to torture me as a schoolboy would devote a rapturous half hour to watching the agonies of an impaled beetle, or as a ferret in a blind burrow might glue himself comfortably to the neck of a rabbit. The burden of his conversation was that there was no escape "of no kind whatever" and that I should stay here till I died and was "thrown onto the sand." If it were possible to forejudge the conversation of the damned on the advent of a new soul in their abode, I should say that they would speak as Gunga Dass did to me throughout that long afternoon. I was powerless to protest or answer, all my energies being devoted to a struggle against the inexplicable terror that threatened to overwhelm me again and again. I can compare the feeling to nothing except the struggles of a man against the overpowering nausea of the Channel passage—only my agony was of the spirit and infinitely more terrible.

As the day wore on, the inhabitants began to appear in full strength to catch the rays of the afternoon sun, which were now sloping in at the mouth of the crater. They assembled by little knots and talked among themselves without even throwing a glance in my direction. About four o'clock, so far as I could judge, Gunga Dass rose and dived into his lair for a moment, emerging with a live crow in his hands. The wretched bird was in a most; draggled and deplorable condition, but seemed to be in no way afraid of its master. Advancing cautiously to the river-front, Gunga Dass stepped from tussock to tussock until he had reached a smooth patch of sand directly in the line of the boat's fire. The occupants of the boat took no notice. Here he stopped, and with a couple of dexterous turns of the wrist, pegged the bird on its back with outstretched wings. As was only natural, the crow began to shriek at once and beat the air with its claws. In a few seconds the clamour had attracted the attention of a bevy of wild crows on a shoal a few hundred yards away, where they were discussing something that looked like a corpse. Half a dozen crows flew over at once to see what was going on, and also, as it proved, to attack the pinioned bird. Gunga Dass, who had lain down on a tussock, motioned to me to be quiet, though I fancy this was a needless precaution. In a moment, and before I could see how it happened, a wild crow who had grappled with the shrieking and helpless bird was entangled in the latter's claws, swiftly disengaged by Gunga Dass, and pegged down beside its companion in adversity. Curiosity, it seemed, overpowered the rest of the flock, and almost before Gunga Dass and I had time to withdraw to the tussock, two more captives were struggling in the upturned claws of the decoys. So the chase—if I can give it so dignified a name—continued until Gunga Dass had captured seven crows. Five of them he throttled at once, reserving two for further operations another day. I was a good deal impressed by this, to me, novel method of securing food, and complimented Gunga Dass on his skill.

"It is nothing to do," said he. "Tomorrow you must do it for me. You are stronger than I am."

This calm assumption of superiority upset me not a little, and I answered peremptorily, "Indeed, you old ruffian? What do you think I have given you money for?"

"Very well," was the unmoved reply. "Perhaps not tomorrow, nor the day after, nor subsequently; but in the end, and for many years, you will catch crows and eat crows, and you will thank your European God that you have crows to catch and eat."

I could have cheerfully strangled him for this, but judged it best under the circumstances to smother my resentment. An hour later I was eating one of the crows, and, as Gunga Dass had said, thanking my God that I had a crow to eat. Never as long as I live shall I forget that evening meal. The whole population were squatting on the hard sand platform opposite their dens, huddled over tiny fires of refuse and dried rushes. Death, having once laid his hand upon these men and forborne to strike, seemed to stand aloof from them now, for most of our company were old men, bent and worn and twisted with years, and women aged to all appearance as the Fates themselves. They sat together in knots and talked—God only knows what they found to discuss—in low equable tones, curiously in contrast to the strident babble with which natives are accustomed to make day hideous. Now and then an access of that sudden fury which had possessed me in the morning would lay hold on a man or woman; and with yells and imprecations the sufferer would attack the steep slope until, baffled and bleeding, he fell back on the platform incapable of moving a limb. The others would never even raise their eyes when this happened, as men too well aware of the futility of their fellows' attempts and wearied with their useless repetition. I saw four such outbursts in the course of that evening.

Gunga Dass took an eminently businesslike view of my situation, and while we were dining—I can afford to laugh at the recollection now, but it was painful enough at the time—propounded the terms on which he would consent to "do" for me. My nine rupees, eight annas, he argued, at the rate of three annas a day, would provide me with food for fifty-one days, or about seven weeks; that is to say, he would be willing to cater for me for that length of time. At the end of it I was to look after myself. For a further consideration—*videlicet* my boots—he would be willing to allow me to occupy the den next to his own and would supply me with as much dried grass for bedding as he could spare.

"Very well, Gunga Dass," I replied; "to the first terms I cheerfully agree, but as there is nothing on earth to prevent my killing you as you sit here and taking everything that you have" (I thought of the two invaluable crows at the time), "I flatly refuse to give you my boots and shall take whichever den I please."

The stroke was a bold one, and I was glad when I saw that it had succeeded. Gunga Dass changed his tone immediately and disavowed all intention of asking for my boots. At the time it did not strike me as at all strange that I, a civil engineer, a man of thirteen years' standing in the service, and, I trust, an average Englishman, should thus calmly threaten murder and violence against the man who had, for a consideration it is true, taken me under his wing. I had left the world, it seemed, for centuries. I was as certain then as I am now of my own existence that in the accursed settlement there was no law save that of the strongest, that the living dead men had thrown behind them every canon of the world which had cast them out, and that I had to depend for my own life on my strength and vigilance alone. The crew of the ill-fated *Mignonette* are the only men who would understand my frame of mind. "At present," I argued to myself, "I am strong and a match for six of these wretches. It is imperatively necessary that I should, for my own sake, keep both health and strength until the hour of my release comes—if it ever does."

Fortified with these resolutions, I ate and drank as much as I could and made Gunga Dass understand that I intended to be his master and that the least sign of insubordination on his part would be visited with the only punishment I had it in my power to inflict—sudden and violent death. Shortly after this I went to bed. That is to say, Gunga Dass gave me a double armful of dried bents, which I thrust down the mouth of the lair to the right of his, and followed myself, feet foremost, the hole running about nine feet into the sand with a slight downward inclination and being neatly shored with timbers. From my den which faced the river-front, I was able to watch the waters of the Sutlej flowing past under the light of a young moon and compose myself to sleep as best I might.

The horrors of that night I shall never forget. My den was nearly as narrow as a coffin, and the sides had been worn smooth and greasy by the contact of innumerable naked bodies, added to which it smelt abominably. Sleep was altogether out of the question to one in my excited frame of mind. As the night wore on, it seemed that the entire amphitheatre was filled with legions of unclean devils that, trooping up from the shoals below, mocked the unfortunates in their lairs.

Personally I am not of an imaginative temperament—very few engineers are—but on that occasion I was as completely prostrated with nervous terror as any woman. After half an hour or so, however, I was able once more to calmly review my chances of escape. Any exit by the steep sand walls was, of course, impracticable. I had been thoroughly convinced of this some time before. It was possible, that I might, in the uncertain moonlight, safely run the gauntlet of the rifle-shots. The place was so full of terror for me that I was prepared to undergo any risk in leaving it. Imagine my delight, then, when after creeping stealthily to the river-front I found that the infernal boat was not there. My freedom lay before me in the next few steps!

By walking out to the first shallow pool that lay at the foot of the projecting left horn of the horseshoe, I could wade across, turn the flank of the crater, and make my way inland. Without a moment's hesitation I marched briskly past the tussocks where Gunga Dass had snared the crows, and out in the direction of the smooth white sand beyond. My first step from the tufts of dried grass showed me how utterly futile was any hope of escape, for as I put my foot down I felt an indescribable drawing, sucking motion of the sand below. Another moment, and my leg was swallowed up nearly to the knee. In the moonlight the whole surface of the sand seemed to be shaken with devilish delight at my disappointment. I struggled clear, sweating with terror and exertion, back to the tussocks behind me, and fell on my face.

My only means of escape from the semicircle was protected with a quicksand!

How long I lay I have not the faintest idea, but I was roused at the last by malevolent chuckle of Gunga Dass at my ear. "I would advise you, Protector of the Poor" (the ruffian was speaking English), "to return to your house. It is unhealthy to lie down here. Moreover, when the boat returns, you will most certainly be rifled at." He stood over me in the dim light of the dawn, chuckling and laughing to himself. Suppressing my first impulse to catch the man by the neck and throw him onto the quicksand, I rose sullenly and followed him to the platform below the burrows.

Suddenly, and futilely as I thought while I spoke, I asked, "Gunga Dass, what is the good of the boat if I can't get out *anyhow?*" I recollect that even in my deepest trouble I had been speculating vaguely on the waste of ammunition in guarding an already well-protected fore-shore.

Gunga Dass laughed again and made answer, "They have the boat only in daytime. It is for the reason that *there is a way.* I hope we shall have the pleasure of your company for much longer time. It is a pleasant spot when you have been here some years and eaten roast crow long enough."

I staggered, numbed and helpless, towards the fetid burrow allotted to me and fell asleep. An hour or so later I was awakened by a piercing scream—the shrill, high-pitched scream of a horse in pain. Those who have once heard that will never forget the sound. I found some little difficulty in scrambling out of the burrow. When I was in the open, I saw Pornic, my poor old Pornic, lying dead on the sandy soil. How they had killed him I cannot guess. Gunga Dass explained that horse was better than crow, and "greatest good of greatest number is political maxim. We are now republic, Mister Jukes, and you are entitled to a fair share of the beast. If you like, we will pass a vote of thanks. Shall I propose?"

Yes, we were a republic indeed! A republic of wild beasts penned at the bottom of a pit to eat and fight and sleep till we died. I attempted no protest of any kind, but sat down and stared at the hideous sight in front of me. In less time almost than it takes me to write this, Pornic's body was divided in some unclean way or other; the men and women had dragged the fragments onto the platform and were preparing their morning meal. Gunga Dass cooked mine. The almost irresistible impulse to fly at the sand walls until I was wearied laid hold of me afresh, and I had to struggle against it with all my might. Gunga Dass was offensively jocular till I told him that if he addressed another remark of any kind whatever to me I should strangle him where he sat. This silenced him till silence became insupportable, and I bade him say something.

"You will live here till you die, like the other Fer-inghee," he said coolly, watching me over the fragment of gristle that he was gnawing.

"What other Sahib, you swine? Speak at once, and don't stop to tell me a lie."

"He is over there," answered Gunga Dass, pointing to a

burrow-mouth about four doors to the left of my own. "You can see for yourself. He died in the burrow as you will die, and I will die, and as all these men and women and the one child will also die."

"For pity's sake tell me all you know about him. Who was he? When did he come, and when did he die?"

This appeal was a weak step on my part. Gunga Dass only leered and replied, "I will not—unless you give me something first."

Then I recollected where I was, and struck the man between the eyes, partially stunning him. He stepped down from the platform at once, and cringing and fawning and weeping and attempting to embrace my feet, led me round to the burrow which he had indicated.

"I know nothing whatever about the gentleman. Your God be my witness that I do not. He was as anxious to escape as you were, and he was shot from the boat, though we all did all things to prevent him from attempting. He was shot here." Gunga Dass laid his hand on his lean stomach and bowed to the earth.

"Well, and what then? Go on!"

"And then—and then, your Honour, we carried him into his house and gave him water, and put wet cloths on the wound, and he laid down in his house and gave up the ghost."

"In how long? In how long?"

"About half an hour after he received his wound. I call Vishnu to witness," yelled the wretched man, "that I did everything for him. Everything which was possible, that I did!"

He threw himself down on the ground and clasped my ankles. But I had my doubts about Gunga Dass's benevolence and kicked him off as he lay protesting.

"I believe you robbed him of everything he had. But I can find out in a minute or two. How long was the Sahib here?"

"Nearly a year and a half. I think he must have gone mad. But hear me swear, Protector of the Poor! Won't your Honour hear me swear that I never touched an article that belonged to him? What is your Worship going to do?"

I had taken Gunga Dass by the waist and had hauled

him onto the platform opposite the deserted burrow. As I did so I thought of my wretched fellow prisoner's unspeakable misery among all these horrors for eighteen months and the final agony of dying like a rat in a hole, with a bullet-wound in the stomach. Gunga Dass fancied I was going to kill him and howled pitifully. The rest of the population, in the plethora that follows a full flesh meal, watched us without stirring.

"Go inside, Gunga Dass," said I, "and fetch it out."

I was feeling sick and faint with horror now. Gunga Dass nearly rolled off the platform and howled aloud.

"But I am Brahmin, Sahib—a high-caste Brahmin. By your soul, by your father's soul, do not make me do this thing!"

"Brahmin or no Brahmin, by my soul and my father's soul, in you go!" I said, and seizing him by the shoulders, I crammed his head into the mouth of the burrow, kicked the rest of him in, and sitting down, covered my face with my hands.

At the end of a few minutes I heard a rustle and a creak, then Gunga Dass in a sobbing, choking whisper speaking to himself, then a soft thud—and I uncovered my eyes.

The dry sand had turned the corpse entrusted to its keeping into a yellow-brown mummy. I told Gunga Dass to stand off while I examined it. The body—clad in an olive-green hunting-suit much stained and worn, with leather pads on the shoulders—was that of a man between thirty and forty, above middle height, with light, sandy hair, long moustache, and a rough, unkempt beard. The left canine of the upper jaw was missing, and a portion of the lobe of the right ear was gone. On the second finger of the left hand was a ring—a shield-shaped bloodstone set in gold, with a monogram that might have been either "B. K." or "B. L." On the third finger of the right hand was a silver ring in the shape of a coiled cobra, much worn and tarnished. Gunga Dass deposited a handful of trifles he had picked out of the burrow at my feet, and covering the face of the body with my handkerchief, I turned to examine these. I give the full list in the hope that it may lead to the identification of the unfortunate man:

1. Bowl of a brierwood pipe, serrated at the edge, much worn and blackened, bound with string of the screw.

2. Two patent-lever keys, wards of both broken.

3. Tortoiseshell-handled penknife, silver or nickel, name-plate marked with monogram "B. K."

4. Envelope, postmark undecipherable, bearing a Victorian stamp, addressed to "Miss Mon—" (rest illegible)—"ham'—'nt."

5. Imitation crocodile-skin notebook with pencil. First forty-five pages blank; four and a half illegible; fifteen others filled with private memoranda relating chiefly to three persons—a "Mrs. L. Singleton," abbreviated several times to "Lot Single," "Mrs. S. May," and "Garmison," referred to in places as "Jerry" or "Jack."

6. Handle of small-sized hunting-knife. Blade snapped short. Buck's horn, diamond-cut, with swivel and ring on the butt; fragment of cotton cord attached.

It must not be supposed that I inventoried all these things on the spot as fully as I have here written them down. The notebook first attracted my attention, and I put it in my pocket with a view to studying it later on. The rest of the articles I conveyed to my burrow for safety's sake, and there, being a methodical man, I inventoried them. I then returned to the corpse and ordered Gunga Dass to help me to carry it out to the river-front. While we were engaged in this, the exploded shell of an old brown cartridge dropped out of one of the pockets and rolled at my feet. Gunga Dass had not seen it; and I fell to thinking that a man does not carry exploded cartridge-cases, especially "browns," which will not bear loading twice, about with him when shooting. In other words, that cartridge-case had been fired inside the crater. Consequently there must be a gun somewhere. I was on the verge of asking Gunga Dass, but checked myself, knowing that he would lie. We laid the body down on the edge of the quicksand by the tussocks. It was my intention to push it out and let it be swallowed up—the only possible mode of burial that I could think of. I ordered Gunga Dass to go away.

Then I gingerly put the corpse out on the quicksand. In doing so—it was lying face downward—I tore the frail and rotten khaki shooting-coat open, disclosing a hideous cavity in the back. I have already told you that the dry sand had, as it were, mummified the body. A moment's glance showed that the gaping hole had been caused by a gunshot wound; the gun must have been fired with the muzzle almost touching the back. The shooting-coat, being intact, had been drawn over the body after death, which must have been instantaneous. The secret of the poor wretch's death was plain to me in a flash. Someone of the crater, presumably Gunga Dass, must have shot him with his own gun—the gun that fitted the brown cartridges. He had never attempted to escape in the face of the rifle-fire from the boat.

I pushed the corpse out hastily and saw it sink from sight literally in a few seconds. I shuddered as I watched. In a dazed, half-conscious way I turned to peruse the notebook. A stained and discoloured slip of paper had been inserted between the binding and the back, and dropped out as I opened the pages. This is what it contained: "Four out from crow-clump; three left; nine out; two right; three back; two left; fourteen out; two left; seven out; one left; nine back; two right; six back; four right; seven back." The paper had been burnt and charred at the edges. What it meant I could not understand. I sat down on the dried bents, turning it over and over between my fingers, until I was aware of Gunga Dass standing immediately behind me with glowing eyes and outstretched hands.

"Have you got it?" he panted. "Will you not let me look at it also? I swear that I will return it."

"Got what? Return what?" I asked.

"That which you have in your hands. It will help us both." He stretched out his long, birdlike talons, trembling with eagerness.

"I could never find it," he continued. "He had secreted it about his person. Therefore I shot him, but nevertheless I was unable to obtain it."

Gunga Dass had quite forgotten his little fiction about the rifle-bullet. I heard him calmly. Morality is blunted by consorting with the dead who are alive.

"What on earth are you raving about? What is it you want me to give you?"

"The piece of paper in the notebook. It will help us both. Oh, you fool! You fool! Can you not see what it will do for us? We shall escape!"

His voice rose almost to a scream, and he danced with excitement before me. I own I was moved at the chance of getting away.

"Do you mean to say that this slip of paper will help us? What does it mean?"

"Read it aloud! Read it aloud! I beg and I pray to you to read it aloud."

I did so. Gunga Dass listened delightedly and drew an irregular line in the sand with his fingers.

"See now! It was the length of his gun-barrels without the stock. I have those barrels. Four gun-barrels out from the place where I caught crows. Straight out; do you mind me? Then three left. Ah! How well I remember how that man worked it out night after night. Then nine out, and so on. Out is always straight before you across the quick-sand to the north. He told me so before I killed him."

"But if you knew all this, why didn't you get out before?"

"I did *not* know it. He told me that he was working it out a year and a half ago, and how he was working it out night after night when the boat had gone away, and he could get out near the quicksand safely. Then he said that we would get away together. But I was afraid that he would leave me behind one night when he had worked it all out, and so I shot him. Besides, it is not advisable that the men who once get in here should escape. Only I, and *I* am a Brahmin."

The hope of escape had brought Gunga Dass's caste back to him. He stood up, walked about, and gesticulated violently. Eventually I managed to make him talk soberly, and he told me how this Englishman had spent six months night after night in exploring inch by inch the passage across the quicksand, how he had declared it to be simplicity itself up to within about twenty yards of the river-bank after turning the flank of the left horn of the horseshoe. This much he had evidently not completed when Gunga Dass shot him with his own gun.

In my frenzy of delight at the possibilities of escape I recollect shaking hands wildly with Gunga Dass after we had decided that we were to make an attempt to get away that very night. It was weary work waiting throughout the afternoon.

About ten o'clock, as far as I could judge, when the moon had just risen above the lip of the crater, Gunga Dass made a move for his burrow to bring out the gun-barrels whereby to measure our path. All the other wretched inhabitants had retired to their lairs long ago. The guardian boat had drifted downstream some hours before, and we were utterly alone by the crow-clump. Gunga Dass, while carrying the gun-barrels, let slip the piece of paper which was to be our guide. I stooped down hastily to recover it, and as I did so, I was aware that the creature was aiming a violent blow at the back of my head with the gun-barrels. It was too late to turn round. I must have received the blow somewhere on the nape of my neck, for I fell senseless at the edge of the quicksand.

When I recovered consciousness, the moon was going down, and I was sensible of intolerable pain in the back of my head. Gunga Dass had disappeared, and my mouth was full of blood. I lay down again and prayed that I might die without more ado. Then the unreasoning fury which I have before mentioned laid hold upon me, and I staggered inland towards the walls of the crater. It seemed that someone was calling to me in a whisper—"Sahib! Sahib! Sahib!" exactly as my bearer used to call me in the mornings. I fancied that I was delirious until a handful of sand fell at my feet. Then I looked up and saw a head peering down into the amphitheatre—the head of Dunnoo, my dog-boy, who attended to my collies. As soon as he had attracted my attention, he held up his hand and showed a rope. I motioned, staggering to and fro the while, that he should throw it down. It was a couple of leather punkah-ropes knotted together, with a loop at one end. I slipped the loop over my head and under my arms, heard Dunnoo urge something forward, was conscious that I was being dragged, face downward, up the steep sand-slope, and the next instant found myself choked and half-fainting on the sand-hills overlooking the crater. Dunnoo, with his face ashy grey in the moonlight, implored me not to stay, but to get back to my tent at once.

It seems that he had tracked Pornic's footprints fourteen miles across the sands of the crater, had returned and told my servants, who flatly refused to meddle with anyone, white or black, once fallen into the hideous Village of the Dead; whereupon Dunnoo had taken one of my ponies and a couple of punkah-ropes, returned to the crater, and hauled me out as I have described.

[First published in 1885.]

BAA BAA, BLACK SHEEP

❦

Baa baa, black sheep,
Have you any wool?
Yes sir, yes sir, three bags full.
One for the master, one for the dame—
None for the little boy that cries down the lane.
Nursery Rhyme

THE FIRST BAG

When I was in my father's house, I was in a better place.

They were putting Punch to bed—the *ayah* and the *hamal*
and Meeta, the big *Surti* boy with the red and gold tur-
ban. Judy, already tucked inside her mosquito-curtains,
was nearly asleep. Punch had been allowed to stay up for
dinner. Many privileges had been accorded to Punch
within the last ten days, and a greater kindness from the
people of his world had encompassed his ways and works,
which were mostly obstreperous. He sat on the edge of his
bed and swung his bare legs defiantly.

"Punch-baba going to bye-lo?" said the *ayah* sug-
gestively.

"No," said Punch. "Punch-baba wants the story about

the Ranee that was turned into a tiger. Meeta must tell it, and the *hamal* shall hide behind the door and make tiger noises at the proper time."

"But Judy-baba will wake up," said the *ayah*.

"Judy-baba is waked," piped a small voice from the mosquito-curtains. "There was a Ranee that lived at Delhi. Go on, Meeta," and she fell fast asleep again while Meeta began the story.

Never had Punch secured the telling of that tale with so little opposition. He reflected for a long time. The *hamal* made the tiger noises in twenty different keys.

" 'Top!" said Punch authoritatively. "Why doesn't Papa come in and say he is going to give me *put-put?*"

"Punch-baba is going away," said the *ayah*. "In another week there will be no Punch-baba to pull my hair anymore." She sighed softly, for the boy of the household was very dear to her heart.

"Up The Ghauts in a train?" said Punch, standing on his bed. "All the way to Nassick where the Ranee-Tiger lives?"

"Not to Nassick this year, little Sahib," said Meeta, lifting him on his shoulder. "Down to the sea where the cocoanuts are thrown, and across the sea in a big ship. Will you take Meeta with you to *Belait?*"

"You shall all come," said Punch from the height of Meeta's strong arms. "Meeta and the *ayah* and the *hamal* and Bhini-in-the-Garden, and the salaam-Captain-Sahib-snake-man."

There was no mockery in Meeta's voice when he replied, "Great is the Sahib's favour," and laid the little man down in the bed, while the *ayah*, sitting in the moonlight at the doorway, lulled him to sleep with an interminable canticle such as they sing in the Roman Catholic Church at Parel. Punch curled himself into a ball and slept.

Next morning Judy shouted that there was a rat in the nursery, and thus he forgot to tell her the wonderful news. It did not much matter, for Judy was only three and she would not have understood. But Punch was five, and he knew that going to England would be much nicer than a trip to Nassick.

Papa and Mamma sold the brougham and the piano,

and stripped the house, and curtailed the allowance of crockery for the daily meals, and took long council together over a bundle of letters bearing the Rocklington postmark.

"The worst of it is that one can't be certain of anything," said Papa, pulling his moustache. "The letters in themselves are excellent, and the terms are moderate enough."

"The worst of it is that the children will grow up away from me," thought Mamma; but she did not say it aloud.

"We are only one case among hundreds," said Papa bitterly. "You shall go home again in five years, dear."

"Punch will be ten then, and Judy eight. Oh, how long and long and long the time will be! And we have to leave them among strangers."

"Punch is a cheery little chap. He's sure to make friends wherever he goes."

"And who could help loving my Ju?"

They were standing over the cots in the nursery late at night, and I think that Mamma was crying softly. After Papa had gone away, she knelt down by the side of Judy's cot. The *ayah* saw her and put up a prayer that the Memsahib might never find the love of her children taken away from her and given to a stranger.

Mamma's own prayer was a slightly illogical one. Summarized it ran: "Let strangers love my children and be as good to them as I should be, but let *me* preserve their love and their confidence forever and ever. Amen." Punch scratched himself in his sleep, and Judy moaned a little.

Next day they all went down to the sea, and there was a scene at the Apollo Bunder when Punch discovered that Meeta could not come too, and Judy learned that the *ayah* must be left behind. But Punch found a thousand fascinating things in the rope, block, and steam-pipe line on the big P. & O. steamer long before Meeta and the *ayah* had dried their tears.

"Come back, Punch-baba," said the *ayah*.

"Come back," said Meeta, "and be a *Burra Sahib*" (a big man).

"Yes," said Punch, lifted up in his father's arms to wave good-bye. "Yes, I will come back, and I will be a *Burra Sahib Bahadur*" (a very big man indeed).

At the end of the first day Punch demanded to be set
down in England, which he was certain must be close at
hand. Next day there was a merry breeze, and Punch was
very sick. "When I come back to Bombay," said Punch
on his recovery, "I will come by the road—in a broom-
gharri. This is a very naughty ship."

The Swedish boatswain consoled him, and he modified
his opinions as the voyage went on. There was so much to
see and to handle and ask questions about that Punch
nearly forget the *ayah* and Meeta and the *hamal*, and with
difficulty remembered a few words of the Hindustani,
once his second speech.

But Judy was much worse. The day before the steamer
reached Southampton, Mamma asked her if she would
not like to see the *ayah* again. Judy's blue eyes turned to
the stretch of sea that had swallowed all her tiny past and
said, "*Ayah!* what *ayah?*"

Mamma cried over her, and Punch marvelled. It was
then that he heard for the first time Mamma's passionate
appeal to him never to let Judy forget Mamma. Seeing
that Judy was young, ridiculously young, and that
Mamma, every evening for four weeks past, had come
into the cabin to sing to her and Punch to sleep with a
mysterious rune that he called "Sonny, My Soul," Punch
could not understand what Mamma meant. But he strove
to do his duty, for the moment Mamma left the cabin, he
said to Judy, "Ju, you bemember Mamma?"

" 'Torse I do," said Judy.

"Then *always* bemember Mamma, 'r else I won't give
you the paper ducks that the red-haired Captain Sahib cut
out for me."

So Judy promised always to "bemember Mamma."

Many and many a time was Mamma's command laid
upon Punch, and Papa would say the same thing with an
insistence that awed the child.

"You must make haste and learn to write, Punch," said
Papa, "and then you'll be able to write letters to us in
Bombay."

"I'll come into your room," said Punch, and Papa
choked.

Papa and Mamma were always choking in those days.
If Punch took Judy to task for not "bemembering," they

choked. If Punch sprawled on the sofa in the Southampton lodging-house and sketched his future in purple and gold, they choked; and so they did if Judy put her mouth up for a kiss.

Through many days all four were vagabonds on the face of the earth—Punch with no one to give orders to, Judy too young for anything, and Papa and Mamma grave, distracted, and choking.

"Where," demanded Punch, wearied of a loathsome contrivance on four wheels with a mound of luggage atop—"*where* is our broom-*gharri?* This thing talks so much that *I* can't talk. Where is our *own* broom-*ghari?* When I was at Bandstand before we comed away, I asked Inverarity Sahib why he was sitting in it, and he said it was his own. And I said, 'I will *give* it you'—I like Inverarity Sahib—and I said, 'Can you put your legs through the pulley-wag loops by the windows?' And Inverarity Sahib said no and laughed. *I* can put my legs through *these* pulley-wag loops. Look! Oh, Mamma's crying again! I didn't know I wasn't not to do *so*."

Punch drew his legs out of the loops of the four-wheeler; the door opened and he slid to the earth in a cascade of parcels, at the door of an austere little villa whose gates bore the legend "Downe Lodge." Punch gathered himself together and eyed the house with disfavour. It stood on a sandy road, and a cold wind tickled his knickerbockered legs.

"Let us go away," said Punch. "This is not a pretty place."

But Mamma and Papa and Judy had left the cab, and all the luggage was being taken into the house. At the doorstep stood a woman in black, and she smiled largely with dry, chapped lips. Behind her was a man, big, bony, grey and lame as to one leg; behind him a boy of twelve, black-haired and oily in appearance. Punch surveyed the trio and advanced without fear, as he had been accustomed to do in Bombay when callers came and he happened to be playing in the veranda.

"How do you do?" said he. "I am Punch." But they were all looking at the luggage—all except the grey man, who shook hands with Punch and said he was "a smart little fellow." There was much running about and banging of boxes, and Punch curled himself up on the sofa in the dining-room and considered things.

"I don't like these people," said Punch. "But never mind. We'll go away soon. We have always went away soon from everywhere. I wish we was gone back to Bombay *soon*."

The wish bore no fruit. For six days Mamma wept at intervals and showed the woman in black all Punch's clothes—a liberty which Punch resented. "But p'raps she's a new white *ayah*," he thought. "I'm to call her Antirosa, but she doesn't call *me* Sahib. She says just Punch," he confided to Judy. "What is Antirosa?"

Judy didn't know. Neither she nor Punch had heard anything of an animal called an aunt. Their world had been Papa and Mamma, who knew everything, permitted everything, and loved everybody—even Punch when he used to go into the garden at Bombay and fill his nails with mould after the weekly nail-cutting, because, as he explained between two strokes of the slipper to his sorely tried father, his fingers "felt so new at the ends."

In an undefined way Punch judged it advisable to keep both parents between himself and the woman in black and the boy in black hair. He did not approve of them. He liked the grey man, who had expressed a wish to be called Uncleharri. They nodded at each other when they met, and the grey man showed him a little ship with rigging that took up and down.

"She is a model of the *Brisk*—the little *Brisk* that was sore exposed that day at Navarino." The grey man hummed the last words and fell into a reverie. "I'll tell you about Navarino, Punch, when we go for walks together; and you mustn't touch the ship, because she's the *Brisk*."

Long before that walk, the first of many, was taken, they roused Punch and Judy in the chill dawn of a February morning to say good-bye; and, of all people in the wide earth, to Papa and Mamma—both crying this time. Punch was very sleepy and Judy was cross.

"Don't forget us," pleaded Mamma. "Oh, my little son, don't forget us, and see that Judy remembers too."

"I've told Judy to bemember," said Punch, wriggling, for his father's beard tickled his neck. "I've told Judy—

ten—forty—'leven thousand times. But Ju's so young—
quite a baby—isn't she?"

"Yes," said Papa, quite a baby, and you must be good
to Judy, and make haste to learn to write—and—and
—and—"

Punch was back in his bed again. Judy was fast asleep,
and there was the rattle of a cab below. Papa and
Mamma had gone away. Not to Nassick; that was across
the sea. To some place much nearer, of course, and
equally of course they would return. They came back after dinner-parties, and Papa had come back after he had
been to a place called The Snows, and Mamma with him,
to Punch and Judy at Mrs. Inverarity's house in Marine
Lines. Assuredly they would come back again. So Punch
fell asleep till the true morning, when the black-haired
boy met him with the information that Papa and Mamma
had gone to Bombay and that he and Judy were to stay at
Downe Lodge "forever." Antirosa, tearfully appealed to
for a contradiction, said that Harry had spoken the truth
and that it behooved Punch to fold up his clothes neatly
on going to bed. Punch went out and wept bitterly with
Judy, into whose fair head he had driven some ideas of
the meaning of separation.

When a matured man discovers that he has been
deserted by Providence, deprived of his God, and cast,
without help, comfort, or sympathy, upon a world which
is new and strange to him, his despair, which may find expression in evil living, the writing of his experiences, or
the more satisfactory diversion of suicide, is generally
supposed to be impressive. A child, under exactly similar
circumstances as far as its knowledge goes, cannot very
well curse God and die. It howls till its nose is red, its
eyes are sore, and its head aches. Punch and Judy,
through no fault of their own, had lost all their world.
They sat in the hall and cried, the black-haired boy
looking on from afar.

The model of the ship availed nothing, though the grey
man assured Punch that he might pull the rigging up and
down as much as he pleased; and Judy was promised free
entry into the kitchen. They wanted Papa and Mamma
gone to Bombay beyond the seas, and their grief while it
lasted was without remedy.

When the tears ceased the house was very still. Antirosa had decided that it was better to let the children
"have their cry out," and the boy had gone to school.
Punch raised his head from the floor and sniffed
mournfully. Judy was nearly asleep. Three short years
had not taught her how to bear sorrow with full knowledge. There was a distant dull boom in the air—a repeated heavy thud. Punch knew that sound in Bombay in
the Monsoon. It was the sea—the sea that must be tra-
versed before anyone could get to Bombay.

"Quick, Ju!" he cried. "We're close to the sea. I can
hear it! Listen! That's where they've went. P'raps we can
catch them if we was in time. They didn't mean to go
without us. They've only forgot."

"Iss," said Judy. "They've only forgotted. Less go to
the sea."

The hall door was open, and so was the garden gate.

"It's very, very big, this place," he said, looking cautiously down the road, "and we will get lost; but *I* will
find a man and order him to take me back to my house—
like I did in Bombay."

He took Judy by the hand, and the two ran hatless in
the direction of the sound of the sea. Downe Villa was almost the last of a range of newly built houses running out,
through a field of brick-mounds, to a heath where gypsies
occasionally camped and where the Garrison Artillery of
Rocklington practised. There were few people to be seen,
and the children might have been taken for those of the
soldiery who ranged far. Half an hour the wearied little
legs tramped across health, potato-patch, and sand-dune.

"I'se so tired," said Judy, "and Mamma will be angry."

"Mamma's *never* angry. I suppose she is waiting at the
sea now while Papa gets tickets. We'll find them and go
along with. Ju, you mustn't sit down. Only a little more
and we'll come to the sea. Ju, if you sit down I'll *thmack*
you!" said Punch.

They climbed another dune and came upon the great
grey sea at low tide. Hundreds of crabs were scuttling
about the beach, but there was no trace of Papa and
Mamma, not even of a ship upon the water—nothing but
sand and mud for miles and miles.

And Uncleharri found them by chance—very muddy

and very forlorn—Punch dissolved in tears, but trying to divert Judy with an "ickle trab," and Judy wailing to the pitiless horizon for "Mamma, Mamma!"—and again "Mamma!"

THE SECOND BAG

Ah, well-a-day, for we are souls bereaved!
Of all the creatures under heaven's wide scope
We are most hopeless, who had once most hope,
And most beliefless, who had most believed.

The City of Dreadful Night

All this time not a word about Black Sheep. He came later, and Harry the black-haired boy was mainly responsible for his coming.

Judy—who could help loving little Judy?—passed, by special permit, into the kitchen, and thence straight to Aunty Rosa's heart. Harry was Aunty Rosa's one child, and Punch was the extra boy about the house. There was no special place for him or his little affairs, and he was forbidden to sprawl on sofas and explain his ideas about the manufacture of this world and his hopes for his future. Sprawling was lazy and wore out sofas, and little boys were not expected to talk. They were talked to, and the talking to was intended for the benefit of their morals. As the unquestioned despot of the house at Bombay, Punch could not quite understand how he came to be of no account in this his new life.

Harry might reach across the table and take what he wanted; Judy might point and get what she wanted. Punch was forbidden to do either. The grey man was his great hope and stand-by for many months after Mamma and Papa left, and he had forgotten to tell Judy to "bemember Mamma."

This lapse was excusable, because in the interval he had been introduced by Aunty Rosa to two very impressive things—an abstraction called God, the intimate friend and ally of Aunty Rosa, generally believed to live behind the kitchen range because it was hot there, and a dirty brown book filled with unintelligible dots and marks. Punch was always anxious to oblige everybody. He therefore welded the story of the Creation onto what he could recollect of his Indian fairy-tales, and scandalized Aunty Rosa by repeating the result to Judy. It was a sin, a grievous sin, and Punch was talked to for a quarter of an hour. He could not understand where the iniquity came in, but was careful not to repeat the offense, because Aunty Rosa told him that God had heard every word he had said and was very angry. If this were true, why didn't God come and say so, thought Punch, and dismissed the matter from his mind. Afterwards he learned to know the Lord as the only thing in the world more awful than Aunty Rosa—as a Creature that stood in the background and counted the strokes of the cane.

But the reading was, just then, a much more serious matter than any creed. Aunty Rosa sat him upon a table and told him that AB meant ab.

"Why?" said Punch. "A is a and B is bee. *Why* does AB mean ab?"

"Because I tell you it does," said Aunty Rosa, "and you've got to say it."

Punch said it accordingly, and for a month, hugely against his will, stumbled through the brown book, not in the least comprehending what it meant. But Uncle Harry, who walked much and generally alone, was wont to come into the nursery and suggest to Aunty Rosa that Punch should walk with him. He seldom spoke, but he showed Punch all Rocklington, from the mud-banks and the sand of the back-bay to the great harbours where ships lay at anchor, and the dockyards where the hammers were never still, and the marine-store shops, and the shiny brass counters in the offices where Uncle Harry went once every three months with a slip of blue paper and received sovereigns in exchange, for he held a wound-pension. Punch heard too from his lips the story of the battle of Navarino, where the sailors of the fleet for three days afterwards were deaf as posts and could only sign to each other. "That was because of the noise of the guns," said Uncle Harry, "and I have got the wadding of a bullet somewhere inside me now."

Punch regarded him with curiosity. He had not the least idea what wadding was, and his notion of a bullet was a dockyard cannon-ball bigger than his own head. How could Uncle Harry keep a cannon-ball inside him? He was ashamed to ask, for fear Uncle Harry might be angry.

Punch had never known what anger—real anger—meant until one terrible day when Harry had taken his paint-box to paint a boat with, and Punch had protested. Then Uncle Harry had appeared on the scene, and muttering something about "strangers' children," had with a stick smitten the black-haired boy across the shoulders till he wept and yelled, and Aunty Rosa came in and abused Uncle Harry for cruelty to his own flesh and blood, and Punch shuddered to the tips of his shoes. "It wasn't my fault," he explained to the boy, but both Harry and Aunty Rosa said that it was, and that Punch had told tales, and for a week there were no more walks with Uncle Harry.

But that week brought a great joy to Punch.

He had repeated till he was thrice weary the statement that "the Cat lay on the Mat and the Rat came in."

"Now I can truly read," said Punch, "and now I will never read anything in the world."

He put the brown book in the cupboard where his school-books lived, and accidentally tumbled out a venerable volume, without covers, labelled "Sharpe's Magazine." There was the most portentous picture of a griffin on the first page, with verses below. The griffin carried off one sheep a day from a German village, till a man came with a "falchion" and split the griffin open. Goodness only knew what a falchion was, but there was the griffin, and his history was an improvement upon the eternal cat.

"This," said Punch, "means things, and now I will know all about everything in all the world." He read till the light failed, not understanding a tithe of the meaning, but tantalized by glimpses of new worlds hereafter to be revealed.

"What is a 'falchion'? What is a 'e-wee lamb'? What is a 'base ussurper'? What is a 'verdant me-ad'?" he demanded with flushed cheeks, at bedtime, of the astonished Aunty Rosa.

"Say your prayers and go to sleep," she replied, and

that was all the help Punch then or afterwards found at
her hands in the new and delightful exercise of reading.

"Aunty Rosa only knows about God and things like
that," argued Punch. "Uncle Harry will tell me."

The next walk proved that Uncle Harry could not help
either, but he allowed Punch to talk, and even sat down
on a bench to hear about the griffin. Other walks brought
other stories as Punch ranged further afield, for the house
held large store of old books that no one ever opened—
from *Frank Fairlegh* in serial numbers, and the earlier poems of Tennyson, contributed anonymously to *Sharpe's
Magazine* to '62 *Exhibition Catalogues*, gay with colours
and delightfully incomprehensible, and odd leaves of *Gul-
liver's Travels*.

As soon as Punch could string a few pot-hooks together, he wrote to Bombay, demanding by return of post
"all the books in all the world." Papa could not comply
with this modest indent, but sent *Grimms' Fairy Tales*
and a Hans Andersen. That was enough. If he were only
left alone, Punch could pass, at any hour he chose, into a
land of his own, beyond reach of Aunty Rosa and her
God, Harry and his teasements, and Judy's claims to be
played with.

"Don't disturve me, I'm reading. Go and play in the
kitchen," grunted Punch. "Aunty Rosa lets *you* go there."
Judy was cutting her second teeth and was fretful. She appealed to Aunty Rosa, who descended on Punch.

"I was reading," he explained, "reading a book. I *want*
to read."

"You're only doing that to show off," said Aunty Rosa.
"But we'll see. Play with Judy now, and don't open a
book for a week."

Judy did not pass very enjoyable playtime with Punch,
who was consumed with indignation. There was a petti-
ness at the bottom of the prohibition which puzzled him.

"It's what I like to do," he said, "and she's found out
that and stopped me. Don't cry, Ju—it wasn't your fault—
please don't cry, or she'll say I made you."

Ju loyally mopped up her tears, and the two played in
their nursery, a room in the basement and half underground, to which they were regularly sent after the
midday dinner while Aunty Rosa slept. She drank

wine—that is to say, something from a bottle in the cellaret—for her stomach's sake, but if she did not fall asleep she would sometimes come into the nursery to see that the children were really playing. Now, bricks, wooden hoops, nine-pins, and chinaware cannot amuse forever, especially when all Fairyland is to be won by the mere opening of a book, and, as often as not, Punch would be discovered reading to Judy or telling her interminable tales. That was an offence in the eyes of the law, and Judy would be whisked off by Aunty Rosa, while Punch was left to play alone, "and be sure that I hear you doing it."

It was not a cheering employ, for he had to make a playful noise. At last, with infinite craft, he devised an arrangement whereby the table could be supported as to three legs on toy bricks, leaving the fourth clear to bring down on the floor. He could work the table with one hand and hold a book with the other. This he did till an evil day when Aunty Rosa pounced upon him unawares and told him that he was "acting a lie."

"If you're old enough to do that," she said—her temper was always worse after dinner—"you're old enough to be beaten."

"But—I'm—I'm not a animal!" said Punch, aghast. He remembered Uncle Harry and the stick and turned white. Aunty Rosa had hidden a light cane behind her, and Punch was beaten then and there over the shoulders. It was a revelation to him. The room door was shut, and he was left to weep himself into repentance and work out his own gospel of life.

Aunty Rosa, he argued, had the power to beat him with many stripes. It was unjust and cruel, and Mamma and Papa would never have allowed it. Unless perhaps, as Aunty Rosa seemed to imply, they had sent secret orders. In which case he was abandoned indeed. It would be discreet in the future to propitiate Aunty Rosa, but then again, even in matters in which he was innocent, he had been accused of wishing to "show off." He had "shown off" before visitors when he had attacked a strange gentleman—Harry's uncle, not his own—with requests for information about the griffin and the falchion, and the precise nature of the tilbury in which Frank Fairlegh rode—

all points of paramount interest which he was bursting to understand. Clearly it would not do to pretend to care for Aunty Rosa.

At this point Harry entered and stood afar off, eyeing Punch, a dishevelled heap in the corner of the room, with disgust.

"You're a liar—a young liar," said Harry with great unction, "and you're to have tea down here because you're not fit to speak to us. And you're not to speak to Judy again till Mother gives you leave. You'll corrupt her. You're only fit to associate with the servant. Mother says so."

Having reduced Punch to a second agony of tears, Harry departed upstairs with the news that Punch was still rebellious.

Uncle Harry sat uneasily in the dining-room. "Damn it all, Rosa," said he at last, "can't you leave the child alone? He's a good enough little chap when I meet him."

"He puts on his best manners with you, Henry," said Aunty Rosa, "but I'm afraid, I'm very much afraid, that he is the black sheep of the family."

Harry heard and stored up the name for future use. Judy cried till she was bidden to stop, her brother not being worth tears; and the evening concluded with the return of Punch to the upper regions and a private sitting at which all the blinding horrors of hell were revealed to Punch with such store of imagery as Aunty Rosa's narrow mind possessed.

Most grievous of all was Judy's round-eyed reproach, and Punch went to bed in the depths of the Valley of Humiliation. He shared his room with Harry, and knew the torture in store. For an hour and a half he had to answer that young gentleman's questions as to his motives for telling a lie, and a grievous lie, the precise quantity of punishment inflicted by Aunty Rosa, and had also to profess his deep gratitude for such religious instruction as Harry thought fit to impart.

From that day began the downfall of Punch, now Black Sheep.

"Untrustworthy in one thing, untrustworthy in all," said Aunty Rosa, and Harry felt that Black Sheep was delivered into his hands. He would wake him up in the night to ask him why he was such a liar.

"I don't know," Punch would reply.

"Then don't you think you ought to get up and pray to God for a new heart?"

"Y-yess."

"Get out and pray then!" And Punch would get out of bed with raging hate in his heart against all the world, seen and unseen. He was always tumbling into trouble. Harry had a knack of cross-examining him as to his day's doings, which seldom failed to lead him, sleepy and savage, into half a dozen contradictions—all duly reported to Aunty Rosa next morning.

"But it *wasn't* a lie," Punch would begin, charging into a laboured explanation that landed him more hopelessly in the mire. "I said that I didn't say my prayers *twice* over in the day, and *that* was on Tuesday. *Once* I did. I *know* I did, but Harry said I didn't," and so forth, till the tension brought tears, and he was dismissed from the table in disgrace.

"You usen't to be as bad as this," said Judy, awe-stricken at the catalogue of Black Sheep's crimes. "Why are you so bad now?"

"I don't know," Black Sheep would reply. "I'm not, if I only wasn't bothered upside down. I knew what I *did*, and I want to say so; but Harry always makes it out different somehow, and Aunty Rosa doesn't believe a word I say. Oh, Ju! Don't *you* say I'm bad too."

"Aunty Rosa says you are," said Judy. "She told the vicar so when he came yesterday."

"Why does she tell all the people outside the house about me? It isn't fair," said Black Sheep. "When I was in Bombay, and was bad—*doing* bad, not make-up bad like this—Mamma told Papa, and Papa told me he knew, and that was all. *Outside* people didn't know too—even Meeta didn't know."

"I don't remember," said Judy wistfully. "I was all little then. Mamma was just as fond of you as she was of me, wasn't she?"

" 'Course she was. So was Papa. So was everybody."

"Aunty Rosa likes me more than she does you. She

says that you are a Trial and a Black Sheep, and I'm not to speak to you more than I can help."

"Always? Not outside of the times when you mustn't speak to me at all?"

Judy nodded her head mournfully. Black Sheep turned away in despair, but Judy's arms were round his neck.

"Never mind, Punch," she whispered. "I *will* speak to you just the same as ever and ever. You're my own own brother, though you are—though Aunty Rosa says you're bad, and Harry says you're a little coward. He says that if I pulled your hair hard, you'd cry."

"Pull then," said Punch.

Judy pulled gingerly.

"Pull harder—as hard as you can! There! I don't mind how much you pull it *now*. If you'll speak to me same as ever I'll let you pull it as much as you like—pull it out if you like. But I know if Harry came and stood by and made you do it, I'd cry."

So the two children sealed the compact with a kiss, and Black Sheep's heart was cheered within him, and by extreme caution and careful avoidance of Harry he acquired virtue, and was allowed to read undisturbed for a week. Uncle Harry took him for walks and consoled him with rough tenderness, never calling him Black Sheep. "It's good for you, I suppose, Punch," he used to say. "Let us sit down. I'm getting tired." His steps led him now not to the beach, but to the cemetery of Rocklington, amid the potato-fields. For hours the grey man would sit on a tombstone, while Black Sheep read epitaphs, and then with a sigh would stump home again.

"I shall lie there soon," said he to Black Sheep one winter evening when his face showed white as a worn silver coin under the light of the lich-gate. "You needn't tell Aunty Rosa."

A month later he turned sharp round, ere half a morning walk was completed, and stumped back to the house. "Put me to bed, Rosa," he muttered. "I've walked my last. The wadding has found me out."

They put him to bed, and for a fortnight the shadow of his sickness lay upon the house, and Black Sheep went to and fro unobserved. Papa had sent him some new books, and he was told to keep quiet. He retired into his own world and was perfectly happy. Even at night his felicity was unbroken. He could lie in bed and string himself tales of travel and adventure while Harry was downstairs.

"Uncle Harry's going to die," said Judy, who now lived almost entirely with Aunty Rosa.

"I'm very sorry," said Black Sheep soberly. "He told me that a long time ago."

Aunty Rosa heard the conversation. "Will nothing check your wicked tongue?" she said angrily. There were blue circles round her eyes.

Black Sheep retreated to the nursery and read *Cometh Up as a Flower* with deep and uncomprehending interest. He had been forbidden to open it on account of its "sinfulness," but the bonds of the universe were crumbling, and Aunty Rosa was in great grief.

"I'm glad," said Black Sheep. "She's unhappy now. It wasn't a lie, though. *I* knew. He told me not to tell."

That night Black Sheep woke with a start. Harry was not in the room, and there was a sound of sobbing on the next floor. Then the voice of Uncle Harry, singing the song of the Battle of Navarino, came through the darkness:

> Our vanship was the Asia—
> The Albion and Genoa!

"He's getting well," thought Black Sheep, who knew the song through all its seventeen verses. But the blood froze at his little heart as he thought. The voice leapt an octave and rang shrill as a boatswain's pipe:

> And next came on the lovely Rose,
> The Philomel, her fire-ship, closed,
> And the little Brisk was sore exposed
> That day at Navarino.

"That day at Navarino, Uncle Harry!" shouted Black Sheep, half wild with excitement and fear of he knew not what.

A door opened, and Aunty Rosa screamed up the staircase, "Hush! For God's sake hush, you little devil. Uncle Harry is *dead!*"

The Third Bag

Journeys end in lovers' meeting,
Every wise man's son doth know.

"I wonder what will happen to me now," thought Black
Sheep when semi-pagan rites peculiar to the burial of the
dead in middle-class houses had been accomplished, and
Aunty Rosa, awful in black crape, had returned to this
life. "I don't think I've done anything bad that she knows
of. I suppose I will soon. She will be very cross after
Uncle Harry's dying, and Harry will be cross too. I'll keep
in the nursery."

Unfortunately for Punch's plans, it was decided that he
should be sent to a day-school, which Harry attended.
This meant a morning walk with Harry, and perhaps an
evening one; but the prospect of freedom in the interval
was refreshing.

"Harry'll tell everything I do, but I won't do anything,"
said Black Sheep. Fortified with this virtuous resolution,
he went to school only to find that Harry's version of his
character had preceded him and that life was a burden in
consequence. He took stock of his associates. Some of
them were unclean, some of them talked in dialect, many
dropped their H's, and there were two Jews and a Negro,
or someone quite as dark, in the assembly. "That's a
hubshi," said Black Sheep to himself. "Even Meeta used
to laugh at a *hubshi*. I don't think this is a proper place."
He was indignant for at least an hour, till he reflected that
any expostulation on his part would be by Aunty Rosa
construed into "showing off," and that Harry would tell
the boys.

"How do you like school?" said Aunty Rosa at the end
of the day.

"I think it is a very nice place," said Punch quietly.

"I suppose you warned the boys of Black Sheep's character?" said Aunty Rosa to Harry.

"Oh, yes," said the censor of Black Sheep's morals.
"They know all about him."

"If I was with my father," said Black Sheep, stung to

the quick, "I shouldn't *speak* to those boys. He wouldn't let me. They live in shops. I saw them go into shops— where their fathers live and sell things."

"You're too good for that school, are you?" said Aunty Rosa with a bitter smile. "You ought to be grateful, Black Sheep, that those boys speak to you at all. It isn't every school that takes little liars."

Harry did not fail to make much capital out of Black Sheep's ill-considered remark, with the result that several boys, including the *hubshi*, demonstrated to Black Sheep the eternal equality of the human race by smacking his head, and his consolation from Aunty Rosa was that it served him right for being vain. He learned, however, to keep his opinions to himself, and by propitiating Harry in carrying books and the like, to get a little peace. His existence was not too joyful. From nine till twelve he was at school, and from two to four, except on Saturdays. In the evenings he was sent down into the nursery to prepare his lessons for the next day and every night came the dreaded cross-questionings at Harry's hand. Of Judy he saw but little. She was deeply religious—at six years of age religion is easy to come by—and sorely divided between her natural love for Black Sheep and her love for Aunty Rosa, who could do no wrong.

The lean woman returned that love with interest, and Judy, when she dared, took advantage of this for the remission of Black Sheep's penalties. Failures in lessons at school were punished at home by a week without reading other than school-books, and Harry brought the news of such a failure with glee. Further, Black Sheep was then bound to repeat his lessons at bedtime to Harry, who generally succeeded in making him break down, and consoled him by gloomiest forebodings for the morrow. Harry was at once spy, practical joker, inquisitor, and Aunt Rosa's deputy executioner. He filled his many posts to admiration. From his actions, now that Uncle Harry was dead, there was no appeal. Black Sheep had not been permitted to keep any self-respect at school; at home he was of course utterly discredited, and grateful for any pity that the servant-girls—they changed frequently at Downe Lodge because they too were liars—might show. "You're just fit to row in the same boat with Black Sheep," was a sentiment that each new Jane or Eliza might expect to hear before a month was over from Aunt Rosa's lips; and Black Sheep was used to ask new girls whether they had yet been compared to him. Harry was "Master Harry" in their mouths; Judy was officially "Miss Judy"; but Black Sheep was never anything more than Black Sheep *tout court*.

As time went on and the memory of Papa and Mamma became wholly overlaid by the unpleasant task of writing them letters, under Aunty Rosa's eye, each Sunday, Black Sheep forgot what manner of life he had led in the beginning of things. Even Judy's appeals to "try and remember about Bombay" failed to quicken him.

"I can't remember," he said. "I know I used to give orders and Mamma kissed me."

"Aunty Rosa will kiss you if you are good," pleaded Judy.

"Ugh! I don't want to be kissed by Aunty Rosa. She'd say I was doing it to get something more to eat."

The weeks lengthened into months, and the holidays came; but just before the holidays Black Sheep fell into deadly sin.

Among the many boys whom Harry had incited to "punch Black Sheep's head because he daren't hit back" was one, more aggravating than the rest, who, in an unlucky moment, fell upon Black Sheep when Harry was not near. The blows stung and Black Sheep struck back at random with all the power at his command. The boy dropped and whimpered. Black Sheep was astounded at his own act, but feeling the unresisting body under him, shook it with both his hands in blind fury and then began to throttle his enemy, meaning honestly to slay him. There was a scuffle, and Black Sheep was torn off the body by Harry and some colleagues and cuffed home tingling but exultant. Aunty Rosa was out; pending her arrival, Harry set himself to lecture Black Sheep on the sin of murder, which he described as the offence of Cain.

"Why didn't you fight him fair? What did you hit him when he was down for, you little cur?"

Black Sheep looked up at Harry's throat and then at a knife on the dinner-table.

"I don't understand," he said wearily. "You always set

him on me and told me I was a coward when I blubbed. Will you leave me alone until Aunty Rosa comes in? She'll beat me if you tell her I ought to be beaten, so it's all right."

"It's all wrong," said Harry magisterially. "You nearly killed him, and I shouldn't wonder if he dies."

"Will he die?" said Black Sheep.

"I dare say," said Harry, "and then you'll be hanged and go to hell."

"All right," said Black Sheep, picking up the table-knife. "Then I'll kill *you* now. You say things and do things, and—and *I* don't know how things happen, and you never leave me alone—and I don't care *what* happens!"

He ran at the boy with the knife, and Harry fled upstairs to his room, promising Black Sheep the finest thrashing in the world when Aunty Rosa returned. Black Sheep sat at the bottom of the stairs, the table-knife in his hand, and wept for that he had not killed Harry. The servant-girl came up from the kitchen, took the knife away, and consoled him. But Black Sheep was beyond consolation. He would be badly beaten by Aunty Rosa; then there would be another beating at Harry's hands; then Judy would not be allowed to speak to him; then the tale would be told at school; and then—

There was no one to help and no one to care, and the best way out of the business was by death. A knife would hurt. but Aunty Rosa had told him a year ago that if he sucked paint he would die. He went into the nursery, unearthed the now disused Noah's ark, and sucked the paint off as many animals as remained. It tasted abominable, but he had licked Noah's dove clean by the time Aunty Rosa and Judy returned. He went upstairs and greeted them with: "Please, Aunty Rosa, I believe I've nearly killed a boy at school, and I've tried to kill Harry, and when you've done all about God and hell, will you beat me and get it over?"

The tale of the assault as told by Harry could only be explained on the ground of possession by the devil. Wherefore Black Sheep was not only most excellently beaten, once by Aunty Rosa and once, when thoroughly cowed down, by Harry, but he was further prayed for at family prayers, together with Jane, who had stolen a cold rissole from the pantry and snuffled audibly as her sin was brought before the Throne of Grace. Black Sheep was sore and stiff, but triumphant. He would die that very night and be rid of them all. No, he would ask for no forgiveness from Harry, and at bedtime, would stand no questioning at Harry's hands, even though addressed as "young Cain."

"I've been beaten," said he, "and I've done other things. I don't care what I do. If you speak to me tonight, Harry, I'll get out and try to kill you. Now you can kill me if you like."

Harry took his bed into the spare room, and Black Sheep lay down to die.

It may be that the makers of Noah's arks know that their animals are likely to find their way into young mouths, and paint them accordingly. Certain it is that the common, weary next morning broke through the windows and found Black Sheep quite well and a good deal ashamed of himself, but richer by the knowledge that he could, in extremity, secure himself against Harry for the future.

When he descended to breakfast on the first day of the holidays, he was greeted with the news that Harry, Aunty Rosa, and Judy were going away to Brighton, while Black Sheep was to stay in the house with the servant. His latest outbreak suited Aunty Rosa's plans admirably. It gave her good excuse for leaving the extra boy behind. Papa in Bombay, who really seemed to know a young sinner's wants to the hour, sent that week a package of new books. And with these and the society of Jane on board-wages, Black Sheep was left alone for a month.

The books lasted for ten days. They were eaten too quickly in long gulps of twelve hours at a time. Then came days of doing absolutely nothing, of dreaming dreams and marching imaginary armies up and down stairs, of counting the number of banisters, and of measuring the length and breadth of every room in hand-spans—fifty down the side, thirty across, and fifty back again. Jane made many friends, and after receiving Black Sheep's assurance that he would not tell of her absences, went out daily for long hours. Black Sheep would follow

the rays of the sinking sun from the kitchen to the
dining-room and thence upward to his own bedroom until
all was grey dark, and he ran down to the kitchen fire and
read by its light. He was happy in that he was left alone
and could read as much as he pleased. But later he grew
afraid of the shadows of window-curtains and the flapping
of doors and the creaking of shutters. He went out into
the garden, and the rustling of the laurel-bushes
frightened him.

He was glad when they all returned—Aunty Rosa,
Harry, and Judy—full of news, and Judy laden with
gifts. Who could help loving loyal little Judy? In return
for all her merry babblement, Black Sheep confided to her
that the distance from the hall door to the top of the first
landing was exactly one hundred and eighty-four hand-
spans. He had found it out himself.

Then the old life recommenced, but with a difference,
and a new sin. To his other iniquities Black Sheep had
now added a phenomenal clumsiness—was as unfit to
trust in action as he was in word. He himself could not
account for spilling everything he touched, upsetting
glasses as he put his hand out, and bumping his head
against doors that were manifestly shut. There was a grey
haze upon all his world, and it narrowed month by
month, until at last it left Black Sheep almost alone with
the flapping curtains that were so like ghosts and the
nameless terrors of broad daylight that were only coats on
pegs after all.

Holidays came and holidays went, and Black Sheep
was taken to see many people whose faces were all exactly alike, was beaten when occasion demanded and
tortured by Harry on all possible occasions, but defended
by Judy through good and evil report, though she thereby
drew upon herself the wrath of Aunty Rosa.

The weeks were interminable, and Papa and Mamma
were clean forgotten. Harry had left school and was a
clerk in a banking-office. Freed from his presence, Black
Sheep resolved that he should no longer be deprived of
his allowance of pleasure-reading. Consequently, when he
failed at school he reported that all was well, and
conceived a large contempt for Aunty Rosa as he saw
how easy it was to deceive her. "She says I'm a little liar

when I don't tell lies, and now I do she doesn't know,"
thought Black Sheep. Aunty Rosa had credited him in the
past with petty cunning and stratagem that had never. entered into his head. By the light of the sordid knowledge
that she had revealed to him, he paid her back full tale.
In a household where the most innocent of his motives,
his natural yearning for a little affection, had been inter-
preted into a desire for more bread and jam or to ingrati-
ate himself with strangers and so put Harry into the background, his work was easy. Aunty Rosa could penetrate
certain kinds of hypocrisy, but not all. He set his child's
wits against hers, and was no more beaten. It grew
monthly more and more of a trouble to read the school-
books, and even the pages of the open-print story-books
danced and were dim. So Black Sheep brooded in the
shadows that fell about him and cut him off from the
world, inventing horrible punishments for "dear Harry" or
plotting another line of the tangled web of deception that
he wrapped round Aunty Rosa.

Then the crash came and the cobwebs were broken. It
was impossible to foresee everything. Aunty Rosa made
personal inquiries as to Black Sheep's progress and received information that startled her. Step by step, with a
delight as keen as when she convinced an underfed housemaid of the theft of cold meats, she followed the trail of
Black Sheep's delinquencies. For weeks and weeks, in
order to escape banishment from the bookshelves, he
had made a fool of Aunty Rosa, of Harry, of God, of all
the world! Horrible, most horrible, and evidence of an utterly depraved mind.

Black Sheep counted the cost. "It will only be one big
beating, and then she'll put a card with 'Liar' on my back,
same as she did before. Harry will whack me and pray for
me, and she will pray for me at prayers and tell me I'm a
child of the devil and give me hymns to learn. But I've
done all my reading, and she never knew. She'll say she
knew all along. She's an old liar too," said he.

For three days Black Sheep was shut in his own bedroom—to prepare his heart. "That means two beatings.
One at school and one here. *That* one will hurt most."
And it fell even as he thought. He was thrashed at school
before the Jews and the *hubshi* for the heinous crime of

bringing home false reports of progress. He was thrashed at home by Aunty Rosa on the same count, and then the placard was produced. Aunty Rosa stitched it between his shoulders and bade him go for a walk with it upon him.

"If you make me do that," said Black Sheep very quietly, "I shall burn this house down, and perhaps I'll kill you. I don't know whether I *can* kill you—you're so bony—but I'll try."

No punishment followed this blasphemy, though Black Sheep held himself ready to work his way to Aunty Rosa's withered throat and grip there till he was beaten off. Perhaps Aunty Rosa was afraid, for Black Sheep, having reached the Nadir of Sin, bore himself with a new recklessness.

In the midst of all the trouble there came a visitor from over the seas to Downe Lodge, who knew Papa and Mamma and was commissioned to see Punch and Judy. Black Sheep was sent to the drawning-room, and charged into a solid tea-table laden with china.

"Gently, gently, little man," said the visitor, turning Black Sheep's face to the light slowly. "What's that big bird on the palings?"

"What bird?" asked Black Sheep.

The visitor looked deep down into Black Sheep's eyes for half a minute, and then said suddenly, "Good God, the little chap's nearly blind!"

It was a most businesslike visitor. He gave orders, on his own responsibility, that Black Sheep was not to go to school or open a book until Mamma came home. "She'll be here in three weeks, as you know of course," said he, "and I'm Inverarity Sahib. I ushered you into this wicked world, young man, and a nice use you seem to have made of your time. You must do nothing whatever. Can you do that?"

"Yes," said Punch in a dazed way. He had known that Mamma was coming. There was a chance, then, of another beating. Thank heaven Papa wasn't coming too. Aunty Rosa had said of late that he ought to be beaten by a man.

For the next three weeks Black Sheep was strictly allowed to do nothing. He spent his time in the old nursery looking at the broken toys, for all of which account must

be rendered to Mamma. Aunty Rosa hit him over the
hands if even a wooden boat were broken. But that sin
was of small importance compared to the other rev-
elations so darkly hinted at by Aunty Rosa.

"When your mother comes and hears what I have to
tell her, she may appreciate you properly," she said
grimly, and mounted guard over Judy lest that small
maiden should attempt to comfort her brother, to the
peril of her soul.

And Mamma came—in a four-wheeler—fluttered with
tender excitement. Such a mamma! She was young, frivo-
lously young, and beautiful, with delicately flushed
cheeks, eyes that shone like stars, and a voice that needed
no appeal of outstretched arms to draw little ones to her
heart. Judy ran straight to her, but Black Sheep hesitated.

Could this wonder be "showing off"? She would not
put out her arms when she knew of his crimes. Meantime
was it possible that by fondling she wanted to get anything out of Black Sheep? Only all his love and all his
confidence, but that Black Sheep did not know. Aunty
Rosa withdrew and left Mamma, kneeling between her
children, half laughing, half crying, in the very hall where
Punch and Judy had wept five years before.

"Well, chicks, do you remember me?"

"No," said Judy frankly, "but I said, 'God bless Papa
and Mamma,' ev'vy night."

"A little," said Black Sheep. "Remember I wrote to
you every week, anyhow. That isn't to show off, but
'cause of what comes afterwards."

"What comes after? What should come after, my darling boy?" And she drew him to her again. He came awk-
wardly, with many angles.

"Not used to petting," said the quick mother-soul.
"The girl is."

"She's too little to hurt anyone," thought Black Sheep,
"and if I said I'd kill her, she'd be afraid. I wonder what
Aunty Rosa will tell."

There was a constrained late dinner, at the end of
which Mamma picked up Judy and put her to bed with
endearments manifold. Faithless little Judy had shown her
defection from Aunty Rosa already. And that lady
resented it bitterly. Black Sheep rose to leave the room.

"Come and say good night," said Aunty Rosa, offering a withered cheek.

"Huh!" said Black Sheep. "I never kiss you, and I'm not going to show off. Tell that woman what I've done, and see what she says."

Black Sheep climbed into bed feeling that he had lost heaven after a glimpse through the gates. In half an hour "that woman" was bending over him. Black Sheep flung up his right arm. It wasn't fair to come and hit him in the dark. Even Aunty Rosa never tried that. But no blow followed.

"Are you showing off? I won't tell you anything more than Aunty Rosa has, and *she* doesn't know everything," said Black Sheep as clearly as he could for the arms round his neck.

"Oh, my son—my little, little son! It was my fault—*my* fault, darling—and yet how could we help it? Forgive me, Punch." The voice died out in a broken whisper, and two hot tears fell on Black Sheep's forehead.

"Has she been making you cry too?" he asked. "You should see Jane cry. But you're nice, and Jane is a born liar—Aunty Rosa says so."

"Hush, Punch, hush! My boy, don't talk like that. Try to love me a little bit—a little bit. You don't know how I want it. Punch-baba, come back to me! I am your mother—your own mother—and never mind the rest. I know—yes, I know, dear. It doesn't matter now. Punch, won't you care for me a little?"

It is astonishing how much petting a big boy of ten can endure when he is quite sure that there is no one to laugh at him. Black Sheep had never been made much of before, and here was this beautiful woman treating him—Black Sheep, the child of the devil and the inheritor of undying flame—as though he were a small God.

"I care for you a great deal, Mother dear," he whispered at last, "and I'm glad you've come back; but are you sure Aunty Rosa told you everything?"

"Everything. What *does* it matter? But"—the voice broke with a sob that was also laughter—"Punch, my poor, dear, half-blind darling, don't you think it was a little foolish of you?"

"*No.* It saved a lickin'."

Mamma shuddered and slipped away in the darkness
to write a long letter to Papa. Here is an extract:

> ... Judy is a dear, plump little prig who adores
> the woman and wears with as much gravity as her
> religious opinions—only eight, Jack!—a venerable
> horse-hair atrocity which she calls her bustle! I have
> just burnt it, and the child is asleep in my bed as I
> write. She will come to me at once. Punch I cannot
> quite understand. He is well nourished, but seems to
> have been worried into a system of small deceptions
> which the woman magnifies into deadly sins. Don't
> you recollect our own upbringing, dear, when the
> fear of the Lord was so often the beginning of false-
> hood? I shall win Punch to me before long. I am
> taking the children away into the country to get
> them to know me, and on the whole I am content, or
> shall be when you come home, dear boy, and then,
> thank God, we shall be all under one roof again at
> last!

Three months later Punch, no longer Black Sheep, has
discovered that he is the veritable owner of a real, live,
lovely mamma, who is also a sister, comforter, and friend,
and that he must protect her till the father comes home.
Deception does not suit the part of a protector, and when
one can do anything without question, where is the use of
deception?

"Mother would be awfully cross if you walked through
that ditch," says Judy, continuing a conversation.

"Mother's never angry," says Punch. "She'd just say,
'You're a little *pagal*'; and that's not nice, but I'll show."

Punch walks through the ditch and mires himself to the
knees. "Mother dear," he shouts, "I'm just as dirty as I
can pos-*sib*-ly be!"

"Then change your clothes as quickly as you pos-*sib*-ly
can!" Mother's clear voice rings out from the house.
"And don't be a little *pagal!*"

"There! Told you so," says Punch. "It's all different
now, and we are just as much Mother's as if she had
never gone."

Not altogether, O Punch, for when young lips have

drunk deep of the bitter waters of Hate, Suspicion, and Despair, all the Love in the world will not wholly take away that knowledge, though it may turn darkened eyes for a while to the light, and teach Faith where no Faith was.

[First published in 1888.]

RUDYARD KIPLING was born in Bombay, India, on December 30, 1865. Seven years before, the rule of the British East India Company had ended and the government of India had been assumed by the British Crown. Bombay was becoming a prosperous city and, indeed, most of India had profited since it had entered the dominion status.

John Lockwood Kipling and his wife, Alice, had gone from England to Bombay in the spring of the year when he had accepted an appointment as teacher of architectural sculpture in the Bombay School of Art. Rudyard was their first child.

In their bungalow the boy spent his first five years. He was completely happy. He learned English and the vernacular of the servants simultaneously and spoke them interchangeably. The Indian boy Meeta taught him much about native ways and mores, legends and worship, that he never forgot.

But it was the custom for the English in the Indian service to send their children to England for their education and to adapt them to English manners. So Rudyard at six and his three-year-old sister were sent to live with a family in Southsea and there began for him a life of misery, relieved only when, at Christmastime, he would spend a few weeks with his mother's relatives, the Burne-Joneses. He was beaten almost as a matter of routine, ac-

211

cused constantly of lying, of hypocrisy, of the sin of "showing off," and referred to always as the "black sheep" of the household. The story he later wrote, "Baa Baa, Black Sheep," is one of the few bits of autobiography that Kipling has ever given us; it tells the details of what were perhaps the worst six years of his life. In 1877 his mother rescued him and he was sent to the school "Westward Ho!" which was part of the United Services College. There he came under the tutelage and guidance of Cormell Price, a sympathetic schoolmaster who encouraged his passion for reading. Westward Ho! was the scene of *Stalky and Co.*, and the boys there were its characters. In school he read deeply of the Bible, the Elizabethans, and Defoe, but especially the English poets.

He was only seventeen when he went back to India to join the staff of the *Civil and Military Gazette* in Lahore. Soon the poems and editorial articles he wrote for the paper found their way back to England. His *Departmental Ditties* in 1886 and his stories in the next two years created an immense sensation in the literary world of London; "Who is this Rudyard Kipling?" was the question that was asked throughout England. In the year 1888, the twenty-three-year-old Kipling published seven volumes of stories: *Plain Tales From the Hills, Soldiers Three, The Story of the Gadsbys, Under the Deodars, The Phantom 'Rickshaw, Wee Willie Winkie,* and *In Black and White.* Since Dickens, no writer had achieved such sudden celebrity.

In 1889 he traveled to London via Japan and the United States, writing of all he observed on the way. In London he met the American journalist Wolcott Balestier, with whom he collaborated on *The Naulahka,* published in 1892. That same year he married Balestier's sister, Caroline. With her he went to live in Brattleboro, Vermont, and after four years, ending in a bitter feud with his brother-in-law Beatty Balestier, took his wife and their children back to England. However, in the winter of 1898–1899 he visited the United States again; and while he was in New York, he and his daughter, Josephine, suffered severe attacks of pneumonia, of which the little girl died. In 1902 he settled in Burwash, England, and for the first time fell in love with the English country. It was then that he wrote the best of his English stories and then too that he became an ardent imperialist, for which he was so harshly criticized by a younger generation that had turned toward democracy and against colonialism.

Kipling never became inflated by the adulation that was accorded him on every side. When he was offered the laureateship, he refused. Personal publicity so often distressed him that he was called shy. He had many enemies, both because of his political opinions and because he consistently refused to join groups or societies that wished to honor him. He did, however, accept the Nobel Prize for Literature, which was awarded him in 1907.

Kipling was deeply distressed by the First World War, in which he lost his son, John. In his bitterness against the Germans he wrote some poems and stories that were often hysterical or brutal. After the war, until his death in 1936, he was increasingly ill and suffered almost continuous pain from a duodenal ulcer, which the English physicians of those days knew little about.

ROGER BURLINGAME